The Ebb and Flow

David Edwards

IndePenPress

First published in Great Britain by Indepenpress

All paper used in the printing of this book has been made from wood grown in managed, sustainable forests.

ISBN13: 978-1-78003-326-6

Printed and bound in the UK

Indepenpress Publishing Limited

25 Eastern Place

Brighton

BN2 1GJ

A catalogue record of this book is available from the British Library

Cover design by Jacqueline Abromeit and Chandler Design Associates Ltd

Acknowledgements

My book was written for you Frances Bridget.

In the two places that we love.

You taught me not to justify and not to judge.

To give and not to take.

With mercy and compassion.

To live life now.

To live for us.

David Edwards

The media baptised him 'the riches to rags author' under his pseudonym of Jack George Edmunson. Jack had huge success with his controversial first book, The Sun Sharer.

Whilst travelling around the UK in his caravan home in 2010, he received enormous attention from the BBC and regional newspapers entranced by the millionaire who gave up everything to become an author in 2007.

David remarried at Christmas 2011 and now lives a simple life in an ancient homestead on Anglesey where he continues to write.

You can contact him via his website: www.theebbandflow.co.uk

David E.

Contents

Anglesea late 1700s

Menai Straits

Holyhead • Bull Bay • Amlwch • Copper Mountain • Red Wharf Bay • Priestholm • Conwy • Beaumaris • Lavan Sands • Sychnant Pass • Aber • Bangor • Llangefni • Porthaethwy • Llanfoeli • Slate mine • Aberffraw • Malltraeth • Brynsiencyn • Newborough • Caernarfon

To England

--------------------- Main routes

Menai Straits

Bull
Inn

Earls
Hill

Ferry to
sands

The
Attack

Llanfairpwllgwyngyll

The
Column

Gorad
Goch

Bangor

The Walk

Plas
Newydd

Moel Y Don

Ferry

Felinheli

Plas
Coch

Mermaid
Inn

Caernarfon

Lovers'
Island

The translucent cover depicts the '4 sisters'. The stark skeleton of an old barge rests on the bank of the Menai Straits washed by the ebb and flow of the tide. It was used to transfer the sandstone to rebuild the Elizabethan house called Plas Coch, 'the red place', which lies in the meadow above. The stone was quarried beyond the white cottage, behind the heronry.

Hidden by the trees is Saint Edwen's church, purely lit inside by candlelight. Beyond the peninsular sits magnificent Plas Newydd, 'a home shaped by love and loss', owned by The Marquis of Anglesey and frequented by Royalty.

This beautiful and secret spot is where the Romans invaded in AD 60 and massacred the Druids on pyres of yew. It is also where Edward I's army was repelled by the men of Anglesey in 1282. The Moel-y-Don ferry ran between here and Felinheli and was used by the slate miners on their weekly commute to the quarries under the shadow of Snowdon.

The cover evokes the Georgian invasion by seven English families who came to buy North Wales and the spirit of the sea as they smuggled and traded in a place you will love – the Menai Straits.

Prologue

1822

Taid could barely see the creaking stairs as he spiralled slowly to the top of the new limestone column. He was sweating profusely but felt clammy and cold as he pushed against the door at the summit. Bending double, he stumbled into the welcoming sunlight, a human eclipse darkening the dim interior. He staggered two steps to the wrought iron railing and collapsed with his arms hanging over the balustrade. As his vision stabilised, he sucked in shallow draughts of air, clinging onto the last gasps of his life as he surveyed the dying world below.

The serpentine band of the Menai Straits glinted in the afternoon glare. It looked insignificant, 250 feet beneath, but the waters had defied the encroachment of the mountains of North Wales for ten million years and protected his beloved island of Ynys Môn from many invaders. To his left he could see the ships anchored off Beaumaris and Bangor, marooned until the treacherous Lavan Sands would again be covered by the shallow sea. The boats floated on the near horizon drifting into the blue smudge which was all he could see of the Great Orme at Llandudno. The indistinct vistas were distant memories of a life that was now ebbing away.

Taid stared at the bulging veins on his hands as he gripped the straight spindles and then hung the flag of Saint George from the railing. Before he could tie it fast, the pain crushed his chest and he slowly slipped downwards. His left arm was crooked rigidly over the iron as he fought the agony that conducted down to his hand; his grey weathered face pressed hard against the bars. He watched the flag waft seawards, a last defiant act as he fought for breath and the ultimate examination of his stewardship.

Despite the bright September sunlight, the slate mines hewn out of Mount Snowdon were hidden in the grey shadows of the distance. The scars blended into the blackness of the mountain's shadow high above the lake of Llyn Peris. Taid's grip loosened as he watched the steaming ferry low down to his right. It battled into an invisible current that was stealing between the castle at Caernarfon and the ever changing sand dunes of New Borough. The tide was unclenching its watery hands that grasped the island, caressing the heart of Wales bound by the aorta of the straits. The belches of black smoke from the ferry's stack were sucked horizontally by the inevitable strong westerly. A feeble opposition to the streaming waters representing a fluid declaration by nature against Man's "progress". Anglesey, Ynys Môn, "the mother of Wales", but a parent who had lost her only child. She had a fabled past as "the dark island", an ancient name immortalised by the Druids and now applicable to the shadowy deeds of the handful of ruling English landlords.

Taid slumped to the paving, his left cheek resting on the cool surface and his arms trapped under the dead-weight of his body. The signal to his watching friends had fluttered to the water, a superfluous action but a final celebration of their united freedom. So he was content to die surrounded by beauty, the land of his fathers. A haunting harp playing resounded softly in his head but with a slowing pluck of the strings. He remembered Lady Elizabeth standing in the drawing room at Plas Coch, singing the words to *Pererin Wyf* in English: "Amazing Grace", vibrant and spiritual, and as beautiful as the young woman herself. An imagining of the one he had always loved, but now there was no air left to mouth the gentle lyrics.

At the top of the column was an empty plinth supporting the clear blue sky. There was no bronze of the Marquess of Anglesey to coldly stare down at him. No hero to inspire him to defy inevitable death, but he had shown the same courage as the Marquess at the Battle of Waterloo and so it was a fitting place.

A final vision shrouded Taid's reality; amidst a thickening sea mist he pictured the country house of Plas Coch adjacent to the straits. It merged to nothingness with its red walls set against the burnt autumn colours of the surrounding beech trees. It had been his home for 50 years as a retainer, a friend and a lover but never a true father or a husband.

Taid, or "grandfather" in English, was a term of endearment, a measure of respect from his benefactors latterly used instead of the impersonal call of 'steward' or 'Tudur'. He had given everything to the Littleton-Joneses and nothing to their enemies. He had given his life to the English family and they in turn had given him a better life. Owen Tudur floated above the large mansion, drawn towards the reddening sun setting over Ynys-y-Cranc and Lover's Island. He was sure the house smiled with sorrow, but then it was gone; his last thought about Ynys Môn in the year 1822.

Chapter I

Ynys Môn - 1767

A spritely young man called Owen Tudur strode towards the country house of Plas Coch. He approached with an escort of newly planted beech trees down the wide avenue on the western side of the house. They were already up to his shoulder and were bursting from brown to green as the virgin growth heralded the longer days of May. The new owners had also ordered him to plant a replica avenue on the eastern approach that led to the busy lane joining Moel-y-don and Llanfairpwll. Numerous carts, gigs, animals and their owners trundled down this gentle hill each day as they headed towards the ferry that crossed the Menai Straits to deposit them at Aberpwll on the mainland of Wales. The human swell mimicked the tide streaming into Bangor, or out towards Caernarfon, but there was a stronger ebb and flow on each Monday and Friday as the slate workers commuted between their homes and the quarries that surrounded Mount Snowdon.

Moel-y-don means "hill of the wave" in Welsh, but Sir John Littleton-Jones and his wife, Lady Elizabeth, didn't speak the language of their new country. Therefore, they were deaf to the jibes of the locals who were incensed about the country estate they had created over the last two years. Although dwarfed by their neighbours in magnificent Plas Newydd, it was certainly more open and hospitable than the Marquess of Anglesey's house, where the Paget family closeted their heritage in the walled estate to the east. Theirs was a bland Georgian mansion, abrupt and cold with its grey blocks in direct contrast to the warm sandstone of Plas Coch. This "Red Place" was built in an Elizabethan style by the Sherriff of Anglesey and still retained its ornate crow-stepped gables, but substantial additions had been made by the Littleton-Joneses during the two years that Owen had been acting steward. The Elizabethan north walls had been taken down and reused to create a third tower. Every window had been fitted with a paned gothic casement but shrunk to reduce taxation, and the dome had been replaced with a striking square turret to house the new clock and its bell. This modernity sounded six times as he approached, but the loud chimes were absorbed by the valley's grass walls, so that it announced the start of work on the estate with a certain lethargy.

Owen was a big man even at the age of 22. Six foot three and lean, he commanded respect by his presence, a trait that would lead to the nickname Taid many years later. He had wiry black hair and a wide smile that was always present and although young, his deep sense of responsibility and his inquiring intelligent nature made him a natural leader. His slate-coloured eyes glinted with excitement as he walked to work on that spring day in 1767. The steward was about to meet his English employer, Sir John Littleton-Jones, face-to-face for the first time. The business magnate from Liverpool and his two brothers owned a fifth of Jamaica. Sir John and his family were rich because of their African slaves and the sugar they harvested in the Caribbean, a sweetness that flowed home to England on the family's ships. The schooners then completed the triangular trade route by heading south to Africa before returning to the West Indies. This had brought the magnate and his brothers a wealth that compared favourably with the hereditary Georgian Peers who owned most of England. But wealth alone did not make them as powerful as they desired.

It was dry for the first time in months, with no hint of rain in the flat grey sky. The term May was derived from Maia, the mother of Mercury. It was the Romans who made a sacrifice on the first day of this month and it was the Romans who had killed so many Welshmen in the nearby fields of *Maes Mawr Gad*, or "the plain of the great army". Owen trod a new path on his approach from his home village of Brynsiencyn where he shared a dark and damp stone cottage with his father Lewis, his sister Aeronwy and her new husband Cadell Thomas. The outside of their low cottage was a depressing grey colour, including the slate roof that had come from the tiny mine in Llyn Peris, newly purchased by the English incomers. The inside of the Tudur home was darker still, a cramped hovel that would seem smaller once Aeronwy's twins were born. The entire Welsh family served the rich English who had earned their wealth from the obscene slave trade. A trade they wanted to fashionably distance themselves from in order to gain a modern respectability but without realising they were recreating it much closer to home. Cadell worked for the Earl of Beaumaris as overseer in his new slate quarries and Lewis held the same position for Sir John. Owen was the steward of the Plas Coch estate and his sister, Aeronwy, practised her skills as a herbalist with most of the gentry on Anglesey. They were truly the new Welsh slaves.

Owen's father's face at 40 years old was as grey as the Tudur family's life; partly because of the dormant cancer, a consequence of the years ingesting slate dust but also due to pure fatigue. The father looked like his son, hewn from the same rock but with two exceptions. Firstly, the black hair had turned silver-grey from the years of stress and poverty. Secondly, he had a hunch on his upper back created by the heavy lifting on the galleries of the mines since the age of 12. Lewis only returned home to the cottage at weekends as he and his colleagues stayed in the barracks high above Llyn Peris. This quarry was a new find, set on one of six farms purchased by the master to extricate premium slate in the harshest of environments. For many years Lewis used to arrive home full of joy to see his young boy and his wife Olwen, but his boy was now a man and his wife had died of consumption ten years earlier. So Lewis worked and existed. He loved his son and had treated him harshly to make him into a man. But he also hated; he loathed the English as they had bought his country and expunged the ancient royal boundaries. They had created new parishes like New Borough close to his home at Brynsiencyn and now they thought that they could buy the rest of Wales; but Lewis was one of many who believed they could never buy the nation. They would never destroy his heritage drawn from the Princes of Wales who lived at Aberffraw within this new borough, nor could they cast aside its people like the waste heaped on the slopes of the mountain beneath the slate workings.

As Owen closed on the house, he passed the substantial stables to his left where his colleagues were now stirring. Elis Wirion was known as "silly Elis" by all the locals. Ostensibly the groom, he functioned as the steward's "leg-man", someone who did what he was told without question, no matter what the task, and in complete secrecy. Elis was a giant of a man who felt no pain. He had no conscience and few thoughts, which made him utterly loyal to Owen. Nominally, Elis reported to the new coachman, Duncan Thomas, but since the coachman's arrival at Plas Coch, there had been a good understanding about Elis's duties with the steward. Thomas himself was a quiet man who worked without complaint. An ex-soldier from Warrington, he had witnessed so much suffering in the wars that had ravaged Europe that he was thankful to be in such a beautiful place with a safe and secure job. At 35 years old he was tall and strong with ginger hair, and although totally reliable and responsible he was regarded by his peers as a trifle dull. The third man who lived above the stables was Andrew, a young Negro from the master's Jamaican plantation, who shared Duncan's peace with life and never spoke. Andrew acted as postilion on the coach as a symbol of the master's power, but most of the time he performed the dirty or hard jobs in the stables as dictated by the coachman.

Owen paused on the new sandstone bridge with its eight arches spanning the stream that the locals called "The Spout". This fed a large lake which languished in the original quarry where the sandstone had been extracted to build the renaissance mansion. On his left was a path that skirted the lake between the rear of the house and the new kitchen garden, which still lay barren. This had been created half a mile away from the house by erecting two new walls to enclose a bare area in front of the 30-foot high quarry faces. The rush of ducks over his right shoulder startled him as the mallards completed an early morning flight to splash into the still waters. The silvered surface rippled and lost the luminous look of "Phlegethan", the place where the waters run with flames in the classical underworld. However, there would be no sun to light the watery fires today. The significance of the disturbance was lost on Owen who only dwelt within the practicalities of each day. He laughed at the noisy calls of the ducks as they paddled to the bank to forage in the light undergrowth. They were always an easy catch to supplement the lamb and pork diet of the estate's inhabitants and by far the cheapest meat available when compared to the expensive and rare taste of the black Anglesey cattle.

Owen opened the imposing studded door that led into the kitchen at the rear of the house.

'Good morning Cook.'

'Don't think you are going to bother me for any breakfast, steward.'

Owen smiled as he warmed himself in front of the giant open fire. He watched the suckling pig's snout slowly turn to look up at him from the spit which was mechanically driven by the upward draught of the fire. The kitchen was immaculate as usual. Siân Jones and her two scullery maids had been awake since 5am, hours ahead of the family and still well before any of the other household staff. The copper pots gleamed red then orange, reflecting the flames of the coal brought in by the weekly wagon from the Halkyn mines near Chester. On the scrubbed oak table in the centre of the room were earthenware pots full of steaming porridge waiting for the dozen household staff to call in and devour their measly breakfast. Anticipated vultures armed with pewter porringers instead of beaks, to greedily cream the gruel from the pot. It was still too early for bread, but the ovens in the large black range secreted the wonderful smell of freshly baked white loaves made from the finest Irish wheat, which was a luxury in itself.

Owen watched Siân bustle around. She had become his friend and ally over the two years they had both been installed in their jobs.

The cook was slightly older than him and already thickening at the waist. Her white apron bulged as she leaned forward to roll some pastry. He studied the kitchen roof ten feet above him as she turned to see if he were looking at her. She hoped he was but quickly bowed her cherub-like face over her work after vainly brushing away an odd red curl that had managed to escape the plain white bonnet. Owen was the one to "catch" out of all the eligible men living along the Menai and it was a beautiful and intelligent farmer's daughter called Beth Cadwallader that had hooked him three years previously.

Beth had lived on a farm close to Brynsiencyn which was part of the master's estate and had often met Owen as a child when he fetched jugs of milk for his mam and tad. Many a kiss had been exchanged between the youngsters whilst collecting mussels on the seashore and three years ago the parents had consented to them lying together. This was a tradition when a man and his future bride could spend the night in bed together in one of the parents' homes but strictly leaving on all their clothes whilst cuddled beneath the covers. Beth and Owen had snuggled, giggling within the heat of the blankets and spent most of the night awake in an amorous embrace which repeated their secret sexual antics on the seashore. But shortly afterwards, Owen had been given new responsibilities as the provisional steward and in his ambitious future, he had no time for a wife and so he declined to marry her. It wasn't considered unusual, as he was going to make something of himself and that was more important. This tradition of a trial night together nullified many potential but convenient marriages and was considered a benefit to the community.

When Beth realised she was pregnant, her father had asked the master's agent to find her work in England. She was lucky; by transferring to the master's Liverpool house as a maid, any gossip was avoided and she was considered "free of the wagon". Luckier still, her ladyship had favoured her. Many other young girls on the island had moved away to avoid the shame of a child outside of marriage but ended up as prostitutes, "dolly mops", in the big cities.

'I just said good morning Mrs.' Owen was smiling but only Jenifer, the scullery maid, smiled back as she scuttled in and out of the massive kitchen. Her alder clogs were noisy and echoed on the floor, but they saved her feet from the cold and wet as she completed scrubbing the granite slabs, parking the heavy brush by heaving it into the alcove alongside the water boiler. The indomitable cook turned to the steward and seductively wiped her hands down her apron, leaving grease marks on the clean white cotton.

'Good morning indeed, sir. I believe you have a meeting with the master today?'

'In half an hour,' Owen checked his fob watch, 'and I cannot be late, even if you do tempt me,' he paused, 'with some of your delightful food.'

She laughed at the tease. 'Maybe so, but you may have another meeting that is far more stressful.'

He looked at her with his hands placed on his strong hips. 'And?'

'She's back.' He didn't require any clarification. "She" was Beth Cadwallader who had been installed as the new mistress's head housekeeper, promoted by Lady Elizabeth in the year after her enforced absence. Owen nervously pulled at his starched collar.

'That won't be an issue Mrs.'

She clamped up, his past wasn't her concern; she was more interested in their possible joint future. She dreamed of him touching her, she wanted his body and to share in his status, a handsome man of power. However, the chances were slim and so she had also been encouraging Duncan Thomas in his advances. Almost any man would suffice as she approached the age of 26 years old.

The steward placed his bowler hat on his head and nervously adjusted his dark blue necktie against the white round collar. Siân admired the fine man in his black suit who nervously bid his goodbyes and marched out of the kitchen door. 'Probably never,' she sighed under her breath and recommenced preparing the family's breakfast.

Owen took a deep breath as he stood in front of the main entrance and stared at the Hughes coat of arms and the date, 1569. The carved stone was set above a large porch commanding the view to the Menai Straits and the emerald mountains beyond. His meeting was in the study immediately to the left of the oak door. To the right were wide mahogany stairs leading to the drawing room and the separate bedrooms of the master and mistress. The nanny and children's bedrooms were pushed as far away from these as possible and resided at the end of the dark corridor. On the third floor were the servant's quarters, where he occasionally slept on a truckle bed covered with unforgiving huckaback linen. A chamber maid always wheeled this into a quiet location if Owen were due to stay, as instructed by Roger Nash, the new butler. This was well away from the butler's tiny bedroom, as Nash treated Owen with disdain. He had started his employment four months earlier and already had a bad reputation. He was a haughty man who was vindictive with all the staff, in contrast to the much loved steward. Whenever their paths crossed, the conversations were always polite but never friendly. A small, slight and bald man of 40 years, the butler wheedled his way through conversations with his peers and superiors whilst constantly berating his underlings.

Owen stepped inside the seemingly deserted house. In the hall was an oval oak table, four Russia leather chairs that stank of birch bark oil, a settle and a small three-footed salt chest. To his left he saw there was no one in the great parlour. The black japanned table, square oak tea table and cane chairs awaited their first visitors and would remain unused until the Littleton-Joneses were accepted into Anglesey's social circle.

Already rotund at 42 years old, Sir John stood by his black mahogany bureau to meet steward Tudur. The former Yorkshire squire had a bright ruddy face due to the copious amounts of alcohol he imbibed each evening. This was enhanced by the stark white of his powdered wig. The rest of his attire was jingoistic: a red velvet waistcoat, a white ruff shirt and dark blue knickerbocker trousers above contemporary white stockings. The archetypal English gentleman held out a steady hand towards Owen who approached with confidence.

'Glad to meet you, sir. My agent informs me that you have performed admirably in these last two years.' Owen bowed his head deferentially.

'Thank you Sir John, it is my pleasure to serve and Mr Smith is too kind.' Owen made a mental note to thank his friend William who had spent many weeks with him as they had created the new estate. William Smith was 30 years old and had served the family for the last five years. A man of science, he was used in many ways by the three brothers within their businesses and was trusted implicitly. His skills as an agent had been honed in Jamaica, but he had been glad to leave the island. He had told Owen that he had been disgusted by the degrading treatment of the slaves and since that conversation, they had become firm friends, sharing the same principles in life. The rich Englishman stepped delicately behind his large oak desk and then sat heavily.

'Sit steward.' He motioned with his hand. 'I am pleased with the renovation sir and now we have more work to do. The base is provided and now the cannon can fire, what!' Owen remained silent, puzzled whether he should answer. 'You are clever enough to wonder why an Englishman from Liverpool has bought extensive lands in Wales.' He looked shrewdly at the new man in his service. 'And I will tell you the answer tomorrow if you give me a solemn undertaking before you become my permanent steward.' The master leaned forward and his jowls wobbled as he placed his elbows on the desk and clasped his hands together as if praying.

'Sir?' Owen wanted to remain in the job forever. The power experienced in the previous two years was a delicious food to his starved personality. Sir John appraised the man for a few moments and then made his decision.

'I require a pledge of loyalty. To be a steward in my new domain, I need loyalty to myself and my family until the day you die. Are you prepared to give me that pledge Owen Tudur?'

'No matter what the circumstances, master?'

'No matter what! You will hear, see, and speak no evil against us.' The steward remained motionless and returned the master's unblinking stare.

'That asks me to give you my soul, Sir John.'

'Precisely. Nothing less will suffice sir. You treat me as God and my family as my angels. Besides, you owe me your soul already...'

Owen sat rock still as he replied. 'Why, Sir John?'

'We looked after the Cadwallader girl. You know the penalty for killing your own child is death and it could easily have gone that way?' He coughed into his hand. 'A principled and upright woman, what!'

Owen realised he knew very little about the last two years but felt the threat instead of the kindness. His heart was beating faster now that the master had confirmed his first love had been pregnant when she left. He asked a simple question. 'Do you think I should give you that depth of loyalty sir?'

The master was adamant. 'Yes, because you cannot possibly understand my every whim or its nuance, nor each action I undertake, and that is no different from your understanding of God. Therefore, you must believe in me too, without thought and with blind faith until the day you die.' He brought the meeting to a head. 'Is it agreed then Mr Tudur? Are you a God-fearing man of the Anglican church?'

Owen stood slowly and stared past Sir John. The mountains of Moel Rhiwen and Moel-y-Ci stood guarding the entrance to the Llyn Peris pass that yawned into the hazy distance. He wanted power and would be well rewarded. The flavour of his personal god was success and being Anglican or non-conformist was immaterial. It was a chance for his current and future family to crawl out of their pitiful existence and join the echelons of the handful of English 'rich' who were buying North Wales. He stepped two paces forward and held out his hand to shake on the bargain with god and hoped Sir John wasn't in fact the devil.

'I accept my responsibilities without any doubts.'

Sir John smiled warmly. 'Any last questions?'

'What do you mean by a new domain sir? I presume it will affect my duties?'

'Because my two brothers and I have been planning where to place our wealth for more than five years and North Wales is our base for these new ventures. Tomorrow morning, we leave at eight for the Dinorwic quarry with agent Smith and then you will learn more. Have three horses ready outside.' He was summarily dismissed. As

Owen opened the study door, the master gave him his second direct order. The steward turned to listen. 'And introduce yourself to Lady Elizabeth as you must serve her every need. I believe she is in the drawing room.' Owen softly closed the door on his old life and went upstairs to meet the new.

He paused outside the door of the drawing room. Firstly, to muster his inner strength to face Beth and secondly to listen to the most beautiful sound he had ever experienced.

> *Amazing grace how sweet the sound*
> *That saved a wretch like me.*
> *I once was lost, but now I'm found;*
> *Was blind, but now I see...*

The door creaked as he entered the room and the moment was lost. It was transcended by the image of a woman standing silhouetted in a bay window with the lake behind her. She appeared to be an angel walking on the waters, but he couldn't see her face due to the glare. No matter, the delicious outline amplified the song and for a moment it stopped both his breath and his thoughts. The vision stepped forward. A blonde with ringlets, about 25 years old, and bedazzling in a simple blue satin dress. She had slender arms emerging from the capped sleeves showing her perfect alabaster skin but as he closed on her, he was entranced by the deep violet eyes which enhanced an already beautiful woman.

'So you have accepted my husband's offer Mr Tudur?'

'Indeed, Lady Elizabeth.' As he bowed slightly, he noticed the second angel. A fashionable replica but brunette this time and dressed in green satin. Owen turned to Beth. 'Miss Cadwallader.'

Her ladyship was amused as she saw his discomfort. She smiled at the head housekeeper who spent much of her time as her confidant.

'I believe you have met Beth before?'

'Yes your ladyship.' He glanced nervously between the two women.

'Don't worry steward, your secrets are safe with me. I was surprised that you didn't marry such an intelligent and beautiful woman.' This time she turned her back on Owen, to give a second but secret smile at Beth. Owen decided that a new steward ought to show some spunk.

'Indeed, she has many qualities and I am a poor man for failing her.' The two ladies nodded their heads in appreciation. 'But,' he paused for effect, 'but love is meant to be and should never be manufactured from circumstances. Maybe we lived too close to each other and were too young at the time. Therefore, I felt honour bound to break her heart and not to disrespect her future life.' Her ladyship delicately clapped her hands in delight.

'I see we have a steward who is gallant as well as clever.'

Beth added her own compliment. 'A "real" man that women chase throughout Ynys Môn but nobody catches. Good day Owen Tudur, I hope you are in good health?' Owen nodded shyly. 'In which case, you can entertain our ladyship with the Welsh version of *Pererin Wyf.*' He shifted on his feet, uncomfortable with beautiful women especially those who shared his secrets. Attack seemed the best form of defence.

'A brief verse for two ladies, as I have many duties to attend.' He focused on the mirror-like lake for a few moments and then he sang in a deep and moving baritone that reflected his emotions.

> *Pererin wyf mewn anial dir,*
> *Yn crwydro yma a thraw;*
> *Ac yn rhyw ddisgwyl bob yr awr*
> *Fod ty fy Nhad gerllaw.*

As he started verse two, her ladyship joined in. A harmony of sound resounding with notes that was emotionally deeper. Beth clasped her hands in front of her mouth in awe of the moment. As the song died, it was her turn to clap with delight. She gushed.

'How delightful! A Scottish hymn sung in English and Welsh. Do any of the countries have the right to such a beautiful unison ma'am?'

Elizabeth looked into Owen's eyes as she replied, 'Maybe not in the serenade, but possibly in the emotions of their people.' Owen bowed deeply and excused himself as he was taking two steps backwards. He turned quickly on his heel and disappeared through the drawing room door. He smiled to himself as he closed it behind him and heard the first titters of laughter.

Elizabeth and Beth stood by the window and admired Owen as he strode back over the sandstone bridge towards the coach house.

'I can see the attraction, Beth; he has a depth to his persona.'

'And he is handsome and successful,' she coyly replied.

'Does he know about the child?' Elizabeth turned to her companion.

'No and he never will, at least not from me, but my little Amy is happy and loved in your house in London and that is all that matters, my Lady. Thank you again for your kindness.' Beth dropped her head, but Elizabeth gently lifted her chin with a finger so that she could look into Beth's eyes.

'I would never see a child abandoned or hurt in my household and there are no favours in friendship. We need to take courage and stand up against these brutal men.' Her ladyship turned away to contemplate her private thoughts about her loveless marriage, convenient within the Establishment but totally unfulfilling. A maid entered the room to tend the fire and bobbed in front of Beth with a curt 'madam' but completely ignored Lady Elizabeth as per protocol.

Later that afternoon the two ladies were playing cards, a game of piquet with halfpenny bets. Beth was sixpence down and knew it would be deducted from her wages at the end of the month. She used an expression she had seen in The London Gazette.

'Madam, you are lucky at cards and therefore you will be unlucky in love.'

As Elizabeth formulated a reply Sir John marched into the room. 'I've asked the nanny to send in the children, ma'am.'

'Thank you Sir John.' Her reply was polite and cool as expected after five years of an arranged marriage. He sat on an oak settle and crossed his arms. An order had been given and he required it to be carried out immediately.

'Strewth and zounds, how long does the woman take?' He was impatient within a minute and Beth glanced at Elizabeth to see if she should leave. A slow shake of the head and brief eye contact was enough for Beth to continue the game of cards. The door creaked open and a small blonde boy dressed in a blue velvet suit was silhouetted alone until the nanny emerged from behind carrying the baby. The boy was tall and strong at 4 years old, but baby Victoria, at five months, was weak and not expected to live long. Their first child, Charles, had died at birth, much to Sir John's annoyance as he desired several male heirs to offset the high mortality rate.

The master spoke to his son. 'Come here boy!' George slowly tottered across the room and stood to attention in front of him. 'Do you like your new home?' The nanny had nervously followed George and leaned down to whisper advice in the child's ear.

George responded correctly, 'Yes, Sir John. Thank you, Sir John.'

'And what is the favourite aspect of your new life boy?'

George hesitated then solemnly said, 'The ducks Sir.'

His father sighed and crossed his arms. 'The ducks? Good god, George. What about the ships on the Menai carrying our goods? What about the 30 farms that comprise our estate? The ducks egad!' He stood and left the room with an order to his wife. 'Start his education wife; this place and my new businesses are his future responsibility.'

As soon as he had closed the door, Elizabeth opened her arms and George ran across the room to give her a loving hug. Beth curtsied an immediate goodbye as Victoria was placed in her ladyship's hands. The housekeeper left the room with tears in her eyes. "Love", as defined by the master, was all about duty and responsibility.

* * *

Beth had determined to visit her parents at the first opportunity and took the path towards Brynsiencyn that ran parallel with the straits. The two-mile walk home started on the ridge overlooking Aberpwll on the mainland. She stopped to admire the view and thank God for her life. To her left was the church of Saint Edwen, small but distinct with a square tower topped by a spire. A tranquil place since 640 AD when the Saint had founded her cell on the hillock. The adjoining parishes of Llanidan and Llandeiniol had shared the Christian church during the same period that they were the principal seat of the Druidical priesthood in Wales. The dark mounds of the ancient yew trees covered the sanguinary history of the sacrificial spot and the hills around contained numerous remains of Druidical temples, altars, henges and cromlechs. She shivered in the breeze and turned towards Caernarfon to continue homeward. To her left were large sand banks exposed by the low spring tide, a deceit waiting to be concealed by the cold sea. Four cormorants were flying line astern above the straits and taking evasive action around the single sail of the Moel-y-Don ferry. Purple sandpipers and turnstones noisily strutted across the shingle banks at the edges of the shore. As she relaxed and breathed the invisible ozone, the second path from the estate joined from her right. Owen Tudur was striding towards her and it made her heart jump. He started the conversation as they fell into step, side by side and alone for the first time since she had furtively disappeared.

'I'm sorry Beth, it was never meant to be so hard.'

She touched his arm gently as she replied, 'We're lucky Owen. We have good jobs, our health and our families.'

The steward smiled brightly at her. 'And beautiful memories,' he pointed towards the seashore, a splendour of nature.

'Very happy memories,' she smiled back.

Owen had to ask the question. 'And the child?'

She didn't inquire who had told him. She was too shocked. 'Given away Owen,' she silently shed a tear in the gathering gloom, 'but to a good home, a squire who accepts him as his own.'

'And his name?'

She hesitated before lying again. 'Owen, of course.'

They walked on in silence and parted amicably at the crossroads at the top of their village. Beth turned to the left towards her father's farm and Owen to the right and the slate miners' cottages. A physical path that was forever together but spiritually and eternally apart.

As Beth was welcomed home by her loving parents, the master sat with Elizabeth in front of a roaring fire. The mistress was sat next to her tambour having started a new embroidery. The circular wooden frame had been made in yew by local craftsman and had the finest Indian silk stretched across it. He was reading a weekly batch of *The London Gazette* sent by his brother from his home in the city.

'They have published a writ of election for the county seat here.'

'Are you interested in becoming the MP my dear?'

He ignored her and read further, skipping over the commissions section and then went straight to the royal proclamations recently made by George III.

'All this is boring as usual and the answer is no, not yet, as it is too damned expensive to rock the boat so soon.'

'So you do want to be an MP, Sir John?'

'When I am ready but business comes first and my brothers have MPs and the Treasury in our pockets, so we can wait.'

She was still thinking about Owen which prompted her next question as Sir John drained his second bottle of claret. 'What do you think about the steward now that you have met him?'

'I own him, madam, and that is all you need to know.'

She remained quiet as he drifted off to sleep and then made her escape to her bedchamber, carefully locking the bedroom door after the maid had stoked up the fire for the night.

Aeronwy Tudur was brown-haired, plump and short and the twins inside her would be doubling the unwanted extra weight for another six months. She had been "caught" at the wrong time in her cycle

David Edwards

and had immediately regretted the pregnancy as she did not love her new husband; she obeyed him... mostly. Aeronwy stood with a raised ladle admonishing Cadell for complaining he was hungry again. A blue smoky haze stayed close to the low ceiling, a pervading stench of dried cow dung that caught in the throat if one stood up. The short, thin man wore his peaked cap covering his black curly hair and the dark blue woollen suit that he would wear to work as the overseer at the quarry. He had one other suit which was reserved for Sunday best and two white shirts to go with his two pairs of black hobnailed boots. Lewis, his father-in-law, slept upright on the oak settle beside him. Both men were tired after their weekend at home, which was mostly taken up with planting their vegetable patch or dealing with their three sheep or single cow and pig. Anything to be out of the damp dark cottage and away from Aeronwy, who tended to the animals and plants as a weekday duty. But their fatigue was constant as it was a statement of their lives. She shook the ladle in Cadell's face again.

'Pheasant stew is dangerous enough without your complaints. I told you not to take the bribe at the quarry. No power on earth will restrain the Earl or steward Morgan if they knew what you had done.'

'Be quiet, damn you woman. You know nothing of men's matters.'

'I know the law my man. Only aristocrats can buy or sell game and you could be transported to Virginia for seven years. A fine way for the breadwinner to behave and me pregnant and all!'

Cadell sat pondering as she busied herself scurrying across the scraped earth floor. He scanned the room. Apart from the slate mantle engraved by Lewis to show a dozen types of ship, it was simple. An oak Welsh dresser, three chairs and a bare table set with some pewter mugs and a large enamelled jug of water that she had fetched from the communal well. He was content to be the overseer and happy he had backed Rhodri Morgan, the wily and ruthless steward of the Earl of Beaumaris. Morgan lived in Porthaethwy and attended the same chapel as Cadell. They had been friends from the age of twelve when they were both starting at the slate quarry and he owed his position to Rhodri. The Earl and Rhodri were rivals of

20

the upstart master and his bastard of a brother-in-law. He was also content in himself as he felt superior to Owen but fed-up because of his hormonal and overassertive wife. The door opened for a glimpse of dusk that didn't brighten the austere interior. Owen walked in, and with a silent nod of the head to each of them, he proceeded to light a single tallow candle which he placed on the table. Pulling out a chair he sat down as his father stirred. Lewis opened a single eye to see who had arrived. It was Aeronwy who spoke first; she wanted to know about her brother's momentous day.

'Is she as beautiful as they say, Owen?'

'Beth has always been beautiful.' She gently tapped him across the head with her ladle to obtain the truth. 'There you go then, Lady Elizabeth is an exceptional beauty sister but "above us", disdainful in a nice way.'

Lewis shifted in his seat to lean towards the warm black range as the evening augmented the damp and cold. He rarely spoke at home.

'Did they confirm you as steward, boy?'

'Yes, providing I give them my soul for eternity.' Owen laughed uncomfortably as his tad replied.

'What else do you expect from the English? Isn't that right Cadell? We exist to be kicked and piss'd upon. It is no different from when I worked in Jamaica, two years of hell and that was when I was on the white man's side!' Cadell nodded his assent. Both men detested the English invasion and the bureaucratic Anglican Church. They wanted a non-conformist chapel society and an independent Wales. They believed in the mutual support of the community, a union of minds. Both men were the first to throw coins into a widow's apron outside of their chapel after her breadwinner had died. Owen shared their sentiments, but he and the other two men of the house never agreed about anything. He decided not to cause an argument.

'It's a job, they pay well and I learn more than when I was in the quarries. That is what is important. A better income and a position of power.' Aeronwy served the stew with some hard wheaten bread made two days before and the family ate in silence. There was no further discussion about their jobs. None of the men would divulge any details as they were all in competition with each other, as men and as managers. So milking the cow, shaving using a shared cut-throat razor and reading the Bible took a silent precedence before an early night. Cadell and Lewis would be leaving the cottage at 4am and Owen an hour later. In all cases, a brief splash of the face in a bowl of water and emptying the "guzunder" in the yard would be followed by a mug of buttermilk and the long walk to work. The two slate overseers would march to the ferry and cross the Menai with 60 other men cramped in the bilges of the boat. They would then spend three hours in a wagon as it slowly bumped along the dirt track to the quarries. After four hours hard graft they would sit in the *caban* with their workers and share some lamb and potatoes washed down with a pint of ale before grafting for another four hours. After a long hard day they would then make their way to the "barracks" to sit in a dark, dank cottage with six other men and talk about their dreams and their God. The Welshmen were dour and downtrodden, as hard as the slate they worked. However, Owen had decided he wanted a better life, but his approach lacked their deep inbred resentment of the English.

Chapter 2

Llyn Peris

It was a fine morning as William Smith trotted on his grey past the high walls protecting Plas Newydd and then turned left to head down the hill towards Plas Coch. From his vantage point he could see a froth of wild cowslips cowering in the fields, ready to be picked and made into his favourite ale. Interlacing this abundance of yellow were beautiful pink anemones, white narcissi and purple violas planted by the Marquess's workers as a spring greeting for visitors to the grand house. Smith had made good time from Parys Mountain in the north of the island and was happy as the mineral surveys were encouraging. His job as agent to Sir John would be more secure if the promised riches from the copper finds were turned from theory into fact. His rewards would also be enormous from a grateful patron and the brothers.

The road was soft dirt, mended in places with gravelly sand or shards of slate, but the variance in quality between each parish annoyed the engineer intensely. He shared the master's ambition to build and own new turnpike toll roads that would be essential for their plans to succeed. The existing tracks wouldn't cope if the amount of wagons multiplied a hundred fold. A toll was preferable to each parish badly maintaining their section for a mere four days a year. Even sanctions on the parishes were unscientific to his mind. The Justice of the Peace's overseers demanded improvements to the roads by attending the local church service, where the congregation promptly blamed each other for the bad conditions. He breathed in deeply and laughed at the green peaks appearing on the horizon as he contemplated the backward nature of the area he was starting to love.

Owen was standing next to three horses in front of the main door.

'Tudur my friend, are you now awake to our new industrial situation or are you still worriting after those ignorant farmers?' Owen retained his smile.

'Smith, with your science and my practical application, I do believe that farming could be improved as well as the master's industry.'

They shook hands firmly, but Smith wanted the last word. 'Indeed steward, an area that is still to be reviewed, but if I was half as ignorant as you sir, I would still be twice the person!' Before Owen could grab his bridle to encourage the grey to rear, the agile agent had dismounted.

'So where have you been the last few weeks?'

Smith tapped his nose. 'You will be awake to the situation soon. Watch and learn steward.'

'Meaning what, Englishman?'

'Secrets Owen, secrets and the Littleton-Joneses go hand in hand.' Sir John walked out of the porch and with a curt nod to both men, he mounted his horse.

'Today is a wonderful day men, no power on earth shall restrain us.' He kicked his roan into a walk and without a backward glance he left the two friends to catch up. Smith mounted a fresh horse and they quickly followed. Admiring the landscape, the agent avidly told Owen about the ferric oxide in the outcrops of sandstone near their route, whilst Owen shared his tales about the ducks eating the mulberry cuttings and the thirty goats poisoned by eating the young fir trees planted to create a windbreak. The three men finally came abreast as they passed Saint Edwen's church to their left, perched on its mound that commanded the sea and looking extra divine with a double rainbow arched above it.

The master was ecstatic, 'Look men, even God is predicting a doubling of my fortune. The rainbows end on my new lands at Aberpwll.' The crescent of colours straddled the straits to touch the mainland where a ferry could be seen loading a flock of noisy sheep. The bleats could be heard from a mile away as Owen elaborated on their enlightened destination opposite.

'The locals call it Felinheli, as it is the Welsh word for the salt water-mill you can see near the inlet. On this side is Moel-y-Don, where the Romans burned the Druids who resisted them in 61 AD. Imagine thousands of tribesmen with their staffs raised to heaven, wild-haired, naked and with their bodies painted in the colours of a vivid nightmare as they stood holding burning torches.'

The agent smiled across at him. 'Not much different to now then Tudur!' The master could only "humph" in appreciation of the joke. He rarely spoke to his staff and when he did so it was usually to question or to order.

As the track sloped steeply towards the sea, the meadows on both sides had boundaries marked with four foot tall slates embedded like grey teeth bared between the adjacent landowners. The master asked Owen to tell him more about the Romans.

'Apparently, they were scared of the Welsh at first, but their general, Suetonius Paulinus, couldn't afford for the Emperor Nero to receive any tales of cowardice and so he goaded his troops into battle. They were vicious in their anger and cut down many of the sacred yew groves to burn the Welsh alive.'

'What a waste of good wood on this barren island, what!'

Owen didn't take offence and continued, 'This has always been a place to cross the Menai and which also hosted a battle with the English in 1282.'

The master chuckled before asking who had won on that occasion.

'A Gascon, Luke de Tany was fighting to increase King Edward I's power and had constructed a bridge of boats, but he was too impetuous and with a detachment of troops he crossed early. He depended on the sandbanks instead of his partly completed bridge. We fought the invaders and killed more than two hundred, leaving a single survivor. His error, Sir John, was not understanding the ebb and flow of the tides.'

The master looked imperiously at both men. 'In that case, it is a sound practice that I have you and Smith who do understand the tides! One day, I will introduce you to Captain Ieuan Fardol who advises us on our shipping interests. He persuaded my family to buy most of Aberpwll.'

The master reined in his horse as they swept down to the sea. To their left was a terrace of ferrymens' cottages as the trio pushed onto the phallus of land that was inserted into the vagina of the mother of Wales. Noisy oyster catchers and sandpipers poked their long beaks into the mud surrounding the landing stage where they halted to watch the ferry approach. The crossing at this point of the Menai was short but had 500 yards of hell in the central section whenever the wind roared across the strong tide. However, the start and end of the journey were sheltered by small headlands. These created the shallows where people collected mussels and samphire to supplement their diets. They could see collectors at work with wicker containers on their backs and fishermen standing by their wattle weirs as they emptied the day's herring into baskets standing on the mud. On the bank were swathes of bright green sward and lumps of natural sponge which momentarily floated into the air when disturbed by the horses' hooves. In the distance there were two ferries, the smallest was closing on them, with its tiny sail supplemented by the husband and wife crew who would start to row in the final few hundred yards. The largest ferry that held up to sixty people was only in use at peak periods and so it bobbed unmanned in the Aberpwll inlet. Smith commented quietly to Sir John.

'That is Grace Parry and her husband. They say she is more of a man than he. Owen claims they rowed all the way to Liverpool and back last year. Beware sir, she hates the English and has a foul and abusive mouth.'

'Well tell her from me, that if she insults the King or me, she will never row this route again.'

Smith went ahead to warn the crew and both the ferryman and his loud wife remained quiet during the thirty minute passage. Safely ensconced on the mainland, the men skirted the river below Aberpwll and stopped 200 yards into the valley. The two ferries were floating to their left, moored next to a small boatyard and behind the party was a steep escarpment that ran eastwards. Sir John asked the agent to explain the status quo whilst Owen listened in amazement.

'Everything on the other side of the inlet belongs to the Ashetton's Faenol estate; he has also bought some land next to yours in Llyn Peris. You own this bank and the escarpment to our rear until it reaches the main road between Bangor and Caernarfon.'

The master stared up the hill behind him as he replied, 'We will need a solution for that one day, but the first priority is to widen the inlet and create a small harbour for my ships. The pack horses with their panniers of slate can walk the extra five miles along the valley until we increase production and improve the access to the quarry.' He was staring thoughtfully at the opposite shore. 'I will ask my brothers to talk to Ashetton whilst he is in London and come to some commercial arrangement for jointly developing the harbour. It is pointless wasting money when we can work together to take on the Pennants at the opposite end of the straits.'

Smith replied quietly, so that Owen struggled to hear. 'Richard Pennant is opening up a 100-acre slate quarry about six miles inland from the inlet he bought at Bangor. He has a natural harbour similar to this and has bought a small estate alongside it, called Penrhyn.'

The master smiled. 'That is what I pay you for agent. Solid information that will mean we are not screwed damn hard in a vice. Well done, Smith.'

It was only the second compliment the agent had ever received from him. As they trotted further up the valley, Owen drew alongside his friend. 'The eye of the master does more work than both of his hands, William!'

Sir John overheard and turned to them both. 'You know Felinheli is a good name, steward. The new company that owns this area and the slate quarry is called Dinorwic, but the additional village here, we shall call Felinheli.'

Owen was on a steep learning curve. 'A new village, Sir John?'

'Indeed man, where else will my workers live? We have wharves and dry docks to build so that we can unload coal and load the slate. Later we will have a tramway from here to the quarry when production is sufficient. The cottages will increase my rental income and a couple of coaching houses will make a tidy profit from the new turnpike along the coast.' Sir John could see his steward was shocked. 'Big business, Tudur, needs big decisions. We made those years ago and now we can feed off the crumbs dropping off the high tables of the Pennants, Ashettons and the Pagets. It is all so simple, what!'

They rode for another hour until they reached the river flowing out of the Llyn Peris pass and then turned inland to face the giant valley scraped by the glacier that had slid between the mountains of Snowdon and Elidir Fawr.

'Do you know much about this area steward? Our agent claims Dinorwic has the best quality slate in the area. Easily split and in a variety of colours.'

Smith jumped in before Owen could repeat what he knew from Lewis and Cadell. 'I hope so, Sir John. The initial quarrying has been undertaken in three trial locations, which gives Mr Tudur a dozen new farms to look after.' The master turned a steely eye on Smith.

'Hope is an emotion and therefore not an acceptable situation, sir.'

Owen was learning fast. He enquired, 'I also understand you have new ideas for your farms.'

'Indeed steward, they will be modernised on Anglesey, but I doubt if you can farm anything here except sheep. Therefore, the agent had better be right about the slate; wool won't pay the damn bills!'

He naturally ruled by fear and both his men knew they would be out of work or possibly dead if they underperformed. It was customary for men with secrets to keep a dagger by their bed for protection. Owen was looking at the hills and saw they were covered in birch at their foot by the river and then gorse as the sides kicked higher. Eventually, this dwindled to tufted islands of coarse grass marooned in the bogs nearer the summits. He told Sir John his immediate thoughts. 'Sheep only sir. Nothing else will survive except for dragons.'

The master smiled and his friend laughed out loud.

William goaded him on. 'Dragons, Owen? Another Welsh fable man?'

'No fable, William. *Y Ddraig Coch,* the red dragon, was a supporter on the Tudor monarchs' coat of arms; it faced the English lion.'

The master chided him, 'You're not a nationalist are you Tudur? Have I made a mistake with you, man?'

'No Sir John, I am definitely not, but we are one people in a small country and my ancestors have used the red dragon to symbolise Wales since it was written into the Historia Brittonum in 820 AD. Before that you can read about it in Revelations chapter twelve. The dragon was even a party in the battle of the angels before Lucifer was cast out of heaven.'

The master nodded his head. 'Very apt steward. The simile between good versus evil is not lost on me. However, tell us your fable then, Tudur of the Tudors. It may help me understand you damned Welsh.' Owen gathered his thoughts as they traipsed higher up the left side of the valley leaving the sparkling river rushing below. The view was startling. In front of them was a pass fed by a dozen white waterfalls cascading off the craggy slopes, and to their rear was an expanse of sea curtailed by the sand dunes of New Borough, drawing the eye into the flat green expanse of Ynys Môn.

'The dragon symbol, according to legend, was on the battle standard of King Arthur and other ancient Celtic leaders. The red dragon fought with an invading white beast and his pained shrieks caused women to miscarry, animals to perish and plants to become barren. Lludd, who was King of Britain, went for advice to his brother Llefelys who lived in France. He told him to dig a pit here in *Eryri*, fill it with mead and finally cover it with cloth. So the dragons drank the mead and fell asleep, allowing the King to capture them wrapped in the cloth and to bury them alive. Their last roars are still heard when the wind rushes off Snowdon to chastise Anglesey. Centuries after this, another King called Vortigern tried to build a castle on the burial ground, but every night the foundations were shaken and demolished yet no one could explain why. The King's advisers told him to sacrifice a boy who had no natural father and this would resolve the problem. The boy they selected was called Merlin. On hearing that he was to be put to death to counteract the bad magic, the future wizard told the King about the two dragons. Vortigern then excavated the hill and freed the dragons to continue their fight and finally the red dragon defeated the white. Symbolically, the white Saxon English were defeated by the red Celtic Welsh. We won and then we won again against Edward I .'

The master cleared his throat. 'But now the English control and own Wales, steward.'

The rest of the journey was made in silence apart from the laboured breathing of the three horses as they ascended to the spur of land called Dinorwic and the quarry named "Elizabeth". Beneath them was the lake, Llyn Peris, and on the far shore a ruined tower which was part of Dolbadarn Castle. Alongside this ruin was the main road that joined Caernarfon with the centre of Wales and hence onwards to the Marches at Shrewsbury. The valley was quiet as this route to England was long and arduous, with poor roads and many highwaymen increasing the risks to travellers. It therefore encouraged them to use the easier but longer coastal route across North Wales to Chester and south to London. This was ideal if they were travelling to London from Ireland via Holyhead, but the river crossing at Conwy, the headland of Penmaenmawr and the ferry crossings to Ynys Môn were almost as hazardous as the Welsh mountains. It was the potential for infrastructure changes on these vital routes that was the driving force behind the Georgian English invasion.

And then there was the slate, which would roof the burgeoning cities of England as the Industrial Revolution encouraged people to migrate from the country in search of a better life. Abruptly, the riders entered a small quarry no more than 100 yards square. The hooves of the horses made the slate detritus squeak and crack under their weight.

* * *

'Tad, how are you today?' Owen had seen his father standing by the *caban* as soon as they arrived at the quarry. It was still a small working, hanging precariously on the side of the mountain, 1,000 feet above the lake and employing no more than twenty men. His father took off his bowler hat and wiped his brow as he appraised his son on his fine horse.

'Good day, steward.' He was a hard man of few words.

'Can we make Sir John and William some food and drink please tad?'

'Tell them to come in.' His father gestured over his shoulder before turning to enter the low door of the slate shed. The four men sat drinking stewed tea whilst eating hard cheese with cold mutton. The master motioned a handful of food at the agent and his overseer.

His voice was muffled as he chewed. 'What's the quality of the slate like?'

Lewis shifted the grubby scarf around his neck before answering, 'This is a rich seam, Sir John, and the slates are the best I have ever seen.'

William joined in. 'But we do have an issue on two of the farms further down the valley.'

Sir John pushed away his plate and slurped his tea. His refined manners were put to one side when with his workers. 'What issue might that be?'

William cleared his throat. 'The Earl of Beaumaris has outbid us by fifty per cent.'

The master slurped more tea and wiped the back of his hand across his mouth before answering. 'And your solution, agent?' The master was abrupt, but Lewis rescued the Englishman.

'The Earl has more money than sense, Sir John. The best slate is above us, further up the valley and the agent has secured four more options on farms in that direction.' Sir John stared hard at William. The agent was fearless in his reply.

'Indeed I have. The Earl has a nominal hold on this side of the valley in an area we don't want. He has plumped for land closer to the sea and on the opposite side. My advice is to take up the four options as soon as possible.'

The master was short. 'So?'

'So, he thinks it will be easier to transport his slate, but with a tramway from Aberpwll to here, the costs are dramatically reduced. A tramway can only be built on this side, following our route today.' The master tilted his chair.

'Therefore my agent and overseer suggest we maximise on our territory on this side. We have the most reserves, the best slate and the ideal transport in future. Am I correct?' William and Lewis tentatively nodded their heads in agreement. Lewis also pointed out that in the short term they had better access to boats on the lake that would service the pack horses taking slate to Aberpwll. 'In that case, I am happy gentlemen. Let the Earl think we have been kicked and piss'd upon, egad.'

Lewis looked at his son as he replied, 'Which leaves Owen to deal with Rhodri Morgan; that snivelling, conniving steward who works for the Earl.' Lewis thumped his fist onto the table to end the conversation.

As they ducked out of the *caban*, the master tapped Owen on his back with his riding whip. 'Remember, everything your father tells you, steward. Morgan is an enemy, whilst the Earl is my friend... at least to his face.'

They slowly walked to the edge of the cliff to watch the men working. There was a second gallery 30 feet below them on which two boys were pushing small wooden trucks laden with blocks of stone four feet square and two feet deep. They were moving them to the splitters, who sat in *gwaliau,* small and low sheds with an open sailcloth curtain ready for drawing closed in inclement weather. The tapping of the splitters' hammers was rhythmic and echoed around the quarry and merged with the cracking of slate as men walked across the debris strewn in front of the huts. The gentle first taps across the edge in three places, then the single heavier hit to the centre whilst holding a dirty cold hand to the outside to even out the pressure. Alongside were other men carefully using their dressing knives to shape the slate into tiles; a cacophony of noise with the tapping of hammers, swish of the knives and a high-pitched crackle and squeak as hobnail boots pressed onto the waste. The master watched a man with a giant crowbar thrusting himself into the air as he enticed a huge block to break away from the cliff face. The whole scene was a travesty of angulation.

'Agent, to steal a mountain, we need to adopt modern techniques. Is that agreed?'

William agreed, 'A thunderbolt from heaven might split a few hundred tons in one go.'

The master clasped his hands on his stomach as the worker swung at an angle of 90 degrees, kicking his legs vigorously to increase his purchase.

'Indeed, sir, and as I believe in God, we need to follow his example!'

The agent and overseer were confused. 'Sir John?' they said in unison.

It was Owen who appreciated what was required and as he said it, the master smiled contentedly. 'A massive charge of gunpowder might suffice instead of a thunderbolt?' Sir John turned to William and Lewis.

'Do you have drills and gunpowder for a test?' They hurried off to prove their worth. After a few minutes, Lewis was roped up and being lowered down the cliff face, clutching a hand-drill and horn of gunpowder provided by the agent. Within half an hour the explosion split a block of a hundred tons that plummeted onto the gallery floor, leaving the workers gaping in wonder until they started to clap. When the agent and overseer rejoined Owen and the master, the latter gave two final orders before they set off back to the coast.

'Make sure you perfect the technique and blast safely. I don't want a bad reputation for killing Welshmen before we have started properly.' The agent suggested that a horn was blown on each occasion and blasting only took place at nine minutes past each hour. The group agreed. 'Secondly overseer, reduce the price paid on the bargains with the men to reflect the increased speed of production. Smith can do the calculations so you can implement the cost reduction next month. Is that agreed?'

They all agreed but with a single question from Owen. 'What do you mean by "started properly" master?'

Sir John turned to him. 'Your ignorance proves that I can trust both your friend and your father, as they obviously haven't told you.' Owen gawped and so Sir John smiled as he completed the picture for him. 'Dinorwic will consist of several quarries which will feed my ships at Felinheli. We are going to compete with the Pennants, Ashettons and beat the damned upstart of an Earl. The task, gentlemen, is to create the greatest slate mine in the world.'

Owen was flabbergasted and remained silent for much of the journey home. His friend and landlord discussed tramways, improvements to roads and the new harbour with vigour and Owen listened carefully and learned a lot.

Near the entry to the Aberpwll valley they were riding on the Bangor road when they heard the horn blown by the postilion stood on the rear of an approaching coach. Trotting in front was Rhodri Morgan on his pure white steed, the much hated steward for the Earl of Beaumaris. The Plas Coch men reined to a stop and watched the coach career between the ruts, bucking and tossing as the driver maintained the crazy speed dictated by the occupants. Morgan and the coach stopped adjacent to the riders allowing the Earl of Beaumaris to alight. Edward Lloyd-Williams was dressed like a dandy in a green silk suit and with an immaculately coiffured and very high wig. He ruefully brushed some white powder off his shoulders before giving a minimal bow to Sir John.

'Greetings cousin, it must be several months since I had the pleasure at the ball in London.' Sir John doffed his hat and bowed his head in a polite and dignified response, whilst regretting his own rough appearance with mud stains on his knickerbockers.

'Indeed your lordship, what a pleasure then and what a pleasure it is now.' Owen eyed up the opposing steward. Morgan was short and thin; he had the marks of smallpox on his face and just the one eye since a fight with the captain of a wherry in Porthaethwy. They had met on rare occasions when Morgan had treated Owen with contempt, a lesser mortal working for a mere "Sir".

The Earl continued, 'We have had such a pleasant day reviewing our new land, so cheap for such riches beneath, don't you think Sir John? The farmers are so selective in their choice of landlord.' He had emphasised "selective" as a sneered but subtle insult. The master was incensed by the implication that he had lost out in some way or been shunned by the farmers.

'I hope the Earl receives great rewards from his purchases. Unfortunately, my loss is your gain, but there is little difference between business and war sir.' The words were polite but barbed, encouraging Rhodri Morgan to move his horse a few steps closer to the opposition as a show of strength. Morgan grimaced and then scowled as he touched the pistol in his waistband. Owen urged his own horse forward a pace to position the beast in front of his master's. He stared at Rhodri without expression. The deathly quiet was suddenly dispelled as the window of the coach slid down and a vision of heaven leaned forward to address the men. Lady Charlotte Lloyd-Williams was full mouthed and round faced in the Dutch style and, like her husband, she wore a huge powdered wig. Her heaving bosoms created a favourable impression on the men as she gently spoke.

'Gentlemen, I hate to bother you whilst you argue about boring old business but... time is of the essence. There have been several incidents with highwaymen on this route recently.'

Sir John jumped down from his horse and walked gallantly to the coach to kiss her ladyship's gloved hand.

'I must apologise for your delay, Lady Charlotte. Talking about land and slate are a mere trifling compared to the joy of a conversation with you.'

She smiled sweetly. 'Thank you Sir John. Please tell me, how is my distant cousin, the Lady Elizabeth? Has she settled into her beautiful new house?'

The master talked pleasantries with Lady Charlotte whilst he admired her bust close-up and pointedly ignored the other men. As he remounted his horse, her ladyship promised to visit Elizabeth and the Earl stepped back into the coach.

Rhodri drew close to Owen as it clattered away from them. 'Steward Tudur, if you need any advice on negotiating land deals or controlling farms, I would be pleased to teach you how to do it... like a child in a school.' Morgan spat as he wheeled away, but Owen had the final word.

'Indeed Morgan, when thousands of pupils are writing on our better quality and cheaper slates with their chalk, I look forward to your demotion when you become their teacher.'

The coach sped away towards the ferry near Bangor, which the Earl controlled in direct competition to Sir John's at Moel-y-Don. It was only in the middle of the straits at Porthaethwy that neither man held a monopoly. The increased sea trade through Liverpool and the new riches of merchants like the master was a constant source of antagonism between the two men. The new battlegrounds were the natural resources of North Wales and the Menai crossings, as the Irish question and the importance of Holyhead increased the profits to be made in shipping and roads. The narrowest point on the straits was at Porthaethwy where they had both acquired a patchwork of land and maritime businesses in anticipation of a future bridge. New wharves now allowed three schooners to moor and quickly unload at the narrows before the treacherous Swellies. Two years earlier the turnpike road had been completed to Holyhead, so the days when drovers made their cattle swim across the waters before driving them to market at Abergele were numbered. Equally, the axis of 500 years of English power at Beaumaris, with its castle and Justices of the Peace, was moving eastwards towards Caernarfon. Lady Charlotte talked to her husband as they rocked their way homewards.

'Do I assume you upset my cousin's husband, my Edward?'

The Earl was smiling. 'Indeed ma'am, but assume nothing that is not your business.'

She had seen many new and exciting scenes during the day on her first visit to a slate quarry, suitably named "Charlotte". She had met the overseer, Cadell, and been told he was married to Aeronwy who occasionally visited their home at Earl's Hill. She came to visit his sister called Frances who worked in the mansion as an assistant cook. Charlotte liked the cook and often consulted her about the dinner party menus. She depended on Aeronwy too as she had helped some of the family when ill, by using her skills as a herbalist.

Lady Charlotte asked another question. 'So you "stole" the Earl's prized land and are politicking by employing relatives of his top staff. Correct?'

'Madam, you wanted to come for the air and the air you have had. Do not trouble your pretty head about a man's business. Sir John is a nothing, a nobody, who is like a boil on my arse and one day he will need to be lanced.'

But Lady Charlotte was clever as well as pretty. Like Elizabeth, her marriage was convenient and loveless. All of her babies were created during the legal rapes when the Earl was drunk. Most of the time, he preferred sex with the youngest and prettiest maids. This was something he had in common with the master and their behaviour was the secret bane of both wives.

She rocked with the coach and gazed out of the window considering whether to meet with Lady Elizabeth. To have her as a friend or foe? They were related through their families in Yorkshire where both their fathers had made their money through wool. Elizabeth's dowry was reputedly two thousand guineas, half of her own. She decided to talk to both Frances and Aeronwy about her new neighbour over the next few months and then fell back into a warm contemplation of Sir John's handsome new steward.

The three tired riders could smell the salt and seaweed a mile before they arrived at the Moel-y-Don ferry. The closer they came to the straits, the louder were the calls of hundreds of seabirds heading home to shelter for the night. A raucous kerfuffle that clashed with the rooks ensconced in the tall oaks above the newly named but non-existent village of Felinheli. They could see a single light across the strait on the ferrymen's cottages, a paltry lantern fighting the dominating dusk that was settling across the water. After rowing away from the shore, Grace Parry started singing a popular sea shanty she had learned whilst working in Liverpool and surprisingly the master joined in, happy with his first day's work in his new home. Their voices were loud but quickly drifted away from the small boat and merged into the cooling night air. The words became another secret between the Plas Coch passengers. Spoken but not shared, loud in the ear but fading to nothing until another time and another day.

The men reined in their horses outside the front of Plas Coch in the remnants of twilight. A beautiful face appeared at the study window to appraise the trio. Only Owen noticed Lady Elizabeth and he held her gaze a fraction too long for politeness, before doffing his bowler hat in respect as she dipped her head behind the satin damask of the curtain. Sir John immediately went inside for his dinner and the inevitable bottle of claret and Owen prepared to walk the horses to the stables of the coach house. William put a hand on his shoulder.

'Owen, you have the capacity to be a great steward and today was the first of many new adventures, but one thing I have learned whilst in Sir John's employ is to listen carefully to what he says and do what he asks without question.'

'William, I gave him a pledge from my soul yesterday and I will fulfil it until the day I die.'

'Then you will be a famous steward even on the day you die, but remember one last piece of advice, Owen Tudur... it's what he doesn't say that you really have to listen to...' They shook hands slowly and firmly, then the Englishman went inside to join the staff for dinner in the warm kitchen, whilst the Welshman walked home deep in thought, happy in the dark with his new knowledge and oblivious to the hoots of the owls.

Chapter 3

Beaumaris

Beaumaris means "beautiful marsh" in French. The town and its castle were built in 1294 as an English stronghold on Ynys Môn and the site developed on the open marshland at the eastern end of the Menai Straits to complement Caernarfon in the west. The castle towns penning the Welsh in the middle like a flock of unruly sheep. It was a balance of power with the Menai as the scales, which was recreating itself 500 years later. However, Beaumaris thought itself special. It was a bastion of English law with access to the English markets, using assets ripped from the heart of the Welsh.

The Earl of Beaumaris was therefore a powerful hereditary title and his house at Earl's Hill had been the location of the family's home for more than a century. The architect, Samuel Wyatt, had supervised the recent rebuild bringing the property into alignment with the family's modern outlook and reinforcing their titled identities. Stonemasons charged one shilling for a day's work, but bricklayers were double the amount and so the cost of building in stone at Earl's Hill had been cheaper, especially when the limestone was quarried locally at Penmon. Bricks were also expensive and had to be transported by sea from Liverpool. So their use was avoided except where they were deemed ideal. For example, when creating the arches of the huge wine cellars beneath the mansion. Caverns filled with smuggled wine from France or rum from the Caribbean, both brought into Anglesey by small ships sailing from the offshore tax haven of the Isle of Man.

Footmen with powdered wigs strutted along the corridors of Earl's Hill and maids curtsied and bowed to them with their heads down. The real power was in the hands of the butler inside the house and the land steward outside. However, the numerous servants were ranked in strict seniority. It started with the butler followed by the head housekeeper and through the assistants of assistants, right down to the lowly scullery maids. All were contained within a distinct pecking order and had rigid job functions. Ladies maid, cook, assistant cook, chambermaid, dairy maid, scullery maid... the titles were endless but each deferred to a single superior. That person was the one immediately "above them", dulling their ambitions and keeping them in their place downstairs, whilst the Earl and his family maintained their superiority upstairs. The butler told everyone that their heart should be where their station was – amongst the poor. They were chattels; slaves akin to the Negroes that learned men, like Wilberforce, were endeavouring to give back their humanity. The Welsh would need a similar champion of their rights and for all age groups as the Earl was not alone in encouraging the recruitment of children as young as 10 years old, their families desperate for any measly extra income. He claimed that cheaper was financially sensible, but invariably they were pretty girls groomed to meet his insatiable needs. He would threaten the abused girl afterwards, saying they would lose their jobs if they told anyone about the brutal sex. He sometimes gave them a shilling to buy something nice for Christmas, and to others, he would imply that without references there could be no job within 100 miles. The majority eventually became pregnant and abandoned their child or killed it in shame before joining the ranks of the prostitutes in Liverpool or Chester. A few girls followed the law and were repatriated to their parish of birth, but many parishes objected to caring for the waifs and strays because of the overbearing costs. Lady Charlotte knew what he did, but her own position was just as dependent on sex.

An heir was required and all of her four sons had died young. He raped her occasionally, but more for fun than to procreate, and so she had no more than ten years left before she too would become a superfluous subject.

The seafront at Beaumaris was changing. Sash and dormer windows adorned the five storey Georgian houses that stood tall, the "John Nash" Regency houses were the latest building rage. The rich English and migrant Irish were anticipating improved access by road and sea and were investing heavily in the town. Inside the houses they decorated the tall rooms with fashionable pictures purchased from the newly formed Royal Academy. Turner and Constable gained a following and hung safely in the county town with its garrison of soldiers, Justices of the Peace, and a gaol. It was invariably the silver that was guarded by a servant armed with a pistol each night. So Beaumaris was a sophisticated place to live, with the gentry meeting at the new town hall to prepare addresses to the King about the important events of the time. The two MPs for Anglesey courted the attention of the mayor, two bailiffs and twenty-one burgesses who retained their power by co-option instead of an election. So Sir John had inserted himself into the middle of an Establishment power base as the two MPs were his competitors, the Earl and the Marquess.

Edward Lloyd-Williams and his steward were sat in the library overlooking the extensive grounds of Earl's Hill that rolled right down to the sea. The sun streamed directly through the tall windows and blinded them from seeing the verdant mountains dominating the village of Aber and the orange-yellow expanse of Lavan Sands exposed by a retreating tide. The Earl had learned that Sir John and the Ashetton family were brokering a deal over a new harbour at Aberpwll and was raging against their connivances.

'Damnation on these incomers, Morgan. "New money" upstarts like Sir John make my blood boil. Strewth and zounds man, why didn't you inform me before?'

Rhodri kept his head down as he wheeled, 'The Plas Coch butler is an old hand at selling information, master. He wants more money for each snippet and by trusting the scullery maid as a messenger, he is nervous that he may be discovered by the new steward. Of course we could try and bribe him too?'

The Earl stood and walked around the huge room admiring the shelves full of leather-bound books. 'No, not the steward. They think their money gives them power Morgan, but we have controlled this area for the English aristocracy since the first castle. My god, the next thing they'll want is to challenge for MP. The Pagets and I have had an understanding for years about that.' Rhodri stayed silent and let the Earl rage. He knew the long term war would be over the potential bridge at Porthaethwy as it affected all of their trade. That was why the Earl had made him live above the new warehouse on the wharf, a representative whom people could turn to, and of course sell information. He didn't know what was happening in the Treasury or Parliament in London as the Earl's cronies legally battled with Sir John's brothers and illegally threatened or bribed as necessary. The Earl stopped pacing next to his large mahogany desk and placed a hand on the red leather surface with its gold inlay.

'You must do everything possible to thwart these upstarts on my island. I don't need the details and if one of your...' he hesitated and decided not to use the word henchmen, 'if one of your fellows ends up in the Justices, give me the nod and I will ask my friends to acquit him.'

'And if it is one of the opposition, like Tudur?'

'Tell me as soon as possible Morgan, and I will bury him; that is legally, at least for the moment.' The steward was dismissed and Lady Charlotte gently closed the library door and went back to the quiet of the study.

A few days later and the same topic was under discussion in Sir John's study. Owen sat being given his orders and the person secretly listening in this time was Roger Nash, the butler.

'My brothers have completed some politics in London and will send me some vital documents for signature in three days' time. I want you to take our coach with some men for protection and meet "The Mail" at Tyn-y-Groes near Conwy. Your job is to ensure the letters reach me intact on the final leg of the journey. Understood?'

'Yes Sir. I will leave on Friday with the coachman, Andrew and Wirion with your approval. We can stay at the inn on Friday night and then return during Saturday in the daylight, but it will depend on the arrival time of the coach from London.'

'That sounds safe, steward but I must reinforce the following three things. Firstly, return home via the Sychnant Pass as the one around the head at Penmaenmawr is too tricky with a coach and horses. Secondly, stay on the mainland and cross the straits at Aberpwll on my ferry. Thirdly, you must guard the documents with your life.'

Owen asked a final question. 'It seems like you want me to avoid our competitors and watch out for any skulduggery. Is that correct Sir John?'

'Correct. I have my reasons, steward and you must trust me as per your pledge. I am not paranoid in this matter. My brothers have experienced two burglaries over the last six months at their houses in Wapping and have also had to dismiss three of their staff. Many of the power brokers in Parliament are linked to the English landlords in North Wales. The country is still poor after the Seven Years' War and therefore lawless with a relatively weak King.'

Owen nodded. 'I will be careful, Sir John.'

The same afternoon, Lady Elizabeth had a brief first meeting with Dean Thomas Runcie who controlled three of the six Anglican deaneries on the island. She described him to Beth later that day, as dull, dark and obese with an unsightly face and a bald head. She had agreed that he would provide a service for the family and household every Sunday at 10am in Saint Edwen's Church. This was to be a special favour for Sir John. The extra contribution to the deanery funds was not discussed as the concept was considered vulgar, but Dean Runcie knew it would be forthcoming. Therefore, he was pleased with himself as he left the house, accompanied on his way by the butler. This had been anticipated by Morgan, and the Dean actively encouraged the butler to trust and need him, by preying on his fear of hell and damnation.

'My friends in Beaumaris inform me that you are a God-fearing Anglican and a firm supporter of the King and Whig party. Is that right, Mister Nash?'

Nash stopped in the front porch of the house and closed the heavy door to the main house behind them. 'I am fearless in defending the rights of certain individuals and their friends, Dean Runcie.'

'That is excellent news, Nash as we share many sentiments. In fact, a common bond during my travels throughout Anglesey.'

The butler was wringing his hands as he replied, 'You must know everything that happens across your parishes, all the way from Beaumaris to Holyhead. An envious knowledge and very rewarding in heaven, sir.'

The Dean nodded sagely as he responded. He firmly grasped the butler's shoulder, 'A reward in heaven? Indeed Nash, and sometimes also on this earth. I spread the word of God and God is everything to me. God rewards me for keeping some things privy. An all-knowing God is essential for our world to function properly. Do you understand Nash?' He received a nodded affirmation. 'In which case, let us take a turn around the lake. I find the fresh air helps me to think more clearly and words disappear into the ether. What do you say man?' Roger Nash was weighing up how much money he could demand for his information. He knew the Dean was a power broker and had close contacts with the rich in Beaumaris but didn't want to scare off the potential purchasers with too high an asking price.

He replied positively, 'I do believe a walk will help us understand God's requirements better.' The two men left the house to stroll around the pretty lake, giving the butler time to outline the master's plan for two days hence. The Dean decided the information could be valuable and therefore, after promising to reward the butler well, he sped in his gig as fast as possible to Earl's Hill. By the time he reached there, it was three o'clock in the afternoon and the Earl was seated with Lady Charlotte taking high tea in the drawing room. The butler preceded the Dean to forewarn the Earl about his unexpected visitor. The urgency of the unannounced visit was emphasised quietly into his master's ear. Edward Lloyd-Williams stood to shake the Dean's hand, whilst Lady Charlotte remained seated. However, she did acknowledge him with a slight nod of her head.

The Earl spoke first. 'Dean Runcie, what a pleasure to see you again. Please sit and take some tea.' They made small talk for ten minutes; about the Wesleys and the growth of Methodism in South Wales. About the supposed charity of the New Testament instead of the harshness of the Old. The Dean supported the Earl's dislike of the increase in numbers of non-conformists and their inveigling into education by expanding the Sunday schools in the new chapels. However, Lady Charlotte lamented that too few children were in state schools. She wanted education to be extended throughout the island for the prime purpose of teaching English. This edict was slowly being applied in the bigger mainland towns such as Bangor, where many children were learning by rote as they spoke no English. Any pupil caught speaking Welsh in class was given "the Welsh knot" to hang around their neck and punished at the end of each day with the cane or belt.

The Earl surprisingly softened his stance on the non-conformists. 'The new Minister on Anglesey, Jenkin Evans seems to be a gifted speaker, Reverend. Have you heard of him?'

'Yes, a man of principle but in the wrong religion; a Calvanistic Methodist who thinks "we" Anglicans are too slow in reforming The Church. Damn impertinence, I say.' The Earl excused himself from her ladyship and led the Dean into his study. Rhodri was waiting for them, having also been tipped off by the butler.

The Earl reiterated, 'Evans and his like are useful to us, Dean, although of course I wouldn't trust her ladyship with that information. The non-conformists hold sway with the workers, the common people, and I will use this religious fervour to help our cause. However, please be assured that I will also be supporting you.' He made the Dean feel important, 'we undoubtedly value all your guidance in every way. Is that understood?'

'Yes Sir.' The Dean felt mildly chastened.

'The Methodists do believe in salvation of the soul via personal knowledge of God through the Bible. The problem is they are all nationalists.'

Rhodri expanded on The Earl's view. 'And nationalists number eight out of ten of the local population which we want to control. Nationalists don't like the Tories, for example Sir John, and we can use their hate to further the cause of the Whigs and our businesses.' Dean Thomas Runcie was only worried about his power base and personal fortune. Therefore, The Earl's support was invaluable. Quickly he briefed them both about the conversation with Roger Nash. Rhodri carefully watched the Earl and saw him turn towards the window, inviting his steward to do his dirty work.

Rhodri spoke. 'I think it is important to wheedle further into Sir John's little mind. You will be well rewarded for this information if it proves valuable and you can divide the spoils with Nash as you think fit.'

The Dean smiled; he felt wanted again. 'Not only in heaven I trust?'

'No my good sir. Man needs to exist on this damned earth and useful information can be extremely profitable.'

'Indeed steward, we cannot live by bread alone.'

Rhodri had a further thought. 'In the meantime, a little smoke screen will pay dividends, so we shall court the non-conformists with their nationalistic views and channel their wrath onto the Littleton-Joneses.'

The Earl commented disingenuously. 'Whatever happened to God in all of this, Morgan?'

He replied, whilst maintaining eye contact with the Dean, 'God is always around us but money isn't'. The Dean knew The Church was founded on profits from both the good and the evil wishes of the English landlords and their whims constantly changed, thus requiring a flexible church. He didn't care where the money came from, provided he maintained his position controlling half the parishes on the island. Maybe one day, he would be promoted to a growing city and become an Archdeacon, but only if he was successful. He had already decided that God could take care of the men's sins, when or if they reached heaven. Rhodri led the Dean outside to his gig and then returned to consult with his master.

The Friday morning start for Tyn-y-Groes was delayed until 10am, as Sir John wanted to make a final inspection of his men and the coach. He marched in front of Duncan, silly Elis and Andrew and gave them their last instructions as they stood to attention inside the coach house. He then motioned Owen to walk outside alone to inspect the coach. The giant leaf springs creaked as Sir John mounted the two steps. He motioned Owen to join him from the tilted interior.

'I wanted to show you something, steward.' He leaned between his legs and turned a carved rose, set within a briar that protruded slightly from the oak frame of the seat. A secret compartment about a foot square, silently slid open above his head. 'The men need to be made aware of the potential danger as you leave Tyn-y-Groes but not aware of this. So one last instruction. There are five letters in the mail pouch you will collect at Conwy. They are all addressed to me, but one will have a capital "B" at the end of my name. This one alone should be hidden in the compartment in total secrecy before you leave for home. Defend this document with your life. The rest are expendable and if you place this inside the mail pouch, it may divert attention if found.' He handed Owen a small leather purse. Inside were ten guineas. 'Use them as a bribe if required.' The master squeezed out of the door and marched swiftly back to the house via the small bridge. On the second floor a curtain twitched as Roger Nash confirmed that the coach and the guards had departed on time. He would send Jenifer the maid to visit her sister in Porthaethwy and she could leave a message with Rhodri on her way.

The outward journey over the Sychnant Pass and on towards Conwy was uneventful. The rock lanes were quiet, echoing the backward nature of North Wales. Silly Elis sat inside with Owen but rarely spoke and Andrew stood in his postilion finery perched outside on the rear, and therefore couldn't converse with Duncan who was driving. At the start of the pass Owen noticed a sign on one of the Inns above Penmaenmawr. It read, "before you venture hence to pass, take a good refreshing glass." After the coach had crawled up to the col at two to three miles an hour, it dawned on Owen that the lower parts of the valleys were perfect places for highwaymen to attack. The most dangerous mix would be a dark evening, the cover of trees and a slow moving target. He touched the pistol hidden in a pocket of his long greatcoat. He had never used one in anger but had practised with it the day before. He had also made sure that Andrew had a short cutlass and Elis and Duncan were equipped with bludgeons. He turned to look at the view back towards the Menai, appreciating the stunning beauty before the coach plunged down towards Conwy. His heart rate increased as this was the most dangerous part of their outward journey. Many coaches went out of control if they gathered too much speed on the rough road. However, Duncan was an expert driver and guided them safely down before taking the route south alongside the River Conwy. At this turning point, was another inn and Owen noticed a second sign. "Now you're over, take another, your drooping spirits to recover." He laughed and presumed the landlord must own both premises. By dusk, the three men sat in the inn at Tyn-y-Groes in front of a roaring fire, supping ale and eating a filling meal consisting of potatoes with a rack of lamb. Owen left the others to drink themselves into a stupor and went to bed early. His last thoughts before sleep were about the contents of the letter marked "B". He imagined it was about slate or shipping, but eventually he turned on his side and murmured to himself. 'There is no reason in an English mind. The Welsh must surely do and die.'

Mail coaches were a novelty and only slowly replacing the post boys on horseback. The economic advantages of moving a large quantity had outweighed the security issues as a coach was much easier to attack than a brave and fast horseman. The pickings were also better for the highwaymen as the passengers invariably carried valuables. The party took delivery of the post about five in the afternoon as the mail coach had been delayed by a landslide near Betws-y-Coed. It was Owen's decision to leave immediately rather than stay another night at the inn, but it would mean an ascent of the pass in the dark. He decided that four armed men were more than a match for a highwayman and so he secreted the "B" document in its compartment and placed the ten guineas in the leather satchel that contained the remaining four letters.

They crawled up Sychnant and into the dusk which soon became a starlit night. Orion's belt was high enough to point to a bright Sirius that was just above the horizon. Andrew carried a flambeau to light their way but was forbidden to use it by Owen. The postilion also had a six foot long pole to deter any highwaymen, but it was mainly used to measure the depth of puddles. All the men remained quiet on the climb as they listened to the horses snorting as they drew their laboured breaths. After an hour, they heard hooves catching up with them from the road below and behind. Silly Elis immediately jumped out of the door and clambered up the side of the coach to join Andrew on the rear platform. The two men faced towards the shadow of the approaching lone rider. The unwelcome escort maintained a distance of 100 yards and thus made all the men nervous. Elis whispered over-loudly.

'It must be alright lads, highwaymen always stops coaches from the front and say "stand and deliver!"' It was the wrong time to be silly and his compatriots ignored the comment by hushing him to remain quiet. As the dirt track crossed a small wooden bridge the coach stopped dead, throwing everyone forwards and causing immediate panic. No matter how much Duncan whipped the horses it seemed as if the brake had stuck on. They were all staring back at the horseman in fearful anticipation when a second stalker noisily joined him from their front making the horses snort in fear. As Owen turned to look forwards, he felt rough hands grab him around his neck and he was brutally pulled out of the window. The man pulling was huge, bigger than Elis Wirion and dressed in wet black clothes. As the robber pinned Owen to the dirt, it dawned on the steward that the man had been waiting in the stream under the bridge. Owen could see the logs that had been pushed under the front wheels, as they lay a few feet from his face and then he passed out as a cudgel was smashed hard across the rear of his skull. Elis immediately jumped down to grapple with the giant as the highwayman at the rear closed in on Andrew, but Elis was too late to prevent the blow to Owen's head, which came from a slight man who had been bent double beneath the coach.

'My Owen!' Elis shouted loudly in frustration as the giant turned to meet him, wary of the bludgeon held high above Wirion's head. Before Elis could level the man, the ear splitting sound of a pistol sounded immediately behind Elis. Half turning in fear, he saw Andrew grasping his cutlass but now on his knees with his heart blown out. The postilion's demise allowed the highwayman to prance forward and club Elis over the head, ensuring he fell next to Owen. Duncan, the old soldier, sat calm and still but gripped the reins tight in his anger. There was a pistol held to his head by a fourth man and a muffled voice sounded in his ear. He wouldn't have seen the face even if he had been stupid enough to look. It was covered with a dark hood made more sinister by the slits for the eyes. The highwayman spoke slowly.

'I am going to keep this pistol to your head until the moment you wish to die. That moment may never come; it depends on your actions. Get down slowly and fetch the mail satchel.' Duncan moved towards the coach door; he wasn't scared of death or the robbers, but he wanted to survive to save his friends who lay inert in the mud. Carefully, he handed over the mail and noted the positions of the four men in the ambush party. Their leader was small and thin and deliberately kept at a distance but was obviously controlling the team in a voice too quiet to recognise. The satchel was thrown to this man who went behind the body of the coach to light a candle and examine the contents. Happy with his findings and careless because of the ten guineas inside the satchel, he immediately called his men off. The last thing Duncan saw were all four galloping towards the summit of the pass and the road to Bangor.

The coachman went to Andrew first. He had seen a lot of death in his career, but the unassuming Negro's last smile upset Duncan as he gripped his hands, and then he was gone with a final splutter that sprayed the coachman's face with blood. He wiped it off with his sleeve and then moved across to Elis who was now regaining consciousness.

'Get up you big oaf.' He leaned down and pulled him to his feet.

Elis was always a master of the obvious. 'That bastard giant kicked and piss'd on me, Duncan. Then that bastard came from behind. The bastards.' Elis slowly realised where he was and saw his mentor lying to one side. 'Owen, are you dead Owen? Speak to me.'

Duncan took over. 'You idiot, let me pass and make yourself useful by putting Andrew's body on the floor of the coach.' Silly Elis stood gawping, tears were pouring down his cheeks. He was still a child in his mind and couldn't understand death. 'Move man, get the body inside now!' He moved reluctantly and gently grasped Andrew to lift him into the coach, giving time for Duncan to crouch by Owen and check for a pulse. He checked again holding two fingers to the steward's neck as he could feel nothing on his wrist. If it was there at all, it was weak and so he put his ear close to Owen's mouth. 'Elis be quiet damn you.' Elis stood quietly and watched the shadowy figures ten feet away from him. He was still crying like a baby.

'Bastards, it was my fault, my poor Owen.'

Duncan hissed at him. 'I said be quiet.' After a few seconds that seemed like minutes, he could feel faint breathing on his cheek. Wrapping his neck scarf around the wound he motioned Elis to help and between them they moved the steward onto a seat in the coach. Elis removed the logs that chocked the wheels whilst Duncan whipped the horses into motion and restarted for the col. The coachman remembered the master's instructions and so he didn't stop as he thrashed the horses all the way back to Plas Coch. If Owen died, he was following orders. It was daybreak as the coach careered down the avenue towards the house and the master emerged as soon as he heard the approach of hooves. Elis and Duncan carried Owen into the house and placed him on a bed in the attic. Duncan despatched Elis to fetch Aeronwy as fast as possible, whilst he and Siân made Owen comfortable and cleaned the wound at the back of his head. She was white with worry.

'How bad is it Duncan?' She never called him that, always Thomas. She had an arm around Duncan's neck in a gentle and caring caress.

'He'll be lucky to live Miss Jones. Can you see the dent in the skull? If there are any fragments in the brain... then he is a dead man.' Her grip tightened on Duncan's arm in sympathy. They both liked the steward. The master stumped up the stairs to join them.

'Coachman! My study, now!' Duncan explained what had happened before being ordered to move the coach and dispose of the body. The master showed no sentiment and the coachman expected none. A dead Negro was unimportant and stewards were replaceable. People were used to a short life, caressing their mortality and believing in God. Sir John waited until the door was closed before pulling the secret letter from under a pile of franks in his desk drawer. After replacing the pre-paid postal envelopes, he scanned through the sets of deeds and agreements relating to Porthaethwy and also the land on the opposite bank of the Menai and onwards towards Bangor. His brothers had covered every contingency if there was ever a new bridge or turnpike in the area and secured the support of the right politicians. The bribes would be insignificant compared to the riches the family would earn. He leaned back in his high-backed leather chair and clapped his hands together with glee; at last they had a stranglehold on the development of Anglesey. Taking the strip maps out of his desk drawer, he looked at the current road leading south from Holyhead and then he followed the potential routes towards England. All the business questions were answered, but who had attempted the robbery? He traced his finger from the Sychnant Pass to Lavan Sands and the ferry across the straits to Beaumaris. The slight leader of the robbers could easily have been the Earl's steward. If Owen lived, he would instruct him to bribe the ferrymen and confirm it was the Earl's men led by Rhodri Morgan. It suited him that his man would hate the Earl's steward, that is, if Owen survived.

It was three days before Owen regained consciousness. Aeronwy used all her skills to help him. Feverfew to bring down the high temperature, laudanum to ease his pain as he started to toss and turn and extract of willow bark to reduce the inflammation and swelling of his brain. The natural remedies had been passed down through her mother and grandmother and they kept him alive. Duncan often visited and was the one who strapped him to the bed with leather thongs to prevent him from hurting himself with his unconscious tossing and turning. Siân came and cried, her tears diluting the chicken broth she fed him on occasion. The master and his mistress left him to die. He was just a servant. Two weeks elapsed before he started walking again and immediately he was summoned to see Sir John.

'I trust you are ready to resume your duties?' Owen was not.

'Yes Sir John, I will start again tomorrow.'

'Excellent man, you protected our interests... thank you.' The master moved swiftly on. 'Do you know who it was?'

'I'm sorry, Sir John, it was too dark.'

'I think it was the Earl's men and the steward was their leader. Send someone across the ferries from Beaumaris to Lavan Sands a few times this week and give them five guineas to grease a few palms. That should give us our proof.'

Owen nodded his assent. 'I'm sorry about the other letters being taken. I hope it doesn't affect the slate project sir.'

The master grunted. 'Slate is cheap and common, steward; there are more important things to develop.'

'Do you mean to develop the Roman silver or lead mines?'

'No my countrified steward, power and money are tied to strategy and infrastructure: bridges, shipping rights, roads... all lead to the future. I have no interest in the past.' The master downed a glass of port in two gulps and laughed. Owen was appalled by the master's lack of mercy and compassion; Andrew had died and he had lost valuable letters and come close to death. Elizabeth entered the study and sat next to Owen. She seemed cold and short towards him at first.

'Are you recovered Mister Tudur?'

'Yes thank you ma'am.'

'Excellent, in that case perhaps you can go and see Beth. She sent a message via her father to say she was ill and in bed at the farm. I need her back as soon as possible.'

Owen was disillusioned enough to comment. 'Life is cheap, Lady Elizabeth.'

She didn't take it as an insult, instead she shocked him. 'Not to everyone, certainly not to everyone.' She looked him in the eyes until he stood in embarrassment and left. The master continued to pour glasses of port down his throat and she watched in disgust.

'I am going upstairs to change for dinner, Sir John, please excuse me.' He lurched to his feet and followed her up the wide stairs, but instead of staggering into his own bedroom he followed into hers. She gritted her teeth as he came behind her and placed his hands on her bosom. She was unable to resist as he turned her round and pushed his wet stinking lips onto hers.

'You are a rare beauty, Elizabeth, soft and supple.' His hands lifted her three skirts and underskirt and his fingers found her through the crotchless drawers. Thrusting her back onto the bed, he fumbled his penis out of his trousers and drove it up her. The rape took no more than a minute as he ejaculated into her dry and damaged vagina. The semen and blood were mixed as they dripped onto the blue satin bedspread. And then he left to finish his bottle of port. Elizabeth slowly turned onto her front and crawled up the bed to the pillows. Burying her head she poured tears. It was the first time he had raped her in the new home, taking advantage of the absence of her head housekeeper. The master wanted another son as did the Earl. Lady Charlotte and Lady Elizabeth had a common cross to bear and they bore it in secrecy and with dignity, as required by their peers. The servants in both houses knew, of course, and they also knew about the masters abusing the young girls on their staff. One such person recently abused at Earl's Hill was Frances, the assistant cook, and Cadell's sister. She was tall and thin, blonde and ugly. A gawky girl of 22 years with a pockmarked face, a legacy of smallpox. When she contracted the disease she was working for the Pennants on the opposite side of the estuary and was immediately sacked. Her family had reluctantly taken her home to Llangefni and kept her quarantined in a small damp outhouse that belonged to their neighbour, the wool carder. That was how she had met Aeronwy and it was Aeronwy's talent that helped her through the illness and saved her life. Therefore, when they had met socially at the chapel in Porthaethwy, it was inevitable that her brother Cadell would also meet Aeronwy. It only took a year before they were married. So Frances had gained new employment at Earl's Hill with excellent experience to her credit, and a pockmarked face that ensured she was "clean" enough to employ. But she was too young to be head cook and therefore became the assistant cook. Since then, she had always helped Lady Charlotte plan her menus. She also introduced Aeronwy to Lady Charlotte and therefore food, medicine and slate gave three close ties between the Edward Lloyd-Williamses and the Tudurs. It was via Frances that Owen confirmed the robbery was masterminded by the Earl. It was also via Frances that he knew the Earl was courting the non-conformists. The maid stoking the fire had repeated some of the conversation she had overheard when Jenkin Evans had visited Earl's Hill. He was the new Methodist Minister at the chapel in Llanfairpwll; an inspiring speaker who was trained in Bala. The Minister was a formidable sight. Six foot three with a white beard and receding hair, he never wore a dog collar, just a normal white shirt and black woollen suit. Jenkin had found God after 20 years of working in the slate quarries. He was the essence of fire and brimstone on Ynys Môn; a new breed spreading the word of God and a nationalist, secretly conspiring to give the workers more rights via a Union. The Earl had been condescendingly addressing Evans.

'I think you need to spread the word, Minister and maybe I can help. A new chapel here and there, a new Sunday school, help for your poor. I give you a little help and you can brief me about the workers in my "friends" little businesses.' Rhodri stood and came close to Evans; he dropped a bag of crowns into the Minister's jacket pocket.

Evans talked with a deep, melodious voice. 'I will be glad to spread the word. My only priorities are my people, so I thank you for your aid, sir.' The Earl was pleased with their new understanding.

'And you can help guide the nationalist non-conformists in the "right" direction for me?'

The Minister stroked his long beard. 'I presume that guiding path is away from Beaumaris or the Earl's enterprises?'

'You have the wisdom of Jesus himself, Minister and I have no doubts the flock will follow the right example set by their shepherd.'

'In that case, to help spread the word of God, we must do whatever we possibly can.' The two men shook hands and Rhodri showed the Minister out. They were both quickly followed by the maid who went downstairs to tittle-tattle, making her feel important in her thankless position for one brief moment.

Chapter 4

Upstairs and Downstairs

The glorious summer had passed quickly at Plas Coch. The master was constantly busy and spent more time in Liverpool or London than in his new home. Owen gradually recovered his strength and spent the long sunny days visiting the tenants' farms and William Smith devoted his waking hours to developing the plans for Dinorwic and Felinheli. The Menai and work became natural barriers between the two friends. William was constantly travelling, but he told Owen very little. Somewhere in the north of Anglesey; South Wales or Cornwall; a meeting with Ieuan Fardol and the three Littleton-Jones brothers in Liverpool. There were still secrets between the English and the Welsh.

November was the ninth month of the old Roman year, which begins in March. The title "blood month" alluded to the custom of slaughtering the cattle on Martinmas to ensure there was sufficient meat to last the winter. The culling was inevitable on Anglesey as there was insufficient feed to keep all of the cows alive through the darkest months. However, Sir John had decided to plant turnips in the following year to provide the cattle with winter feed. He believed this would increase the profits from his estate. This was a new concept introduced from the south of England and was his first order to Owen in an attempt to modernise the estate farms. The year of 1767 had been too busy to start cultivating turnips, firstly because the farmers needed to prepare the poor soil by spreading shell sand transported all the way from Red Wharf Bay. Sometimes, they also added local lime and in both cases, the tasks were extremely labour-intensive. Secondly, Sir John wanted more common land enclosed, depriving the nationalistic locals of free grazing for their solitary pig or cow. This was disastrous for the villagers as they relied upon these beasts to feed their families. The natives were angry and their anger had to be assuaged by the land steward. He promised they would share in the success of the larger farms as new ways were adopted. A long term bribe, which they reluctantly accepted from an honest man who was "one of their own".

As the chill grey winter lay on the land, Beth became ill again. She had suffered from various malaises all summer, but on this occasion had taken to her bed at her parents' farm, much to Lady Elizabeth's annoyance. The butler had been given extra duties out of necessity and he constantly grumbled about it. That was why he was alone with the maid called Jenifer on November 11th, the beginning of winter according to the Romans and celebrated as Saint Martin's day on the north coast of Ynys Môn. Jenifer was bending over the mistress's bed changing the sheets, as her ladyship was due home from Liverpool. Roger Nash watched her bottom wiggle, and persuaded himself she was trying to entice him. He put his hands in his pockets and started to feel himself.

'Make sure you keep your mouth shut whenever I ask you to do something girl.' She turned and bobbed to him.

'Yes sir, I never tell "no one" about them messages.' He smirked.

'That's the way then. Are you happy doing things for me, earning those extra pennies, Jenifer?'

'Of course, sir.' He sidled closer as she tucked and pulled at the sheets. Feeling his presence, she moved adeptly towards the head of the bed to attend to the pillowcases. Now he was glad Beth was ill. Looking after the maids had some benefits.

'What's wrong with the Cadwallader woman?'

This time she didn't turn around. 'She has the cough they say. You know, like it might be consumption or summat.'

'No wonder Lady Elizabeth doesn't want her around. Damned nuisance though, it means I have to chase after you maids to make sure you do your jobs properly.' He came closer and spanked her bottom hard. 'Seems like I need to keep you in line, Jenifer. A nice name darling; I believe it means a friend of peace.' He softened his tone. 'All to keep the peace, my little Jenny penny.' He turned her around and pulled her close. She quickly tucked her chin onto her ample chest but could still smell the alcohol on his breath. 'I asked you girl, are you happy with the extra money I give you?' She nodded silently as he fondled her breasts, slipping his hands beneath her white apron. Bending slightly, he forced her to kiss him and reached lower to pull up her skirt and two petticoats. Pushing her back on the bed he forced himself up her and started to thrust. To his delight she was wet and welcoming and started to return his deep kisses as she writhed under him. They both grunted as they came together after a few minutes. She wanted the sex and he was rewarding her well.

'After all,' she thought, 'one cock was the same as another.'

The butler buttoned his trousers after wiping his penis on the clean sheet. 'Remember, say nothing and do what I say or you'll die, yes?' After she replied affirmatively, he gave her a final order. 'And change those sodding sheets again.' He turned and imperiously walked out of the room. Jenifer, the peacemaker shrugged and carried on working. A few extra shillings a year, occasional sex and an odd message to Rhodri Morgan. She believed she was truly a friend of peace, but her deluded actions would fuel a war.

Crimson creepers were like a splash of blood on the front walls of the house and the stone slabs leading to the gravel drive were covered with slippery green algae after weeks of drizzle. The cook was outside enjoying her freedom as she gathered toadstools with Catrin, the second scullery maid. She was day dreaming about

Duncan Thomas whom she had by now secretly met on a couple of occasions.

'Catrin, you can pick the pink ones but not the orange and yellow sulphur tufts.' The maid was a pleasant girl, small and dumpy with brown hair. She was good company on any food gathering trips and was always preferred to Jenifer, who was blonde and bolshy, prettier but loud-mouthed. Catrin was a harder worker and always interested in whatever she was doing.

'Mrs, can I pick the blue-black ones, them over there, growing up that beech tree?'

Siân walked across to look at the pretty species. She put a hand on the maid's shoulder, 'No my lovely, but I think we have enough for tomorrow's breakfast. Sir John and his wife are due back, so I thought we could prepare them a special treat.' They fell in step, side by side as they trudged home. The bramble leaves were brown and the blackberries in the hedgerows had all been picked or sat decomposing on sharp serrated stems. Tall brush-like heads of rose-bay willow herb moved gently in the breeze, shaking their seeds onto the damp ground beneath.

Catrin looked at the cook. 'I like it when Beth is here and in charge; the English can stay away, especially the snobby mistress.' The cook mentored her younger colleague.

'Unfortunately, Beth is very ill. The steward sent Aeronwy to see her last week, so we may have to cope with extra nasty Nash.'

'He's a bastard, Mrs. Takes advantage when Beth ain't around. An English bastard, unlike our nice Mr Tudur.' She was aggrieved. 'Roger the dodger feels my arse he does, and even makes me take the slops out. That's not me job, Mrs.'

'I know lovely, but without a butler the house would stop functioning and all the butlers I have known, have all been bastards. But don't resent the master and Lady Elizabeth. I have seen much worse in my time.'

Catrin was mischievous. 'Does you like our Owen Mrs, or is you fancying Duncan more?'

The cook turned away to look at the bare hedgerow plaited with silver spiderwebs. 'Who wouldn't like him? And his name is Mr Tudur.'

They walked slowly and enjoyed the sun shining in haloes through the half-bare oak trees. A thrush sang sweetly on a leafless bough and tomorrow was Sunday, a day to wear their best clothes and attend Saint Edwen's with the rest of the servants and estate's farmers. A chance to peruse the "available" young men and an opportunity to dream wishful fancies.

Sunday was dry and warm enough for the entire congregation to walk to church, including the incomers. Owen stood outside the gates with the rest of the household as they waited to enter, in respect for the Littleton-Joneses. The butler and steward stood to one side from the rest and casually watched the Paget family enter through the private gate that led to Plas Newydd. Nash nudged Owen in the ribs. 'Heard the rumours steward?'

'Sorry, Mr Nash. I don't know what you mean.'

'Connubial infidelity, Welshman.' The term was used as a slur.

Owen turned and leaned close to the butler. 'And your point is?'

The butler nodded towards the Pagets. 'Common knowledge. Sir John and the Earl are both "tupping" the pretty daughter called Isabel, the one in yellow. A woman shared is a woman bared, I say.' Owen motioned to him to stop, but he ignored him. 'Apparently, she can't go without it, unless it's several times a day.' Nash was smirking.

Owen placed his mouth near the butler's ear, 'Sheep "tup", butler. So never spread rumours about Sir John. If you say one more word, I will show you the graves... from below.'

Roger Nash took the threat seriously enough to leave Owen's side and join the master as he approached. Sir John walked with Nash towards the church to discuss matters of the house and the nanny followed with Victoria and George leaving Elizabeth to walk with Owen. She paused by the black-green yew trees that were soaking up the light in the pretty graveyard sloping towards the Menai.

'These yew trees must be 1,000 years old. No doubt a sacred grove for the Druids. Is that correct Mr Tudur?'

'Correct ma'am but also as a symbol of mourning in a place of the dead over the last 500 years. Maybe they were also used for the bows of the archers who fought the invaders.'

She smiled at him as she replied. 'They are convolved and confused, a little like the history of the Welsh?'

He shrugged, 'Those are true words, ma'am.'

She turned to Owen as they drew closer to the porch. 'Thank you for escorting me steward, it can be a lonely walk.'

He realised she was trying to be friendly but rejected it; he felt uncomfortable when close to her. 'It is my duty, madam and to quote John Milton "order is Heaven's first law"'.

She paused next to a slate gravestone, riven with green copper streaks. 'Duty? That is an interesting concept we could debate, steward.' She pointed to Henry Rowlands name etched into the tall grey slab. 'I have read *Mona Antiqua Restaurata* written by this cleric, in order to understand Anglesey and my new duties. Will it help me, do you think?'

'We like history in this area, your ladyship, and his words will help you. This place is at the heart of Wales – a place of historians, Druids and Romans, royal families and, of course, the inevitable battles with the English.'

'That sounds quite nationalistic coming from a new appointee?'

'No, your ladyship, I know my place and my pledge. Even here in this tiny church we love our history and will only use the 1662 *Book of Common Prayer.*'

'In that case, steward, let us hope the Littleton-Joneses make some exciting new history and leave the use of the prayer book to posterity!' They walked into the church and heaven took priority over order as they were delighted to see the flickering light of three hundred candles. A galaxy of God amidst the dark and earth bound congregation. She and the steward took their respective places after the Pagets had greeted Lady Elizabeth through gritted teeth; after all, the Littleton-Joneses were new money from Liverpool. They all turned in unison as some surprise visitors darkened the doorway.

The Earl and Lady Charlotte gracefully walked towards the pulpit and acknowledged the Pagets and the Dean. They sat in front of the Littleton-Joneses and adjacent to the Marquess, a slight to the former that was deliberate and for all to notice. Dean Runcie proceeded happily with the service, whilst inwardly thinking about the Church's one tenth tithe due from the three rich landowners sat in front of him. Lady Charlotte sneaked an occasional glance behind her to see what Lady Elizabeth was wearing and decided she liked the attire. Twenty-six-year-old Lady Isabel sat playing with her blonde ringlets and dreaming of her new artist friend who had stayed for the summer at Plas Newydd. She was not allowed to mix with the commoners, but art was an acceptable diversion. It was also a relief as she was trapped on her estate with men dreaming of war and dandies wanting to be actors. She loved the artist who had been commissioned to paint portraits of the whole family and also a dramatic frieze covering the whole of the dining room wall. But Isabel loved every man, a nymphomaniac who had also noticed the handsome Owen Tudur.

Once outside in the cold air, the Earl kept away from Sir John who stood talking with the Dean by the Paget mausoleum.

Runcie was pontificating loudly, 'Sir John, I believe some of the Christian needs of the Welsh on this dreadful island can wait whilst progress eradicates their ignorance.'

The master replied, 'My dear Dean, all you must do is save their souls before they die. The mortality rate here is twice that of Liverpool because of that ignorance. My steward keeps telling me about tenants who have died of ague, typhus or consumption. Lead the heathens to God, sir, and keep those who are ill away from me, what!'

The Earl manoeuvred himself closer to the Marquess. He wanted to talk to his peer about the copper finds on the north of the island and encourage a joint business venture. That left Lady Elizabeth free to invite Lady Charlotte and her husband back to Plas Coch for tea. The Earl made his excuses and left on horseback leaving the two ladies to meet back at the house and sit and chat in the drawing room.

Charlotte began, 'I do believe we are distant cousins, Lady Elizabeth?'

'Please call me Elizabeth when we are alone. Yes that is a pleasant thought, isn't it? A relative on this lonely island.'

'Indeed Elizabeth and please call me Charlotte. There must be no boundaries between us.' The women chatted amicably about their houses and their servants and eventually it led to a discourse about the seemingly magical powers of Aeronwy and the delicious delights concocted by Frances.

Charlotte leaned forward, 'I understand from my cook that Aeronwy may be a Druid like her husband and Morgan. How exciting, don't you think?'

Elizabeth clapped her hands together in delight. 'Does that mean she heals people using some witchery? Goodness me, what could she be doing with my head housekeeper at this very moment?'

'No witchery Elizabeth, at least not in my experience. However, she and her brother understand the local folklore and can both be extremely useful to you. Apparently, Aeronwy found a black pippin in a well near here,' she saw Elizabeth's confusion, 'an earthenware mug or a cursing pot with a frog inside. It had been killed by inserting forty pins into its body.'

Elizabeth was horrified, 'That is very gruesome, why would someone do that?'

Charlotte hesitated. 'The tradition is... there is a slate on top of the pippin that contains the sacrificed frog and on the slate is engraved the name of the individual who has been cursed.' She paused.

'What was the name?'

Lady Charlotte pensively placed her hands to the side of her face before replying quietly, 'On top of this particular slate was a wax figurine... and the name was Elizabeth.' She looked so shocked that her new friend came close to comfort her with a gentle hug. 'Don't worry my dear, it is superstitious nonsense. Mere hatred because you are English, I would think.'

'Or I am seen as a competitor?'

'Either or; we have no idea of the significance and it is farcical Druid lore.' But it was enough to end the happy conversation prematurely and so Lady Charlotte departed after promising to meet her again, no matter what the Earl said.

Chapter 5

Being Mortal

Elizabeth felt morbid after the pippin incident. The short days were occupied watching the blue tits from her drawing room window as they stole occasional baubles of red or black from the holly and privet bushes beneath her. The master had commanded Owen to visit Dinorwic with him, and to alleviate her depression Lady Elizabeth had succeeded in being invited along for the first time. After her chat with Lady Charlotte, she too wanted to see the drama of the quarry and also to view the alpine flowers, which were one of her passions. On the morning of the visit, the master was called to an urgent meeting in Holyhead by Captain Fardol after a run-in with a nefarious customs officer called Dai Jones. There was a serious dispute concerning tax on claret imported on the master's schooner via Portrush in Northern Ireland and so the master went with a purse full of guineas to bribe the official who was known to be in the Earl's pocket. Therefore, Elizabeth and Owen made the journey to the quarry without him but took Elis Wirion as both escort and chaperone.

* * *

Grace Parry pulled mightily on the oars to spin the small ferry into the current that would help them cross to Aberpwll. Elizabeth had been silent as the three of them walked their horses down the hill from Plas Coch to Moel-y-Don. She had been relishing the bright sun of the early morning as it glistened on the wet blades of grass and likened the silver drops to the tears of the long dead Druids; but as she topped the rise before the ferry, her breath had been taken away by the stunning flow of beauty as the silver reflections were swept off the flat waters and on towards Caernarfon. Her quiet demeanour was because she was enraptured by the natural beauty surrounding her new home.

The boat rode high and steady on the fast moving tide, reassuring Elizabeth as this was her first crossing on Sir John's new ferry. Grace's husband and Elis sat holding the horses' reins and the animals stood patiently on the raised platform in the centre of the boat. Grace faced Elizabeth and Owen as she rowed. The fiery Welshwoman spat her chewed tobacco over the side in a long and disgusting spurt.

'You can see the pretty lawns of Plas Newydd and Faenol opposing each other, my Lady. Two English well to do's seeing who can fart the loudest whilst shitting on the Welsh.' Owen stared hard at her, a warning to be quiet but to no avail. 'The old money of the hoity-toity Marquess versus the new money of a "mere" Mr Ashetton. Both bleeding the Welsh dry.'

Owen leaned forward to shut her up. 'Without the English money, you would have no food and no house for your family. Give them respect for what they are achieving and shut your yapping woman.'

She looked coy for a minute as she exerted herself to reach the still waters off the opposite bank. 'Without our blood and sweat, steward, they would not be able to develop their new wealth!'

'That is untrue Parry; they have slaves in Jamaica who are treated worse than your mangy dog. Think yourself lucky and pay some respect in front of Lady Elizabeth.' They both fell silent and listened to the repetitive sweeping of oars through the brine as they pondered their freedom whilst jealously gazing at the perfect green lawns of the Georgian super rich. Elizabeth listened and she learned as she was rowed further from her splendid isolation.

They followed the same route to the quarry as before and Lady Elizabeth took the initiative by riding alongside Owen, leaving Elis as point.

'Do you dislike me steward? Have I done something so wrong that you refuse to talk to me?'

'No, my Lady, to both questions. I...'

She tapped his leg with her whip. 'Say it man!'

'I am new to the job and don't know how I should behave with you.' She laughed into the cold air creating plumes of white breath. The wind had increased since their crossing and the clouds now hung ominously on the mountains.

'Explain how you think you should behave.'

He glanced across and was immediately mesmerised by the large violet eyes. 'I know I must respect and obey you at all times, whether you are right or wrong.' She pondered the words for a few hundred yards. They were high above the lake and close to the quarry named after her. She was disappointed that she had seen no wild flowers and decided she would have to make a special trip.

'In that case we need to start again, you and I. You must respect me for what I am and not what I appear to be in "your world", that is to "your people". No one understands me except Beth, and I have missed her company. So Mr Owen Tudur, ex fiancée of my confidant. Remember, I am not the outer person in the public's face, I am the inner woman who does not share all of our master's views.'

Owen nodded his head in understanding. He was pleased she had thawed in private and felt he could now talk to her normally. 'My family have lived around here for generations, my Lady. We were called Twdr then, and four brothers fought with Owain Glyndwr when they stormed Conwy Castle.'

She was interested in the local history. 'Who was Glyndwr?'

'He was the last true Prince of Wales and shook the English throne in the early 1400s as he bravely led the Welsh in a struggle for their independence.'

'Did he succeed, Mr Twdr?'

He laughed at her inference. 'No, he was beaten by the harsh winter of 1408 and the English capture of Harlech Castle. I'll show you his last refuge later.'

'What happened to your descendants? Were they killed?'

'One brother survived, he was called Maredudd and joined the opposition by waging war on France on behalf of Henry V. That's when the name changed to Tudor.'

She was enthusiastic in her reply, 'I know some of the history after Henry's death. The King caught influenza whilst in France and a Regent protected his young son, leaving the boy's mother called Katherine to marry Owain Tudor. Now I understand your royal past sir!'

'We never talk about our history ma'am, but one of their five sons became Henry Tudor and beat King Richard at Bosworth and so ascended to the English throne. You see the broom bush over there? It is sometimes called the goldfinch of the meadow and was on the badge of the vanquished Plantagenets.'

'Well, I am blessed to have ridden with royalty today, Sir Owen Tudor.' She was smiling and joking with him and so he doffed his black bowler and gracefully bowed from his saddle, showing off by sweeping the hat close to the floor.

'And your head housekeeper's ancestor was also part of the Welsh royalty. Her name is a corruption of Cadwaladr who was a local king about AD 650.'

Before she could comment, they turned the corner of the track and heard the crack of an explosion reverberate its way off the valley walls and thunder downwards towards the sea. A few minutes later and they came to a huge scar cut into the mountain above Llyn Peris. The quarry now had five massive galleries each 30 feet tall, and each of the five tiers was manned by at least one hundred men.

'Now that was certainly worth the journey, sir.' Owen was shocked by the massive devastation created in just six months and cast his eye across the new industrial concern. Men hung off ropes roughly triangulated to small wooden platforms so they could place the explosive charges. There were heaps of spoil below each terrace and ten new splitting and cutting *gwaliau* with a substantially larger *caban*. William Smith and Owen's tad walked towards them. As he and Elizabeth dismounted, William politely addressed her. 'Welcome to your quarry ma'am. Is it as big as you imagined?'

'Goodness me Smith, it is like Milton's hell. How do the men cope with such harsh conditions?'

'They just cope; that is the key to survival between the bitter cold of winter and the boiling hot summer. I admire the men as they have such guts and determination, including our own overseer Lewis Tudur.' Lewis stepped forward to meet her. She saw an older version of Owen, proud and handsome.

'I am pleased to meet you, sir. I understand you have intelligence and determination that you have passed onto your son.'

Lewis kept his head down as he replied, 'That may be so, my Lady, but he is still a young whippersnapper. He will shape up no doubt.'

She glanced at Owen, who as always felt like a small child in his father's dominating presence. 'I am sure he will sir, now please let us look around.'

Lewis waved his right arm at a group of forty men who had assembled nearby. 'Before Mr Smith shows you the workings, we would like to welcome you properly. A Welsh welcome, ma'am.'

The men started to sing *Guide me, O thou great Jehovah* but in Welsh, which annoyed Owen intensely. However, her ladyship loved the deep baritone voices harmonising together and then echoing apart as the sounds split off the cliffs of blue and green slate.

Owen formerly addressed Lewis, 'And now, overseer, may we have an English song?' Lewis looked daggers at his son but motioned the choir leader towards him. After a brief interval, a lone man set his bow to his violin and then they started to sing again. This time they enchanted Elizabeth with a rendition from the *Messiah*. Layer upon layer of inspirational notes were set upon each other to build the song, as if there were six choirs instead of one. *And the glory of the Lord shall be revealed* repeated itself endlessly to merge with the next rendition. Procreating a sonorous salute to their God in a place that all the men called heaven.

Lewis turned to Owen, 'Is that good enough for you steward?'

The tension was palpable and it was William who guided Owen and Elizabeth away from the potential argument. She loved the place immediately. The sweat and grime, the cold and damp, it was earthbound and real; a welcome distraction from her cosseted life and one that centred her soul in the depths of mother Wales. They stopped to look at Llyn Peris 1,000 feet below them and Dolbadarn Castle on the opposite side.

William pointed upwards, 'You can't see the summit of Snowdon from here, Lady Elizabeth, but it has been calculated to be 3,500 feet high.'

Owen nudged him before adding, 'Snow hill is the English name. We call it *Y Wyddfa* –the land of the eagles.' They watched a bird circling high above, a small speck in a dark grey sky that could have been any type of predator, even a dragon.

William nudged him in return before speaking to Elizabeth, who was savouring the view from the valley col by turning 180 degrees to the sea at Caernarfon. 'You have to watch out for these nationalists, ma'am. Glyndwr came from these parts and inspired the locals to rise up against the racial laws laid down by the English crown. The Welsh were forbidden to own their own lands and could not even speak their own language in public.'

She looked disconcertingly into his eyes. 'In that case, it was a travesty of justice, agent. We have seen that the People always win in the end. Whether in Europe like in the recent Seven Years' War, when our Prussian allies wavered constantly against the French and Spanish. Or in Ireland, with the current Irish question hanging over the People of the north and south. People win, not politicians and certainly not warmongers. People sir!'

William liked her feisty speech and applauded it. 'Bravo ma'am, I agree, but power and money seem to be shaping a world that none of us can control.' They stood nodding their quiet assents as William turned and moved away.

It was Owen who broke the thoughtful silence. 'That is where Owain is buried.' He pointed at the ruined castle opposite them. 'Clasped between the lover's arms of the lake, with the sweet tinkling of the stream's voice in his ear. He lies beneath the shadow of our greatest mountain and can see "the mother of Wales" floating on the sea on the northern horizon. The highest and lowest reaches of a man's imagination to match the valour of his failed quest.'

She gently touched his arm to break his reverie. 'Did he have a love of his life? A woman with whom he could share eternity?'

Owen waited and then replied thoughtfully, 'The fables say he loved the English Queen and she loved him too, but the endless battles between the nations left them lonely and apart.'

'That is very poignant and very beautiful, but it makes me very sad.' They turned away from the silent call of Owain Glyndwr and walked towards the tethered horses. Two souls united as if one but destined by fate to always be apart.

On their way home, the heavens opened and cold torrential rain soaked through their woollen overcoats. Even silly Elis complained about the discomfort, which was unusual. They had to wait for the ferry, marooned behind a curtain of rain on the wrong side of the straits and so they had been cold and wet for several hours before reaching the warmth and safety of home.

As he took her proffered reins, she turned in the dim light of the porch. 'Goodnight Mr Tudur. I enjoyed my day immensely. Thank you so much for your guidance.' And with that the beauty with the violet whirlpool eyes turned and left him. She needn't have said more, it took all of Owen's willpower to stop thinking about her as he trudged home to his tiny cottage and truculent family.

That week, it was confirmed that Beth had consumption and the chances of her living past Christmas were poor; only the fearless Aeronwy called to see her each day.

'Come on, Beth take this.' Her healer forced the liquid into Beth's mouth as she reclined in the bed placed next to the fire. The patient was so weak she could barely speak.

'What is it that tastes so damned awful?' At least she had some spark of life left. Aeronwy cradled her head against her chest and rocked her like a baby. None of the family came near; they were too scared of catching the contagion.

'It's called orange flower pleurisy root. My grandmother always used it against infections in the lungs. It will help as it allows you to spit out the badness and will stop the spasms my love.' Beth was terrified of dying. She turned and coughed into a bowl while her friend supported her.

She whispered two words. 'Owen? Elizabeth?'

Aeronwy gave her some more of the disgusting medicine before replying. 'Owen is smitten I think. Is that what you mean? Probably not, you just want to know what is happening in the world.' Beth rolled her eyes and gripped Aeronwy's hand tightly. She still loved Owen and she also loved her mistress. 'Anyway, he moons over her; a woman can see it but not Cadell or Lewis. Stupid men. They are tongue-tied and diffident with women of their own class and take advantage of those beneath them, for example, the butler with the maids. That is a good enough reason for you to return to work young lady, to protect those girls. As for Owen, well he is happy working and happiest when he goes up to the house and it is definitely not because he is smitten by the cook...' She paused and wiped Beth's forehead with a cooling damp cloth. 'Now someone has been practising a little black pippin magic against Elizabeth and my guess it is one of the maids or even Siân Jones herself. Yes, I can see she might be jealous enough. So nothing changes Beth, my dear. At the weekends my man and Lewis disappear off into the nights, thinking I am dim-witted.' The hand gripped tighter. 'Where to? I think they are playing at Druids or nationalists, they don't seem to differentiate between the two and they are certainly not fornicating with other woman! Who would have either of them?' She laughed at the thought and then wiped Beth's forehead again before gently prising "the wed" from the corner of her eyes. 'I'll return tomorrow morning and expect to see an improvement.' The hand gripped tightly again. 'Elizabeth? Well I heard Lady Elizabeth was ill in bed yesterday; apparently my brother took her up to Dinorwic and got her soaked and cold. Men are so silly sometimes.' She left Beth warm and loved, which was the best medicine she could give, and now Beth had some motivation to help her recover.

As the head housekeeper made progress, her mistress became worse. The nanny kept the children away from her on Sir John's instructions and that made her depressed. Her husband also refused to be near her in case it was catching and the butler decided it was none of his business. Only Siân had the decency to call in but that was out of duty. The cook sat well away from the bed and watched her mistress. Elizabeth was too weak to eat the chicken broth she had brought and it sat on the side table going cold. Siân hadn't meant to harm her by casting the spell, but now she regretted it. It had seemed harmless, but she had desperately wanted Owen in her life before turning her attentions to Duncan. As a woman, she could see Owen's reactions to Elizabeth whenever she had seen them near each other.

'Can I fetch you anything, Lady Elizabeth?'

The pale woman on the bed coughed and spluttered. 'Fetch the apothecary from Llannerchymedd.' She spluttered again and fell back onto her pillows after the effort of speaking. Siân removed the food and went to find the steward, an act of kindness and also of recompense.

Downstairs, the Dean was sat drinking tea with Sir John. He asked him politely. 'How is Lady Elizabeth today?'

'I think she has consumption like the Cadwallader woman. In fact, we could all have it Dean! Damned inconvenient what! You can go and say a prayer with her if you like?'

The Dean had no inclination to catch anything and was there for business not spiritual relief. 'I think not sir. She needs to rest and not have me bothering her poor little mind. But I will remember her in the prayers at the church service in Beaumaris this evening.' Owen knocked on the study door and entered after Sir John had boomed 'come!'

'Master, her ladyship is asking to see the apothecary. Is it convenient if I fetch the man and attend her ladyship in her bedroom? I thought it best to ask as it may seem improper. I might be able to help with my insight on my sister's knowledge, as everyone else in the house has abandoned her.' He didn't add 'including you', but he thought it. He was more concerned by the lack of care and duty shown by Roger Nash and Siân.

'Of course, steward. I don't want her dead so do anything you want. What a disaster that would be, I would be all alone in society circles. How damn inconvenient what!' Owen turned and left the house riding as fast as possible to fetch some help.

Evan Evans, the apothecary, moved closer to the bed, clutching a handkerchief over his large nose. He resembled a giant dark bird with swept long black hair and humped shoulders that hung his head forward like a crow.

'Apologies madam, but I need to know your symptoms. If it is consumption, let me tell you now that you will probably die.' He was too blunt for Owen who pushed him to one side and sat on the bedspread close to her head. He admired the blonde ringlets strewn across the silk pillowcase.

'Lady Elizabeth, please tell me the symptoms.' He leaned closer to make it easier for her and relayed the words to Evans. 'Extreme pain in the ribs, tightness like influenza and she feels worn out. She can't get her breath and has a cough and fever.' He looked up at Evans the grim reaper with determined hope on his face, despite Elizabeth's coughs that made Evans step backwards in fear. The apothecary advanced his cure.

'First you need to make her vomit by giving her five grains of emetic tartar. An hour later you must give her Sydenham's liquid laudanum to stop the flux and finally some opium for the pain. I will return this afternoon to bleed her profusely.'

Owen had learned many things from his sister. 'Are you mad, Evans? How can you dry out a barrel and expect it to stay watertight?' Owen was angry and the apothecary retaliated.

'Trust me steward, this is not a farming matter and I am held in the highest esteem. Ah yes and for breakfast... if she lives, it should be goat's milk. Dinner can only be white meat and as a drink I recommend barley water with spirits of sulphur. Also give her a little German white wine from the Rhine but sweetened further by adding brown sugar candy.'

Owen was shaking his head negatively and Elizabeth grasped his arm and squeezed to show her support for him. The apothecary had a final flourish. 'I suggest purging using some plant ash mixed with lemon juice, that should sort the bottom end out, my man. My fee is two guineas and is payable before I give you the medicines.'

Owen was irate. 'Get out of here you quack! You have no idea what will cure her, have you?'

Evans turned smartly towards the door. As he left he added over his shoulder. 'My fee for attendance is ten shillings. I expect it to be paid this week. Good day.

Owen walked back to her bed and mopped her pale brow with a damp cloth. 'I am so sorry, my Lady. I hate these people. Aeronwy has taught me so much about medicine that I boil over when these idiots talk their twaddle.'

Her reply was weak. 'Thank you for being here, Owen.'

He patted her arm gently. 'Listen to me. Even in my boyhood I remember seeing a bottle with a famous name called "Witheringay's Lung Tonic". Supposedly, a cure for a hundred ills; just take a good nip four times a day to make one better. Can you believe it? I did at the time. There was no science to illness then and frankly there still isn't!'

'Thank you for caring, Owen'. She was feeling extremely lonely and unloved.

'It is what any caring man would do for his wife.' He stumbled on after this indiscretion. 'You'd have thought he'd got the ingredients from the witches in *Macbeth*: fenugreek seed, pleurisy root, black cohosh, unicorn root, water, and a secret ingredient... money in the pocket.' She smiled gently; at least his humour brightened her day. 'Don't worry ma'am, I will look after you. It may be pleurisy and nothing more; please don't let ignorance of the illness worry you unduly as I will fetch my sister to help.'

Elizabeth touched his arm again. 'Consumption kills one in four, Owen.'

'But who knows what you've got?'

She coughed before speaking again. It was a painstakingly slow and quiet sentence. 'Death is one of the unique aspects of our humanity that sets us apart from all other animals, in all but our baser instincts. We live to die and understand when it is upon us.'

Owen agreed, 'They are fine words, but I will not let you die. You have too much living left, my Lady.'

He left to fetch Aeronwy, who then proceeded to come twice each day. She gave her ladyship the same herbs as Beth and the same warmth of support. She also administered a tincture of poppies, sweetened with a syrup of damsons each night to ease her rest. Owen fetched her extra laudanum from Caernarfon and also a tincture of rhubarb with rose hip syrup, but it was left to Owen to make Elizabeth eat and stay warm in bed as she poured sweat. He visited ten times a day and enjoyed his one way conversations as a way to cheer her up. Sometimes, his subject matter was a little black and too practical for an ill lady, but that was Owen, the salt of the earth and always open and honest. He sat staring at the fire and denied that a miasma, a poisonous cloud containing germs would be the cause of cholera. His theory was that faeces and drinking water should never mix and he cited evidence to support it.

'In Edinburgh, they throw the turds and piss into the hundred closes twice a day, thousands of buckets of slop that run into the lake below the city. And guess where they obtain their drinking water!' He went on for many hours and waged war on an unsupportive and absent Dean and decried that illness was a punishment from God. He was a practical man and was used to nature as he lived with it on the farms on a daily basis. She took heart from his practicality and listened intently to his tales of everyday life in the country and then she prayed, thankful for everything she had, compared to the majority who hadn't. By the fifth day she stank, she had soiled herself despite his coy help with the guzunder and the smell of stale sweat, urine and faeces was putrid.

'Owen, I need a bath. Will you help me please?' It was nearly ten in the evening, the master was drunk and snoring in the study and the servants were in the attic having closed up for the night. Owen always remained close and had taken to sleeping outside her door on his truckle bed so that he could hear her calls. 'Please, don't be shy. You have told me about the practical lives that people lead and you can help me. It is between you and I.' He had to help out of mercy and compassion but was sorely embarrassed. However, he made several trips downstairs to the kitchen to fetch pails of hot water and to pour them into the hip bath. He set a chair next to it and covered it with towels and then he went to Elizabeth.

'Practicalities your ladyship, please bear with me.' He pulled back the bed clothes and threw them onto the floor as they needed to be changed. She looked frail and thin in her white flannelette night dress. As she held her arms up to be carried, she assumed the apparition of an angel. Gently, he carried her to the bath, her head resting close to his face; a baby in need of help. Owen took a deep breath and held it. He rested her feet in the water and as he lowered her on his right arm he used the left to pull the nightdress up and over her head.

'There my Lady.' He was trying to look away as he handed her the soap, but she dropped it in the tepid water.

'Owen please help, don't be embarrassed. This is not emotional, just practical.' And so Owen soaked her and then soaped her with a sponge squeezed softly in his loving, gentle hands. He changed her bed, dried her and carried her back and then he watched her fall asleep. But he didn't go outside; he sat in the chair by her bed all night and held her hands. The loving attention was repeated for the next four days and then she started to recover. Elizabeth asked Owen to read some Shakespeare to her. She chose sonnet number 40. He started slowly, unsure of the words as it was new to him.

'Take all my loves, my love yea take them all;
What hast thou then more than thou hadst before?
No love, my love, that thou mayst true love call;
All mine was thine, before thou hadst this more.'

He glanced up at Elizabeth and she smiled and closed her eyes as he started the second verse.

'Then, if for my love, thou my love receivest.' He stopped reading aloud as she was asleep but read the sonnet to the end. The gentle words seemed to apply to his new life and so he sat and memorised the whole poem.

As she improved further, the staff and master came to visit and he became superfluous. A would-be lover spurned by illness and a difference in upbringing. On his last visit, ten days after she became ill, she managed a few words alone with him.

'Whatever, whenever, I will be your best friend forever. Thank you, Owen.'

'Don't thank me Elizabeth, I had to help.' Then he was gone and was never to return to her bedroom.

Late December, after a muted Christmas, it was bright and clear with a cold wind from the north-east. Beth and Elizabeth played cards and happily chatted once again and a semblance of order was brought to the household. The cook always gave George treats whenever he ventured into the kitchen and he helped to make some of her favourite dishes. However, sometimes his father caught him and with a 'strewth and zounds' he would despatch him on "man's work" to see the farms with Owen. George was a sensitive boy and he missed the joint love of his mother and father. However, they lived separate lives on most days, apart from when they met before dinner. It was therefore natural that he would like Siân and Owen's company as they were fun, unlike the nanny and his new teacher. He liked to hunt with Owen and enjoyed the loud crash of the shots, as teal and partridge suicidally crossed the path of the happy pair as they walked to see the pregnant ewes. He saw the looks and laughs between the cook, the steward and the coachman as she gutted the birds in the warm kitchen and he was involved in a reality that gave him immense pleasure. Young George learned to appreciate that pickled puffin, Jamaican rum and the luxury of iced cream belonged to the few. He went inside the farmers' cottages and saw the poverty. He learned that their dinner of rock venison was a play on words and was actually tough goat's meat. He learned some Welsh and told his mamma about *blawd a dwr*. He described its bland taste after trying the flour and water broth, but it had been quickly washed down with buttermilk. However, some foods he truly enjoyed. The herrings and pickled walnuts with wheaten bread were all very different from the rich food served in Plas Coch. The heavily salted meats were avoided as he knew from his mamma that the salt disguised the flavour of rotten flesh.

One common trait enjoyed by both the rich and the poor was betting. He begged Owen to be taken to a cock fight which was always refused, but he did help papa enter the state lottery on occasion, betting £15 each quarter. He also saw men on the farms constantly playing dice for money and realised it was the same game that entertained mamma and the housekeeper.

The two women had finished playing cribbage and were deciding on which game of dice to play when Sir John walked in.

'Elizabeth, now you are much better, I have decided to stay in London and suggest you accompany me.' She bowed her head.

'In that case my dear, perhaps I could also inhale the sea air at Brighton for a month or two?'

'Dammit, you have enough sea air here, woman!' She deferred to him. Her real aim was to be away from her husband and any location would suffice.

Beth read the situation and opined. 'They say Bath is the ninth largest city in England now and is the place to be.'

The master guffawed, 'Beau Nash died long ago and so there is little fun left in Bath for people recovering from consumption.' However, he was warming to the idea as he strode around the room. One of his business deals was in the port of Bristol and he wanted to view the tin mines in Cornwall and smelting in Swansea. 'However, it might be a place to rest awhile your ladyship. What do you think?'

'I hear the waters are reputedly healthier than somewhere like Llandrindod Wells and it is certainly supposed to be livelier.'

The master turned to go. 'Bath it is then. It was good enough for the Romans, madam, and therefore it is good enough for you. Good day.'

The women were excited by the prospect; Anglesey was beautiful but socially very quiet as the Earl and the Marquess were slow with their invitations.

Before the family departed for London and then Bath, there were two sad events in the house to end a bleak winter. Victoria became weaker in the cold and damp and influenza finally claimed her life. It was taken in everyone's stride and she was quickly buried and forgotten. Infant mortality was high and a death was always around the corner for any sickly child. But it made Lady Elizabeth appreciate her own saviour and so she made a point of walking around the lake to "accidentally" meet him before leaving.

Owen was stood amidst three farmhands who were catching ducks for the household dinner. He broke away from the noisy chase as she approached and left them to casting their nets with a few brief orders. Elizabeth came close to Owen and quietly asked him to walk with her towards the sandstone quarry. They walked slowly side by side and savoured the crispness of the day. The ground was frozen hard underfoot, which was rare so close to the sea. Verdure trails of ivy laced the ground and struggled up parts of the crumbling red cliff. Small wrens and large blackbirds were fighting over the shiny black berries to stave off their hunger on the cold and frosty afternoon.

'I am going to Bath for a few months, steward and I wanted to say goodbye.' He knew she couldn't call him Owen in so public a place. 'I also wanted to thank you for saving my life. It seems so distant now, half-forgotten already and I didn't want to leave without telling you that I will always remember your devotion.'

Owen looked up at the orange and pink clouds drifting on the bright blue background of a winter's sky. He motioned upwards towards the beauty clasped within the clouds. 'That's all that counts, Lady Elizabeth. Seeing the sky each day.'

She smiled warmly at him and his heart turned over. He felt as if he was drawn into her eyes. Each time he looked at her, he was enchanted.

'Practical as always steward. In which case, when I return, I have a project that needs your help.'

He touched his bowler in acquiescence. 'Ma'am, what is that?'

She pointed to the barren cottage garden. 'I want your help to create my garden. You know that flowers are a passion of mine, a love in my life.'

He was happy as he replied, 'I would be delighted to help you in the spring, Lady Elizabeth. Delighted to be of practical help.'

She turned to go and gently touched his arm. 'Look, the patches of blue sky are losing their battle with the clouds, Owen. I think it is a good time for me to leave.'

'The blue continues mistress. If we were buzzards, we could fly above the clouds and follow the sun all the way to the Americas.'

She walked away ten steps and turned to him with one final thought. 'I shall miss this place, Owen Tudur,' and then she quickly left and so she missed his soft reply.

'And I shall miss you, my Elizabeth.' Owen sadly watched every step as she went back to the house and then he filled his life with constant work.

It was to be two years before she returned.

The master was ill, then she was ill again before business consumed the Littleton-Joneses lives in Liverpool and London. The world was turning faster. The Americans went to war for their independence and the French fleet ruled the channel as the old foes threatened to invade England. The family made money from these wars. They created one of the hundreds of new banks with partners in Birmingham and called it Lloyds. It expanded quickly by lending the government millions of pounds at extortionate rates of interest. They financed other landowners with mortgage upon mortgage but always in their strategic areas of interest to secure the company's future. Sir John's brothers played within the politics of the era whilst he created the new commercial interests of their age. They supported the Tories, "the court party", and made the most out of their relationships with the Crown and the landed gentry. They bitterly opposed the Whigs and the great aristocratic families, but the elections were controlled by the elite in both parties. So power in parliament was bought rather than assigned by the popular votes of the people.

A sighing of a great nation still to take a deep breath before leaping into prosperity; a jump that would be powered by its people.

But in North Wales change was much slower. The turnpikes developed and Owen sent more cattle to England for fattening. He shod them before the start of their journey and left them with the drovers at Porthaethwy. They made the cows swim the straits before driving them 20 miles a day via the market at Abergele and hence to Barnet to sell into the London market. Owen used the drovers to take messages and money to the Littleton-Jones brothers. He gave them good news as he developed the farms faster than any other steward on Anglesey by liming and sanding the larger pastures and using turnips for winter feed. He made credit agreements with the reliable drovers and gained their respect and trust. But he also helped his tenants and when they gathered to pay their rents he was always fair, always honest. Each quarter they stood around the leather-topped rent table in the parlour of the house and they would swap ideas over a toddy. So he gained the respect and trust of the absent family allowing them to concentrate on the bigger issues, whilst he ensured the house servants were happy with their £7 a year and that Nash didn't siphon off any expenses. He allowed the servants to borrow in part against their wages to buy boots and clothes when needed and with occasional gratuities, he added to their wage and bought their loyalty. A new steward was developing into an exceptional steward.

Chapter 6

Saint Dwynwen

The name of the month we call April is derived from the Greek word for "opening". The first day has always been associated with sending an unsuspecting person on a worthless or non-existent errand. The "April fool" in England, "hunting the gowk" in Scotland and "poisson d'avril" or April fish in France.

Elizabeth had extracted George away from the nanny and was walking inland towards Bryn Celli Ddu, the Neolithic burial ground high above Plas Coch. Silly Elis walked ten yards behind, ostensibly for their protection. However, he only succeeded in distraction as he was pulling funny faces at the boy to make him laugh. Elizabeth put her arm around George and cosseted him closely.

'Ignore silly Elis for a minute, my little poppet; you can go and see the horses with him later if you like. Look instead at the beautiful island on which we live.' The boy stared innocently at his mother, who was another access to the outside world, a pleasant divergence from the confines of his nanny.

'Can I see Owen too, mamma?' Her heart leapt a beat. The steward had kept his distance since her return.

'Of course you can my love. Silly Elis, horses and Owen, all in one menagerie.' They slowly walked beside a wide gurgling stream and she pointed out to him the natural wonders she hoped he too would love. Yellow wood spurges and purple pasque flowers, delicate wood sorrels and pretty white flowers of the blackthorn hedge that bordered their route. The mother and beloved son stopped to listen to the song of a Chiffchaff until a grinning Elis imitated its call and scared it away. Looking back to the mountains on the mainland, they wondered at the wisps of smoke merging into the blue sky as the farmers burned the gorse to create a patchwork of black near the remnants of white snow.

On reaching the burial mound she decided to turn for home. It lay in dangerous territory, as it stood adjacent to a farm owned by the Earl and that was the moment when Morgan rode up. He shouted loudly at them.

'What are you doing on the Earl's land? Are you poaching young man?' The white horse reared and bucked, scaring George and immediately bringing Elis running forward. Their escort stood between his mistress and the steward and shouted back at him.

'Bugger off you. You should be ashamed of scaring little boys. Pick on someone your own size.'

Rhodri sneered at the backward giant, 'I did once and I won, you oaf.' Rhodri deliberately kicked his horse to make it skittish again, scaring the three pedestrians. 'So madam, am I to fetch a constable or escort you directly to the assizes for trespassing with intent to steal?' Elis moved forward to tackle the vicious steward. He had missed the insinuation that they had fought before, but Elizabeth hadn't and would inform Owen later.

'No Wirion, step back.' She approached the horse, talking gently to it and then stroked the foaming muzzle, which calmed it down. 'Good morning steward, I do believe your land starts at the barrow and follows the stream eastwards to Llanfairpwll. In fact, based on the maps I reviewed with Sir John this morning, I am certain of it.'

Rhodri grimaced; in his view she was too clever for a woman and should obey not question. 'No doubt the maps are out of date, madam. I am certain the Earl has bought more land from under Sir John's arse.'

She smiled sweetly. 'Then please ask your agent to come and see Sir John with a new map and also explain why we haven't been informed. And by the way, send my good wishes to Lady Charlotte when you see her next.'

Morgan swept his horse around and kicked it into a trot. Her ladyship was too connected to upset and so he gave up on his mischief-making.

As the trio resumed their walk, she lavished praise on her son for his courage, who informed her he had only done what Owen would have done. They headed downhill towards the stables and within twenty minutes she had found Owen and told him what had happened. Elis put George bareback onto their quietest horse and walked him around the yard, allowing the two adults to speak. Owen knew that Rhodri was in the wrong, but the law and being in the right were of no protection.

'You should have two men with you at all times, ma'am and ideally you should all be on horseback.'

'Tush steward. If I can't take my son on a nature walk, then what is the point of living?'

'I agree but please remain living. Next time both Wirion and I will accompany you. We have a small pony that I bought in your absence and so Elis will teach George to ride it as soon as possible. Then we can all go together safely.'

She was delighted by the care he showed to her son and his sound advice. The times were lawless and most crimes went unpunished. 'In that case, on the last Sunday of the month you can take us all to see the delights of this New Borough that everyone says is so wonderful. Is that achievable?'

He agreed and then belatedly asked about her trip. Elizabeth made small talk about the dignitaries they had met but confided that small talk with artists and MPs had been boring compared to walks outdoors and feeling part of nature.

She teased him before she returned to the house. 'Beth and I went to see a play in Stratford upon Avon on the way back. Have you heard of the town? It's the home of William Shakespeare, the man who wrote the sonnets I love.'

He was embarrassed as the memory of sonnet number 40 taunted him. 'I remember ma'am, I liked his work.'

'We saw *The Two Gentlemen of Verona*. Do you know it?' He didn't and explained he had little opportunity to read. 'You should read it one day steward.' After they had left, he raced across to the house and hunted for the book in the library. That night, sat next to a single tallow candle he struggled to read it. The print was tiny and the words confusing. One paragraph did stand out as he turned the yellowed pages.

> *Oh how this spring of love resembleth*
> *The uncertain glory of an April day!*
> *Which now shows all the beauty of the sun*
> *And by and bye a cloud takes all away.*

He closed the leather covers and sat listening to the snoring of his sister. The fire flamed briefly illuminating their gloomy existence and then the radiance was gone. Had she meant him to read it or was it fate, a chance occurrence?

It was the perfect seaman's day as William Smith arrived in Caernarfon with Captain Ieuan Fardol. The weather was warmer than normal for spring and a brisk force 4 wind drove the boat across a small chop, spreading clouds of spray off the crests. The 200-ton smack had a crew of sixteen and was carrying coal from the new colliery in Worsley near Manchester. William had hitched a lift down the Mersey after visiting Sir John's coalmine and had spent the last day talking to the captain about the port development at Felinheli. Most of the coal used on Anglesey still came by wagon from Halkyn near Chester as it was cheaper because any coal transported by sea was heavily taxed. But this irrational law was part of their plotting as Fardol's main job for the shipping line concerned "customs and tax avoidance". The agent and captain controlled this endeavour with Sir John's support, but no one called it smuggling. In fact, the biggest local players for many years had been the Marquess and the Earl. They controlled the Justices of the Peace and continued to bribe Dai Jones who was now the comptroller for His Majesty's Customs based in Beaumaris. The advent of the new harbour in the west of the straits would change this eastern dominance. Coal could be shipped in larger quantities at Felinheli and used to power the new James Watt steam engines for pumping water or milling, and both would be needed at Parys Mountain and Dinorwic. One of William's latest tasks as agent was to buy land at the tiny port of Amlwch, in the north east of Ynys Môn. It was only three miles from Parys Mountain and the anticipated wealth from the new copper mine. The master would then have a stranglehold on the sea trade supplying the local industry between Anglesey, Holywell, Liverpool and eventually Swansea, where he had visions of refining his copper ore. As slaving and sugar declined, the industrial mining of minerals in North Wales would increase. A strategic plan that looked 20 years into the future, but the immediate issue required transport by land and that involved meeting Owen and the master.

Fardol was in his element as he steered the small dinghy towards The Mermaid Inn at Tal-y-Foel. They were halfway across the Menai, having left the smack anchored in the port near the castle. He was a blunt man in his forties, ruddy-faced, grey-whiskered and with red rheumy eyes from the years of salt spray and imbibed rum. William was controlling the solitary sail and was taking a drenching from the occasional wave as the captain headed across the straits.

'Good god, Ieuan why couldn't we take a nice big ferry rather than this two penn'orth of a boat?'

The captain leaned forward and slapped him hard on the leg. 'You damn'd landlubber, pull the sail in a little man.' William did as he was told. 'I hope you understand how to build ports because you certainly can't sail boats.' He was laughing at William's quiet discomfort. 'And you have more about you than when you're drinking lad.'

William always pleaded the need for an early night when onboard the captain's ship. Ieuan had drunk himself into oblivion on most nights since the fateful day in Jamaica when the slaves had killed his family. He had three motivations to get up every morning. To drink himself silly, to serve Sir John and to stay at sea as much as possible. William was soaked despite the linen cape made from sailcloth that was impregnated with linseed oil. He started to shiver as the captain asked him another question. 'What's this steward Tudur like?'

'A good man, trustworthy and pledged to the master. One of us Ieuan, a man who has sold his soul to the devil.' They laughed together and kept laughing until they closed on the small sheltered quay by the inn. The captain expertly headed into the breeze and slowed the boat to a crawl so that William could leap out and make fast. They walked quickly towards the inn, ready for a toddy made from brandy with a sip of hot water and sweetened with sugar.

The four men sat drinking in a quiet corner. To their right was a roaring fire and in front were empty trestles and tables. Sir John lecherously watched the 12-year-old waitress as she polished the tabletops with beeswax before rudely telling her to leave them be.

William started briefing Owen on his role after their third round of toddies. 'I know it's a shock to you Owen, but that's what we do. The captain moves his ships in a carefully planned pattern that the customs officers try to keep track of and occasionally one of our boats will drift off course, so to speak. On the night of the new moon, a smack from Dublin will inadvertently anchor off Bull Bay near Cemaes. You must meet Fardol with a team of farmers to take the cargo away from the beach. It's simple!' Ieuan leaned towards Owen, carefully watched by Sir John. This was Owen's biggest test so far. The steward knew everyone on the island smuggled, but for the first time he was the linchpin in a new adventure.

The captain jabbed him in the chest with a massive finger. 'So I look after the diversion to the Isle of Man, load up with claret and rum and make sure the custom's cutter stays miles behind us. All you have to do is lump a few barrels over to this side of the island.'

Owen added morosely, 'And distribute the contraband through the Moel-y-Don ferry to Caernarfon and Bangor, whilst avoiding the customs men, vagabonds and thieves and finally hide the goods from the population of half the island.'

Ieuan clapped him on the knee, 'There you go man, an easy job and on dry land. Just what you do and understand.' He smiled at Owen's discomfort, but the captain already felt he could be trusted and liked him after an hour's drinking together.

The steward looked at Sir John. 'These new farmers I am to manage, can you tell me why you have bought their land near Amlwch and Parys Mountain?'

Sir John crossed his arms. 'A very good question, steward and one I will not answer yet. You do not need to know. Pay them well and they will do a good job, but remember to arm them as we are stepping on a few toes.' Owen pondered on whose feet they belonged but guessed it was the Earl.

'In that case, I will also take a few of my own men from Plas Coch. This time we will not be surprised.' The men merrily drank the afternoon away as they formalised the arrangements. The captain would immediately supply blunderbusses, muskets, cutlasses and pistols from the smack and on the night 47 gallon casks of rum and claret, with an odd chest of tea. He valiantly declared he would only be stopping to take on some "shell sand" at Red Wharf Bay as it was more fertile when dug overnight. He made them all laugh with his tales of customs men and the games he had played with them. Roaring drunk, Owen asked William where he would be on the night.

Ieuan teased the agent whilst pointing out of the opaque window obscured by rivulets of rain. 'Safe and asleep in a prostitute's bed over there in Caernarfon.'

Owen tossed his drink down before he replied. 'Nothing new there Smith; is that how you save money? Sleeping instead of fornicating, it must halve their price!' They all laughed at William's discomfort. 'Saving your money like that will make you as rich as Sir John.'

But Sir John had left the group and taken the young waitress upstairs. He liked young girls and they were cheaper than the disease-ridden prostitutes and more exciting.

The men trusted each other, but when a coachman is having sex with a maid, then secret information about a trip can reach the wrong person. Duncan said too much to Jenifer after humping her against a hay bale and then she received her payment for the information from Roger Nash which included sex for the second time that day. So the Earl knew the time and place for the rendezvous and all he had to decide, was the proportion he would steal and the proportion the customs would declare to validate Sir John's guilt. The court case would be a mockery but having a clever competitor hung would be to his advantage. Neither Sir John nor Duncan would ever feel guilty about their actions. Smuggling contraband or humping servants was normal behaviour whether you were married or single.

Lady Elizabeth received a private note from Lady Charlotte. It was Aeronwy who delivered it to the house as she had been at Earl's Hill earlier in the day to attend to one of the servants. Beth took it into her mistress who was sat in the window seat staring at the lake. The housekeeper sat opposite and waited with bated breath. Elizabeth always shared everything with her. Her ladyship broke the wax seal and carefully opened the letter. The writing was flowery, in blue ink and flowed across the cream paper. But it was succinct and coded.

Dearest Elizabeth,

I am sorry we have not been allowed to meet again, but my husband seems dead set against yours. Men and their business, always fighting over someone or something! Never mind, I enjoyed seeing you cousin and have you in my thoughts.

I also believe we share an interest in Plas Newydd as well as with our distant relations in Yorkshire, but this relationship appears more personal. I wanted to forewarn you as it is already the gossip downstairs, here in Beaumaris.

In passing, I met Lady Isabel Paget the other day. She had called to see my husband about an art commission as she was so pleased with the attentions of her London artist again. I do believe she misses him so. Of course, the Earl is disinterested in art unless the pictures are of horses and hounds, so I think her visit was rather thankless but her interest spans years I gather. Maybe she will also venture from within her walls to visit Plas Coch one fine day to pursue her art.

Well Elizabeth, duty calls us as ever. Duty, children and always being a good and obedient wife, of course. Please do not reply as you need to be confident that any message is confidential.

God be with you,

Charlotte.

Elizabeth stood and walked to the opposite window leaving Beth perplexed. It wasn't the purported infidelity that upset her ladyship, it was the fact that it was common knowledge that the two men had been visiting Isabel Paget, a Marquess's daughter. This was a potential social scandal. Everyone accepted the men had sex with the servant girls, but an aristocrat's daughter was a different proposition.

She tucked the note in her bodice as Beth entreated her, 'Is everything alright, my Lady? You seem so perturbed.'

Elizabeth answered without turning round. 'Perfectly fine, Beth. Lady Charlotte misses some company and our husbands are never around to keep us entertained.' She left it open to interpretation. Beth would hear the rumours soon enough. 'I have asked Owen to escort George and me to see New Borough tomorrow. Would you like to come with us, my dear?'

'I am so sorry, but I must attend the quarterly fair at Llangefni with the cook. We have so many items we must purchase. I can imagine George will be excited by the pony ride and seaside.' She paused, 'Have you heard about Saint Dwynwen, the Welsh patron saint of love?'

'No Beth, what does she have to do with New Borough?' Elizabeth returned to the window seat and sat opposite her friend to listen.

Beth used an example. 'Yesterday, after you sanctioned the marriage of Duncan and Siân, I went to inform them on your behalf. So I asked them both if they truly loved each other before I gave them your blessing. Apparently, she had given him a love spoon on the 14th February and in return, he took her to Llanddwyn Island where there is a lovers' shrine next to the church.'

'How beautiful, I didn't realise the coachman was so romantic!'

'Methinks not Lady Elizabeth, maybe he is just attracted to a pretty girl 20 years his junior. In fact, I think he is attracted to anyone who finds him attractive!' They both giggled. 'However, it is a wild and romantic place to pledge your love and Siân was pleased.'

'Why Llanddwyn?'

Beth continued, 'It's where a princess became a hermit in the fifth century as she was forbidden by her father to marry the one she loved.'

Elizabeth had her hands to her lips as she commented indistinctly, 'Goodness me Beth, do we know if this is true?'

'I, for one, definitely believe the fable ma'am, because the steward told me it was true. It was passed down through his family over the centuries and he should know as he is related to the Welsh royalty. They lived at Aberffraw, which is the village north of New Borough.'

Elizabeth asked dreamily, 'What was the shrine?'

'Not was... is, my Lady. The well of Saint Dwynwen, where if you place a lover's handkerchief over the water, small eels appear from the wall sides and their movements can be interpreted to predict a lover's future.'

Elizabeth clapped in delight. 'You tell such wonderful stories, Beth. What happened when the coachman and his future bride tried it?'

'Nothing, they couldn't afford a handkerchief and so they threw a coin in for good luck.'

'What fun! And the Princess? Did she leave the island and marry?'

Beth had a tear in her eye as she replied. 'She lived there for the rest of her life, all alone with no husband, no children and not even a companion.' She sniffed slightly. 'At her death, she wished that she could gaze at the sun setting over the sea for eternity as then she felt closest to her beau.' The two women hugged each other; they had so much in common despite the difference in class.

The party heading towards the beach made good time on their horses. George had learned to trot his small roan pony and pestered his mamma every ten minutes, informing her she was going too slowly. Elis led the way and Owen hung behind to ensure everyone was safe. Within two hours they reached the small village of New Borough perched a few hundred feet above sea level with breathtaking views towards Caernarfon and Mount Snowdon. From the village they followed a sandy track nestling between outcrops of grey-green rock with acres of bright yellow gorse growing on either side. To their left was the entrance to the Menai Straits, where the sea shallowed to create a tidal garden full of wild flowers and flocks of feeding sea birds. This was sheltered from the Irish Sea by the huge sand dunes hewn into contorted shapes by the battering westerlies, as if the sand were in pain from their onslaught. It was warm, with a bright blue sky, a late April day that was as good as any in the summer. They reached the second part of the village as they neared the sea at the end of the ridge. Owen explained to George and Elizabeth that the men and women they could see in the dunes were called "morass workers" and they were collecting marram grass to make their wares. The group passed the makeshift huts that were the workers' homes during the summer months and could see marram ropes, mats and brushes stacked against the walls. The women outside the huts silently stared at them as they passed. They didn't welcome incomers, especially the English, and especially if they weren't there to buy. The women workers typically wore a long white apron from their waist to their shoes, with a check woollen shawl and a tall peaked hat that always had a highly decorative band. George was beside himself with joy as he heard the sound of the sea and as soon as he caught a glimpse of the shining waters, he kicked his pony so hard in his excitement that it galloped towards it. The others immediately chased after him and Elizabeth's calls for him to slow down were either not heard or ignored. Eventually they all came together as the pony tired and they stopped in a gaggle, laughing heartily whilst the horses excitedly stamped their feet in the shallows.

Owen clapped George on the back, 'Well done young sir, what a fine first gallop!' Elizabeth stopped herself from admonishing her son. She could see how proud he was in front of the steward.

Elis pointed seaward, 'Dolphin, dolphin, look George, lovely dolphins jumping in the sea.'

They all followed his pointed finger and watched five arched shapes leave the shiny surface before plunging below again. George wanted to know why they were so close to the shore and Owen answered as they all watched mesmerised.

'They hunt as a group and at low tide they come in between the sandbanks to catch any "flatties".' He looked kindly at the boy who was puzzled. 'Plaice and the like. Very dainty and sweet compared to the herring you tried in the cottage the other day.' Elizabeth was intrigued. She knew so little about what George did with Owen but was pleased he had a father figure. She looked to her right and saw a spit of land with a small ruined church on top. Llanddwyn Island, separated by shallow water from the mainland at this state of tide.

'Can we go to the church steward?' Little did he know why but he assented. So they trotted a mile through the surf having immense fun and then climbed the shallow hill onto the top of Lovers' Island. Elis and George walked their horses towards the natural harbour on the south side leaving Owen and Elizabeth a few hundred yards away near the church. They dismounted and he started to unpack the food from the saddlebags as she wandered off. Ten minutes later, she had not reappeared and so seeing that Elis and George were happily skimming stones, he walked towards the ruin.

When she had found the well, Elizabeth had glanced behind her to make sure she was alone and then withdrew her cream lace handkerchief and gently laid it on the water. It didn't sink, there was too much air in the fabric and she watched in anticipation but nothing happened.

'Lady Elizabeth!' She started as Owen came up behind her. 'I was worried about you ma'am.'

Her face reddened as she leaned nonchalantly against the crumbling wall of the old well. 'I'm so sorry, it...' she had lost command of the situation, 'I was just... fascinated by the place and forgot the time.'

He peered over her shoulder. 'Shall I remove your handkerchief ma'am?' She didn't answer. 'Or shall we see what the eels do according to an old wives' tale?' Elizabeth turned back to the well and gasped. A dozen or more small eels had emerged from the sides of the well and were twisting together.

She looked back into Owen's face, but his eyes remained on the enchanting scene as she asked, 'What does it mean? You know the local fables.'

He smiled but kept his gaze averted. 'I think you must know a few too, Lady Elizabeth.' He paused and then looked into her eyes. 'A man from the west of the country will meet a woman from the east and become lovers.' They both glanced at the eels as they broke apart and swam aimlessly around the well. 'But they can never be together.' He turned on his heel and walked purposefully back to the food and then went to check that George was safe. She approached Owen as he sat on a rock, angrily cutting chunks of cheese with a long dagger. He had an eyebrow raised and thin lips set in a grimace, but he spoke gently. 'Of course, like many traditions on Ynys Môn, our fables are wrapped in impossibilities.'

Perching beside him, she stared down at her happy son a few hundred yards away. She deliberately changed the subject. 'Like the impossibility of a Welsh nation.'

'No Lady Elizabeth, more like the impossibility of a better life for the poor'.

'I know you care well for our tenants, steward.'

'I try Lady Elizabeth, at least "the have-nots" are a part of the divine order according to the Dean. The cruelty lies within applying the master's rules. Our tenancy agreements are strict but are made flexible to increase his profits.'

'What do you mean?'

'Well, I make an inspection knowing the answer before I perform it. It doesn't matter if they haven't mopped the floor, made walls stock proof or emptied the chamber pots. I just tally up enough excuses to evict them.'

Elizabeth was genuinely shocked. 'So you evict them to close the small farm down and then share the lands between others to increase efficiency?'

'Precisely. The people don't matter. Families who have lived for years in the same cottage. Families with up to eight children.'

'And the master dictates the plan?' Owen nodded and stood to move away. He followed orders but it hurt him. The English landlord hurt the Welsh poor. It was a fact of life.

Their journey home was uneventful. As they left Lovers' Island, Owen glanced into the setting sun at Ynys-y-Cranc, a small rocky outcrop a few hundred yards to the west. The shadowed rock lay like a young man resting on his back, his arms closed upon his chest as if laid to rest. He realised he was in the exact place where Lady Dwynwen used to stare at the sun and wish for her true love. He crossed himself and spoke to his nemesis from a distant past, 'the Father, the Son, the Holy Ghost,' and was thankful to be alive in such a privileged situation.

George was exhausted and rode on Owen's horse perched in front of him. He was safely delivered to the nanny at the house but turned in the porch to thank Owen profusely for his day at the seaside.

Elizabeth added her own thanks as they walked the horses back towards the stables, taking the long route around the lake by her still derelict cottage garden. 'He loved today, steward. You would make a good father one day.' There was a pregnant pause. 'Maybe you and Elis could teach him to swim this summer?'

'I can't swim, ma'am.'

She laughed. 'Everyone can swim!' As he repeated the word 'can't' she pushed him backwards and laughed even louder as he fell into the lake. Owen went under; he couldn't find the bottom with his feet. He went under again and could feel his heart pumping hard against his chest. As he came up for the second time he heard her shouts.

'Kick with your feet and pull with your arms!' He went under a third time and kicked. He wasn't out of air and as his head broke the surface he took a huge breath and grabbed at the water in front of him. Grabbing and kicking for all he was worth, he eventually made the opposing bank 50 yards away and dragged himself out of the water. He stank and was covered in green algae and mud. As he stripped to his underwear he too was laughing and looked across to see a beautiful woman, with her blonde ringlets dancing in the evening sun. She was happy and loudly clapping his success. She was also admiring his hard muscular body and trim waist and realised how badly she wanted him. The hand on the curtain in the window disappeared after Nash had seen enough.

Siân and Beth were excited as they clutched each other's arms whilst sat in the bucking gig driven by silly Elis. A day of buying and an escape from the drudgery of the house was a rare tonic for the two friends.

'"Scaredy" cats, "scaredy" women, faster and faster we goes and coming.' As the excitement escalated into fear, it was Beth who admonished the silliness and made Elis slow the gig to a walk. He did as he was told because he knew she would give him money to spend in the ale house if he behaved. She squeezed the cook's arm.

'Isn't life marvellous Siân? A day out and a wedding to plan!'

The cook stared straight ahead. 'I can't wait to visit the shops my friend.'

Beth turned to look into her eyes. 'Isn't that the wrong priority?'

'No Beth, we are women and have to know our place. Duncan and I will live well in the coach house, but nothing much will change apart from sharing a bed with a man.'

Beth giggled, 'I can't think of anything nicer my lovely!'

Elis rudely interrupted the women, 'Share with me Bethy, share with me, cos Jenifer don't.' He sang the rest. 'Jenny for a penny gives it to many, but she won't give it to silly Eli.' The two women closed their minds to the facts and hushed silly Elis as they approached the town. The harshness of the reality outside the stability of Plas Coch meant any personal inconvenience was acceptable. It was an unavoidable fact of life.

As they drew into the main street of Llangefni they joined a queue of carts and wagons. They were jostling for the prized selling spaces at the side of the hammered dirt road with its margin of rough stones to form a low paving. The stopped traffic created endless towers of tottering baskets, mounted as high as the merchants could safely stack them. The lowest carts contained a mixture of animals restrained by a roof of netting. This allowed a symphony of brays, quacks and barks to merge with the rest of the choir as sheep were driven into temporary corals and horses and cows were tethered together and then anchored to their minders.

Elis left the women to wander the streets and he quickly merged with the groups of men in black suits and bowlers as they argued, raising their walking sticks to reinforce their points or stood with hands in pockets to show their determination to remain aloof from the discussion. The arguments and negotiations became more heated as the market progressed and the amount of ale consumed increased. Beth and Siân were feeling the rolls of fabric stacked next to a tall column of galvanised bath tubs outside a shop when the cook started to voice her concerns.

'I do want to marry Duncan but... well I know he has given cock to a lot of other women, including some of the staff.'

Beth wasn't surprised, 'Everyone knows that. So why are you worried?'

'Because I have never had anyone before.'

'Look Siân. I have had it three times in my life and always with the same man. Trust me, if Duncan is experienced it is for your pleasure my dear.'

Her friend felt reassured. 'If the rumours are true, I can't imagine what drives Lady Isabel to keep doing it with anyone. Egad, the candle maker says most of the gentry on the island have given it her.'

Beth was laughing. 'Well maybe the master and the Earl last longer than the three minutes they take with the maids!'

'Three minutes Beth? You are optimistic; I heard two was normal and nasty Nash holds the record at four!' The women moved on to search for wedding dress material, happy in the knowledge that their reputations remained intact. However, they gossiped with disrespect about everyone, including Owen. They described him as a castrated bull leaning over the fence to look at the most beautiful cow on the farm called Lizzie.

The day was freedom itself and so they stood in front of a shop with its windows full of bottles and posters advertising soap and dye as they watched a short interlude. Two extremely poor families had begged a farmer to let them use his wagon as a stage for their play, but the Plas Coch women moved on before any of the family's children mingled with the crowd to beg for money. The rich and the Methodists didn't like the interludes, but it was a way for the poor to earn a few pennies.

Further down the street some of the local men stood on a table and used it as a stage to attack the injustices of the age with pungent nationalist satire. Again they quickly moved past and browsed the temporary market stalls with their rough canvas roofs that kept the produce in the shade.

There was a final compelling show and this time they stood and watched it all before meeting with Elis to drive home. The last Beaumaris sessions had sentenced six men for crimes committed. Four had already been deported on a ship bound for Virginia, but the remaining two were being hauled around the island as an example to the general public. They felt obliged to watch the first man's whipping as his punishment for stealing cheese. The six strokes "razored" bloody lines across the scars from a week before and the man's cries chilled their hearts. It wasn't that sight that made them turn away and walk to their gig. It was the smell of roasted flesh from the second man as they burnt his hand for stealing a side of beef.

* * *

It was the night of the new moon and a group of twelve shadows stood next to half a dozen wagons overlooking Bull Bay. They watched as a line of phosphorescence clung to the surf as it gently wallowed in and out of the cove. There was a single track hung off the short cliffs that led down to the hard stone beach. All that Owen required was a signal from the smack before they lit their torches to wend their way down to meet the long boats carrying the contraband. He was nervous despite the pre-planning in The Mermaid Inn and his reconnaissance the week before. Apart from Elis he had only met the ten farmers on a couple of occasions over the last month. He hoped their payment would buy their loyalty, half before and half after. A single lantern flashed three times about half a mile out to sea and the troop began their lighted descent.

A mile away, Rhodri Morgan smiled cynically as he and a group of six thugs sat on the headland above Cemaes.

'Such an easy target, Tudur.' He turned to Dai Jones, the customs comptroller. 'Go to your men now and take the smugglers as they reach the top of the cliff on their return. Remember, to leave most of your men escorting Tudur and his team. Reduce the guard on the wagons of contraband to the drivers alone when they reach Llangefni so we can ambush them and take our agreed share.'

Jones face loomed closer, a greyness in the dark topped with a peaked hat. 'Just remember Morgan. No killings. My men have families to go home to.'

The steward sneered back at him, 'Do as you're told scum. Now get away and ambush Tudur. I am relying on you.'

The customs officer slunk off to his horse, ruminating on his personal safety since selling his soul to the Earl.

It took less than an hour to load the casks and chests worth more than a 1,000 guineas onto the wagons sat on the stony beach. As the procession started back up the narrow track, Owen took the torch off Elis and crossed it rapidly three times with his own. Neither the customs men at the top of the cliff nor Morgan's noticed the signal. Elis passed around the slitted hoods and each man quickly donned one as they made a slow ascent. The steward's instruction was to stay by the wagons at all times, maintaining absolute silence but keeping the glaring torches burning bright.

A smiling Dai Jones and ten customs officers formed a semi-circle as the snake of light reached the flat above the bay.

'Halt in the name of the King.' He let off a single shot into the air from his pistol. His instructions were to take Tudur alive. 'Take your masks off immediately.' No one moved. He levelled his pistol at the leading rider. 'I said take off your damn masks!' The wagons had formed a crescent in front of the customs men, encouraging them to mimic the shape. Two files bent away from each other in mutual hatred. The customs men were armed and had the advantage of surprise, but they faced a bright and now totally inanimate and silent semi-circle of smugglers. 'Come on dammit, you bastards. Which one of you is Tudur?' Still no one moved. The silence was deafening.

After a few seconds, it was broken by a rapid series of clicks, the terrifying sound of 20 triggers or more being cocked. Unfortunately for Dai Jones it emanated from the darkness behind him and his men. His immediate thought was of Morgan, but it turned to instant disappointment. The deep English voice at their rear sent a shiver through each and every customs man. They weren't paid to die.

'Drop your weapons on the ground behind you and get off your horses... now.' Within a few minutes every man was tied up and their horses driven away. Duncan had been an expert soldier and remained professional and quiet as instructed as he took control. Owen watched the coachman and his team with smug satisfaction. It was always unpleasant to learn by an experience such as the Sychnant incident but a pleasure to apply the same dark art. Sir John's men collected the assortment of blunderbusses, pistols and cutlasses before disappearing into the darkness as an enlarged group, just in case anyone else was tempted to attack them. The laughter started half an hour later, led by Owen and Duncan, with silly Elis whooping like a wolf in his frenzy of excitement and happiness.

One of Morgan's henchmen trotted close as he stood inert on the headland watching the movement of the torches. 'Are we going to have them steward?'

'Bugger off man, there must be thirty of Sir John's men against our seven. Are you a complete idiot?' He whipped the man across the face in his anger as he stared at the torchlight procession heading towards Amlwch. Rhodri dug his spurs into the stallion and made it rear high in the air before he kicked it viciously to make it gallop towards Beaumaris.

Sir John's men whipped their carthorses into a frenzy to make the barns used for storage before daylight, but Owen stopped and turned. He looked back a few hundred yards towards the headland. He heard the snort of a distressed horse and was sure he caught a glimpse of white as the sound of hooves became quieter in the distance.

He murmured into the night before shouting further encouragement to his men, 'To teach you how to do it... like a child in a school... goodbye teacher. You are never too old to learn, Morgan.'

The Anglo Saxons called June "the dry month", but even on the day of the summer solstice it was raining in the early morning. Rivulets of shiny water flowed in synchronised sheets as they plunged from the edge of the slates on the roof of Saint Edwen's. The staff of Plas Coch stared out of the windows of the house and scoured the skies for a hint of brightness whilst muttering old mottoes. "A dripping June keeps all in tune" and "June damp and warm does the farmer no harm." No one wanted the cook and coachman to be married in the wet. It would spoil the party to be had on the trestle tables outside. However, by 11am the low clouds had scudded away. A fresh breeze heralded the blue sky and a strong sun created an ephemeral mist as the damp evaporated into that poignant day with so little night. The lanes converging on the church were decorated by nature to herald the couple's happiness. Tears of rain hung from the leaves of dusky cranesbill and lesser spearwort. Bouquets of white sat on the crests of wild guelder roses, and pink dog roses hung from the tall hedges interlaced with fragrant honeysuckles, whose flowers resembled lovers' hands entangled forever.

The wedding was part of the normal Sunday service and the local gentry sat patiently inside, excluding the master who was in London and the Earl who didn't need to attend to make a political point again. The Dean's sonorous tones weighed heavily on the congregation.

'Psalm xix 13: Keep back thy servant also from presumptuous sins,' he droned on whilst the farmers considered if the sun would allow them to complete their haymaking in the fields outside. 'Divine providence has placed many in the condition of servants to a master and you should rejoice that he bears your keep, both in body and mind.' They could all hear the buzzing of the bees behind the north wall of the church as they gathered their pollen from the thyme and elder blossom. 'Grief and disturbance to the family is an abomination and brings disgrace upon yourselves and the family.' As he eulogised, the congregation's minds flowed in the freedom of the warm summer day they envisaged outside. It gave them happier thoughts than those dulled by the cold and disciplined interior. Eventually, he laboriously married the couple as many started to yawn.

When the Dean asked if anyone had just cause, that they should not be married, it was Jenifer who whispered to Roger Nash who was sat in front of her.

'I could tell a tale or two.'

He turned slightly and whispered back, 'Like what young missy?'

'Like who satisfied Duncan's needs before the virgin cook turned up trumps. Like who held-up Duncan on the Sychnant Pass. That sort of tale. Information to bribe people with.'

Nash had developed a nervous twitch when he was angry. His head imperceptibly jerked as he leaned further back towards her ear. His voice was sinister between the happy wedding vows. 'Did you... satisfy his needs?'

'Course I did, I got to earn me pennies butler.'

He sat twitching, considering her lack of loyalty as the couple were declared man and wife. It wasn't jealousy that was making him nervous. The week before, he had taken on a pretty new maid of 13 years old called Elizabeth. He knew Sir John would be pleased but when he sat with the girl to instruct her on her duties, she had asked if she could run messages for him to Morgan so that she could see her mother in Porthaethwy. Swearing her to secrecy, he gave her a list of daily tasks and ordered her to report to him directly. He also called her Louise. 'That is your name whilst you work in this household girl. Do you understand?' She did. It was protocol to change the name when it clashed with someone in the family.

As the young men lined up outside the church for the wedding race back to Plas Coch, it gave Lady Isabel time to sidle up to Owen, who had been happily stood alone. His thoughts were with Siân. He hoped she would be content as Duncan's wife as he liked her. He needed her to be happy for the smooth running of the estate.

'Steward, how pleasant to see a couple joined?'

'Indeed Lady Isabel. They are an ideal pairing.' She took his arm and gently guided him towards the low wall that overlooked a small mere filled with water forget-me-knots. Dragonflies danced across the mirror-like surface, gently touching upon the odd violet flower.

'Nature is such a wonderful thing, MrTudur. No doubt the couple will be copulating all night, but what a shame it will be so short!' Owen was deeply embarrassed by the inappropriate comment. He could see Lady Elizabeth had noticed his captor dragging him away from the rest of the company.

'Ma'am.' He was at a loss about how to reply. The woman was hotter than her reputation as she thrust her groin into his hip.

'Yes indeed steward. I can't imagine why a handsome young man like you has not married yet. I would think you could have a dozen brats or more?' He was stunned and stayed silent. She pointed her yellow parasol at two mating dragon flies. 'Maybe you should come and tell me your secrets tomorrow, I would think about noon? You see, I love it when men fight over me like a piece of contraband...' Owen realised she had heard about the run-in with the customs and guessed it was Sir John's contraband. She teased further. 'How much tax do you think I am worth to the Revenue?'

Before he could respond he was saved by Elizabeth, 'We must leave now steward. Pardon me Lady Isabel, always a pleasure to see you, but with my husband away I have so much more to do... although when he is at home he seems to go missing so often. Just when a woman needs a good man yes?' Lady Isabel politely bowed her head and loosened her grip on Owen.

'Well good men need gripping hold of tightly, Lady Elizabeth. I bid good day to you both.' She turned away with a haughty toss of her wig and made her way to a gig.

Elizabeth faced Owen, 'Take care, sir. She seems to have an ardent interest in nature.'

As the second beauty left his side, he realised that he had much to learn about women.

Nash and the Dean were having a quiet conversation inside the vestry when the wedding race began. Siân had taken the wedding band from her finger as soon as she and Duncan had stood outside the porch to be showered with dried flower petals. She held her left hand high in the air and as she placed the ring back on the third finger they were off. Twenty young men leapt away from the church door to run the two miles back to the house and the wedding feast. The first ones back were deemed the most eligible as they were fast and strong. All the single young women clapped and shouted to encourage their favourites and then they followed at a fast walk, suitably slowed by their responsible parents or married sisters.

It was a wonderful wedding feast. The trestle tables on the lawn behind the house groaned under the weight of food and drink. Jugs of ale and milk. Barley bread and cheeses with pickled walnuts. Mussels from Moel-y-Don and roasted lamb and duck. A plethora of abundance that would never have been forthcoming without the generosity of Lady Elizabeth and, of course, the absence of stingy Sir John.

Sometime in the twilight of the activities, the owls and nightjars had called out their warnings but only the stars heard. A buxom servant girl had wandered away from the crowd, encouraged by the promise of money and relaxed by illicit gin. She was seen to leave alone, swaying down the field towards the sea. No one remembered if anyone had left at the same time, departing for a secret rendezvous with a luscious woman.

It was two days before Jenifer's body was found by a morass worker. A cold white piece of meat washed up on New Borough beach, close to Lovers' Island. There was no investigation, the girl was obviously drunk when last seen and must have committed suicide in the straits.

It was a travesty that the kitchen garden lay neglected behind its brick walls. A fantasy of weeds and grasses waiting for love and attention to fashion its heart, to create a place of beauty and peace. Owen walked there on occasion and remembered her promise to plant the seeds and lovingly tend the new growths. She had professed a love of nature and plants, but Elizabeth had been despatched by the master to mix with his new friends in high society and they demanded a two-year trip across Europe. The fashionable new sights and places of France and Italy were deemed more socially acceptable compared to the rugged but unsophisticated joys of Wales. It was in Venice that Lady Charlotte and Lady Elizabeth met and socialised for nearly three months. A secret opportunity to become true friends, sharing their fears and worries about their lives and in particular the brutality of their convenient marriages. The Earl's wife overtly flirted with the dandies of the day, the artists and the composers. She enjoyed the freedom of her infertility as sensitive lovers pleasured her every need, a holiday from brutality and duty. One lover had swum to her window barely above the surface of the Grand Canal, her love enhanced by the romantic moonlight that glinted off the waters. It was a hedonistic lifestyle that gave instant pleasure, but it would never last or lead to anything solid.

But neither Elizabeth nor Beth found an entertaining lover in that society bereft of morals. They kept each other company at the balls and dinners. Men approached them and were rejected as no man could match the true love in their hearts. Neither woman wrote to Owen. Beth had been rejected and Lady Elizabeth could never lower herself to correspond with a steward. Any letter would be a danger to her station as she supported Sir John in his rise to fame. That left Owen feeling unloved and deflated, but he accepted the inexorable grind of his lot. He felt alone in his work, with no support from his divided family as they scraped a life between the slate quarries and the overcrowded cottage in Brynsiencyn. He lived for nature, spending his waking hours outdoors and following the pull of the earth as the seasons changed from hot to cold and wet to dry.

But every five hours the sea surged in opposite directions through the Menai Straits and the trade on the passing ships and ferries inevitably followed its flow. Man was changing nature and therefore even the inevitable can also change in time; when the metal of a mountain is exposed or centuries of domination by the huge straits is belittled by a small bridge.

Chapter 7

Copper Mines Have No Flowers

July used to be the fifth month in the calendar year and therefore the Romans originally called it Quinctilis. The later name of Julius was given in honour of Julius Caesar who was born in this month. A tyrant of a leader, he was hugely successful with fanatical followers and devious enemies. The Anglo Saxons called it "Maed Monad" or mead month after the meadows which are in bloom, but Anglesey has few meadows and was once described as a "a barren and dreary waste away from the wooded banks of the Menai Straits." Parys Mountain could not be further from the beautiful Menai. The blue views across the sea to Westmoreland and Cumberland are startling in their clarity, but the most amazing colours spew from the earth when you invert your gaze. There you see a kaleidoscope of purple, yellow, orange, brown and red, all leached from the iron sulphides deep beneath the surface. However, it is a barren and windswept mountain, a mere pimple compared to its sisters ten miles south. But the wealth hidden beneath the crust was a rarity. Only Parys in Wales, Cornwall in England and Rio Tinto in Spain heralded a bright new age. A time of cheap and plentiful copper.

There was no rain on Saint Swithin's day, but forty more days without rain on Ynys Môn was highly unlikely. It was a yellow day for William, Owen and Sir John as they climbed the track on the west side of Parys Mountain. The bright sunlight had augmented the birdfoot trefoil, cinquefoil and stonecrop flowers they had seen on their ride from Plas Coch and now they rode amidst a profusion of gorse, as shiny as the copper below. This undergrowth covered many of the ancient workings from the Roman and Bronze Age periods and it was one of these that had been newly opened. They stopped by a tiny quarry on the north side. It had a single whimsie to crane material out of its depths and they could see three men working below.

Sir John addressed the agent as he contemplated the land around him, turning through 360 degrees whilst still in the saddle. 'The smelting company in Liverpool has now been established so when exactly are you due in court to finalise ownership from the clergy?'

'Next spring at the sessions in Beaumaris. Everything is prepared since my visit to London last month. Our case cannot fail, but it is slow and tedious with multiple contracts; it's like building a house with playing cards. One slight tremor and the lot would fall.'

Owen interrupted, 'What exactly are you buying here?'

The agent bisected the view with his pointed arm.

'Even more poor farmland for you to worry about, Owen. We will own about five square miles on the north side of here. Our issue is the new Mona Mine Company that borders us on the south as it is owned by the Earl.'

'Why is that?'

'Because bribes and court agreements won't prevent him from tunnelling into our veins. Essentially it is the same deposit and neither of us have managed to obtain total control.'

The master was looking eastward. 'But we do have an advantage, agent. You gave Fardol and me the choices of shipping from the harbours at Cemaes or Amlwch.'

'Did you decide Sir John?'

'It is easy to see the main reason to choose between them. Look north, Cemaes is eight miles away and would be less accessible by tramway when production increases.' His agent and steward could see Amlwch at the foot of the mountain and the Cemaes headland in the distance. 'I also sent the captain into both places in a small wherry in bad weather. It was an easy decision. The southern side of the natural harbour at Amlwch has been bought by a tiny lead mining company in Birmingham. Of course, it doesn't have our family name attached to it in anyway, but it is ours.'

Owen raised his eyebrows and blew loudly. As the master walked around the area, William sidled alongside Owen. 'Impressed?'

'Shocked and impressed. How did all that happen over the last six years?'

'Ten years to be precise.'

'Sorry William, why ten?'

'Because until Sir John bribed me, I was a happy employee of the Earl.'

Now Owen was truly shocked. 'Good god man, if you betrayed the Earl, he will kill you.'

'Well he may suspect, but at the moment he has no proof. Long may it stay like that or I will be taking the first boat to the Americas.' They remounted their horses to reach the highest point of the peak. Sir John gazed around him in ecstasy.

'If this is a success, I will be remembered as one of the great Georgian businessmen.'

Owen dared to ask his strategy. 'Please do not think me impudent Sir John but what made you even consider this enterprise?'

The master felt safe with Owen now and smug enough to let him into his thoughts. 'A chance meeting with Smith after he left our employ in Jamaica started it. My brothers and I were in Liverpool to discuss copper sheathing for the hulls of our merchant ships and then Smith told us about this place. It was all rumours and innuendo, of course, but we backed him, unlike the lily-livered Earl who was poncing about as usual.' William was smiling at the memory; it had changed his life and fortunes. 'Fardol told us about the navy's interest in copper sheathing as it reduces damage to wooden hulls. It stopped the teredo worm attack in the Caribbean and reduced fouling. So we ordered him to perform our own trials. The benefits were incredible steward, damned amazing in fact. A faster speed, easier to manoeuvre and fewer repairs, of course, meaning less time lost in the dockyard. Fundamentally, on each Atlantic crossing we would have fewer dead slaves as it was so much quicker.' He paused to look at Owen who was nodding to show his understanding. 'Tell me Smith, how has the Earl started mining?'

'His plans remain the same as five years ago. I am still bribing the overseer who says Lloyd-Williams wants to take unworkable shortcuts. He is increasing the amount of ore extracted by robbing pillars that are holding up the roof of the shaft. That is an engineering disaster sir! Shafts are six feet high, seven across and ninety deep. They are all roughly timbered, which is an expensive option on a grassy island and they will undoubtedly have many rock falls.'

'Let him pursue the method Smith, hopefully he will sow the seeds of his own destruction by such bad practices.' The master queried further. 'Do you think I need to agree a deal with the Earl?'

'You should consider your options Sir John. Commercially the potential extraction could make you both rich beyond your dreams. Working together will help the economics, especially on transport to Amlwch and towards running the port.'

Sir John couldn't be happier as he asked, 'How rich?'

'You could become the world's largest producer and exporter of copper.'

The master stroked his corpulent chin. He never fudged a decision. 'In that case I need to meet with the Earl but on my terms and at the right time. Now tell me, have our opencast trials been a success?'

'It seems slower as we move so much more rock to reach each vein, but if we change the traditional way we pay the men, I think we can make it cheaper than using the shaft methods. It can be a lottery as it depends on the geology beneath us.'

Sir John asked an obvious question. 'Once the deals with the workers are complete, I was thinking of blasting with gunpowder as at Dinorwic. What do you think?'

Smith was less inclined to use the method this time. 'The rock falls will be less predictable than with slate. I would therefore be concerned for the men's safety, sir.'

'I wanted to know if it could be the easiest and cheapest method?'

The agent didn't hesitate as he knew the master's whims. 'Yes, Sir John.'

'Well if they are trapped by a rock fall, their friends will be more inclined to quickly dig them out and boost production, what!'

'Yes Sir John.'

Owen gave William a knowing look. Lives were cheap in the Littleton-Jones business empire.

The master mounted his horse. 'Let's be off. I want to see Amlwch again.' The tireless agent jumped on his horse to stay close to Sir John and discuss further details, whilst Owen sat at their rear in wonder at the extraordinary energy and foresight of the family. He also struggled with how devious and cunning they had been and how they had placed his friend in danger. Would he ever have that same level of responsibility, the same need for deceit? And would he be prepared to take the ultimate risk as an honest upright man?

It had taken six years before the kitchen garden ideas had become a reality. Elizabeth wore a long black skirt and a white armless blouse, both made of cotton to keep her cool in the July heat, but Beth was dressed to impress in satin. Her ladyship's physic garden design was inspired by a local man called Hugh Davis. Owen had provided men for the hard work, but it was her creation, a dream come true, although Aeronwy had suggested many of the medicinal plants. Bees and red admirals competed for space on two hundred species of annuals and perennials. Carefully planted in between were bulbs of garlic to help recovery, dill to soothe a stomach, arnica for bruises and cannabis for pain relief. Her ladyship was proud of her new knowledge. Hawthorn to reduce tension, echinacea to treat colds, digitalis to soothe the heart or used to kill...

'Remember Beth, a lady demands respect. A man who takes advantage is disrespectful.'

'Ma'am, we have only kissed. If he wants me, he must ask my father for my hand.' Elizabeth threw some raspberries into a basket to take to Siân. She needed to return to the house shortly, before the master returned. He disapproved of the time she spent in the garden, 'ladies are not supposed to exercise, madam, and servants do the doing!' She glanced around her and thought about Beth with William. Surely she must want him badly as she could identify with the feeling; the need to be loved and physically fulfilled. She moved a few steps and took a deep breath. She was pleased how well the seeds of white valerian, marvel of Peru and Prusion-stock had taken. The scents made her giddy with delight; an aphrodisiac on a perfect day when she needed a real man like Beth was going to meet.

'Do you love him Beth?'

The head housekeeper twirled her parasol in the bright sun, making an elongated shadow that flickered across her friend's concerned face.

'What is love, my ladyship? I loved Owen, but it did me no good.'

Elizabeth stood to push aside her thoughts and then kissed her friend's cheeks, whilst carefully keeping her dirty hands from Beth's shimmering dress. 'Love is everything my dear... enjoy your afternoon and be true to your heart.'

A few hundred yards away, two young men in their working prime were slouching over the low bridge wall and staring idly at the ten coots competing for space with three hundred ducks. The coots set about their day in a more assured way, silent and energetic, jerky, but intellectual in their purpose as they crossed the lake. The ducks chased and chattered to each other about nothing. They followed each other and squabbled for the sake of it and with seemingly no real purpose to their lives except to end up on the plates of the watching men.

Smith was excited about the new copper mine he would create for Sir John. 'Do you realise how important this find is for the nation?'

Owen looked at his friend who seemed to be spending much more time at Plas Coch. He had seen how friendly he had recently become with Beth.

'Yours or mine William?'

'Ours, of course! Great Britain. You signed up with Sir John and his family are your family now.'

Owen turned away. He slightly regretted his past, but his true family advocated a different future. 'Wales must be itself one day. You know that, don't you?'

'Of course, my friend. I'm sorry for being so insensitive. Wales will come of age one day but not now and not this century.' Owen watched as Beth approached. She wore a beautiful coral satin dress and carried a white parasol above her head that was held at an enticing angle. He often had regrets when he saw how she had changed and now, in particular, as the vision of beauty came closer. It dawned on him that she was no longer available.

'You seem to be here more than usual William?'

Smith knew the failed relationship was still sensitive so he replied gently. 'I don't want a life of work and giving my soul to the devil through prostitutes and drink Owen.'

Owen looked up and responded negatively, 'You have no choice but to include work in the bargain with the devil.'

Smith smiled. 'Sir John you mean?'

'Of course, but the real question is can you really change? '

'I would for the right woman.'

Owen raised a quizzical eyebrow. 'You can change because of an emotion, an interesting concept for an engineer.' He pushed himself upright. 'In that case, I wish you well but... please take care of her; she has seen enough hardship in her life.'

William clasped his shoulder with a reassuringly strong grip before quickly walking towards his new beau.

Owen slowly walked towards the walled gardens in the distance; it was a favourite place for him to think. As he entered on the south side he could admire the abundance of the netted fruit trees. He leaned closer to inspect the apricots, pears and cherries. At the gable end of the brew-house were quince and raspberries ready for making jam. She was stood by the latter and immediately before the mulberry and orange trees. This end of the garden was protected by the walls in winter and the tender trees were planted next to warm air flues driven by the boiler in the brew-house. He glanced to his right before approaching. It was a long hesitation as he stood and noted that dung was needed around the herbs. The sour smell would repress the sweet ones from the parsley, thyme, sweet marjoram, hyssop and sage. He walked towards her with butterflies in his stomach. She had impressed him with her creation; it was more than a work of art, it was one of thwarted love.

Elizabeth heard his approach as the boots ground into the sandy path laced with seashells. She looked up and spoke quietly. 'I see Beth has found some happiness in her life at last.'

'I am pleased for her ma'am.' He passed her a ball of coarse string.

'And a little jealous maybe?'

'A man should never regret his actions.'

'No indeed, steward but sometimes if a man and woman decide something, then they should both partake and live with that action without any regrets? Correct?'

Owen was thoughtful and hesitated with his reply. 'I think the world in which we live places little responsibility on a man and a lot on a woman. Therefore, the man who regrets something is kind and sensitive in an insensitive period.' He turned and walked away before she could reply. She admired his back as he retreated, the strong straight shoulders under his white shirt, the slim waist and strong legs that kicked up clouds of pink dust.

'That is what makes you unique, Owen Tudur.' She bent and tied a stray raspberry cane into position and adjusted her straw hat to keep the sun off her perfectly white face.

March 1st, Saint David's day in Beaumaris was a non-event. A national celebration would come later that century, but even then it would be essentially for those living in South Wales. It was nearly 1,200 years before, when the Saint had settled on the Lleyn peninsula nearby. The local King had then given him the old Roman fort near Holyhead where he had founded his monastery. But the people around Beaumaris knew more about Saint Cybi who had also lived about the same time. Cybi would always face the sun when travelling to meet his friend Saint Seiriol from the Penmon monastery, east of Beaumaris. Therefore Cybi was always known as "the tanned". Conversely, Seiriol always had his back to the sun on his way to their meeting place at Red Wharf Bay and so he was known as Seiriol "the fair". The pigments of these two local Saints were far more interesting than a patron Saint of Wales, which reinforced the English character of the town.

However, it would still be a memorable day as the quarter sessions were held in the new town hall. The lofty gentry and heavenly clerics gathered under its high ceilings to approve orders for bridge, road and gaol repairs. They pontificated about the care and removal of paupers and the strict application of the bastardy laws. Many of the bastard children were illegitimately procreated by the gentry themselves. Support was withdrawn from families when these children reached the age of 10 years old as they were then deemed able to work for a living. The Justices issued warrants for the arrest of suspected poachers and agreed the lists of officers and men for the local and national militia. A requisite number of locals were paid to join the national force and their wives and families accompanied them around England as necessary. The last item on the meeting's agenda was consideration of land rights on the island. Following minimal discussion, the master's ownership on the north side of Parys Mountain was finalised.

The gentle and good repaired to their rooms in the Bulkeley Arms Hotel and looked forward to an early dinner. Sir John had also booked himself into the hotel and made sure he politely joined them. The meal was carnivorous and eaten greedily. Steaming quarters of lamb, huge sides of veal and blood engorged ox tongue were served with smaller portions of teal, snipe and plover with the lot washed down with the finest French claret. Dessert consisted of pickings tentatively made from the Spanish oranges, Moroccan raisins and currants. These were temptingly set around large portions of iced cream made in the ice house at Bangor and delicate flutes of cloudy gooseberry wine and teak-coloured cognac. Port was served at the end of the meal to ensure that everyone was totally inebriated.

The Earl sidled up to his successful competitor. 'My man Morgan tells me he saw Smith poking around Amlwch this winter past. I can't imagine what he was doing up there, Sir John.'

The master gently clutched the Earl's velvet sleeve, 'Dear Edward, I have some excellent opium in my pouch and wondered whether you would care to take a pipe with me in the smoking room?'

'I would be delighted John, I am always glad to consider the ways of the world with you.'

They moved drunkenly towards a quiet area in the hotel and sat quietly in a blue haze to consider each other. They convivially mulled over the "bastard" Frenchies, the inadequacies of the Treasury to supply enough coin of the realm and their huge interest as fund holders for the national debt. They skirted around the opportunities for the growth in copper mining, slate quarrying and the impact on sea trade if slavery was abolished, but they both agreed that cooperation at Parys Mountain would be much better than confrontation. The impact on the infrastructure at Amlwch and a potential bridge at Porthaethwy were discussed but no firm agreements made. However, they did agree to meet again and secretly formalise their relationship to take the battle to the Pennants and Ashettons on the mainland. A second ounce of opium was smoked whilst Owen and Lady Elizabeth were eating their supper in the fourteenth century Bull Inn on the same street and nearly opposite the relatively new hotel.

It was no coincidence on February 28th that her ladyship asked Owen to escort her on a trip to search for wild flowers. She had insisted that Elis Wirion should accompany them and that they should go on the day following, when Sir John was away on business. She had suggested that they could search for the elusive alpines near Dinorwic, but it was Owen's idea to head east from Aberpwll and explore the valley above the village of Aber on the mainland opposite Beaumaris. He explained it would be quick to reach with all three of them on horseback. He knew it was a beautiful area as he and Aeronwy used to visit her grandmother in a tiny cottage dwarfed by the dell halfway up the valley. She was delighted by his suggestion and so they had departed early on Saint David's Day,

David or "the beloved". She would have been even more delighted if she knew Owen had ordered Elis to remain at least 300 yards behind at all times.

Owen and Elizabeth chatted constantly as they trotted side by side. In his saddlebag he carried her notes that categorised the plants they might find on the mountains of North Wales. They were written by her botanical friend, Hugh Davies, who saw it as his life's work. Her ladyship wore a thick navy mantua beneath her greatcoat; it was made from wool and designed to keep out the cold of the spring day. Owen had also anticipated the early morning cold and therefore donned a suit of duroy. This was made from a local Berber thread from black sheep and spun in Llangefni.

The coastal journey on the brand new turnpike took no more than two hours. They stopped briefly in Bangor for refreshments whilst he told her the city's name meant an enclosure using a fence made of poles with branches woven between. She hung on his every word as they wondered at the change from such a small place into the burgeoning city. But time was of the essence and they didn't delay to explore Saint Deiniol's Celtic monastery or the wide variety of shops. The master always insisted on visiting Caernarfon instead of Bangor for any goods or entertainment as it was 'on his territory.'

The three riders reached Aber and slowly wended their way up the narrow cutting which precedes the green valley. All around them they saw nature bursting into life after a hard winter. Drooping white snowdrops hugged the north side and two-tone yellow narcissi faced them from the warmer south. Stands of alder stood straight, adjacent to the wide but winding stream which cascaded over the dark granite boulders and fell into deep churned pools every 200 yards. Owen explained how the villagers harvested the alder for clogs and charcoal. Sometimes the horses walked through a fetid blue smoke as they passed a charcoal mound surrounded by four workers. As they climbed higher, a dark brown duck with a crested head scampered its way up the stream in parallel to them. It paused on rocks to gaze at the humans before half swimming, half running its way through the next succession of turbulent rapids. Then it would reach a deep pool and wait for them before clambering onto another boulder. The place delighted Elizabeth as she watched red squirrels dig for their secret caches of nuts between carpets of pink and white cyclamen growing under the ivy bound trees. By the time they stood at the foot of the Aber waterfall, her notes and search were forgotten in the rapture of the stunning sight. Waters cascaded from a hundred feet above them, a white gush of icy cold threads that bounced once or twice on an outcrop of shiny rock before stitching themselves together in the finality of a deep hole at the foot.

'Owen, thank you.' They had dismounted and sat on a rock eating bread and cheese a few yards from the waterfall.

'It is my pleasure, Elizabeth. I knew you would be delighted by it.'

'Delight! This is more than delight. In the two years of travelling around Europe I never saw such a beautiful sight.'

They sat mesmerised by the falls for half an hour before crossing the turbulent stream and heading west walking their horses. Elis kept his distance but also kept his eyes open for any trouble.

'Now we must try to find some specimens to take home.' Owen pulled her notes from the saddlebag and read some of the scientific phrases with delicate watercolours of each plant facing each page of notes. 'I can help you with meconopsis cambrica, the Welsh poppy and tufted saxifrage but avens, bogbean and butterwort are outside my experience. I'm so sorry I can't help more.'

'Don't be sorry, Owen, please be happy you are here. The day out is worth a thousand fold more than a few plants.' He relaxed as she smiled at him and took the reins of her horse to make it easier for her to search. As they reached the seaward end of the valley ridge they both paused, looking down at Aber 1,000 feet below and in the middle distance the huge expanse of Lavan Sands. The sun was still bright at 3pm, with a blue sky poised like a halo above the whole of *Yr Ynys Dwyll*, "the dark island".

'God is in his heaven today, Elizabeth. All of that,' Owen stretched his arm and swept it through an arc covering Bangor to Puffin Island, 'makes me want to sing with joy.' Beyond the bright blue sky to their right was a murky horizon. They could see the sea mist building up in banks near Llandudno and thereby obscuring the view of the seaside town. Their horses were almost leaning against each other as she gently touched his arm.

'I believe that feelings are the most important part of life. Without feelings there is no life. We would think to exist and never think to live. It is on a day like this that makes those feelings Owen.'

He didn't need to speak; she knew what he was feeling. Owen kicked his horse towards the steep narrow track that led down to the coastal plain. His manly but haunting tones bounced around the valley, stilling the bird song as he sang in pure joy. It was a hymn by William Williams from the Brecon Beacons, a composer from similar mountains and valleys in the south. "*Gloria in excelsis*" but sung in Welsh. He looked around and saw her delight and so he sang again. "*Lord, Lead Me Through The Wilderness*", translated as the English Hymn "*Guide me, O Thou Great Jehovah*". Songs of the Welsh Methodist revival, strident and true, and from a distance came a joyful echo, as silly Elis joined in with gusto. Owen turned around again to check that she was coping with the descent. She was beaming with joy as she was guided to glory by the only man she wanted in her life.

'These words will inspire our Welsh nation to greatness again, Elizabeth. Greatness madam!'

She shouted back happily, 'As you said Owen, God is in his heaven, and today we feed on the very bread of heaven itself.'

The rest of the descent was made in silence as the horses zigzagged their way down the steep and slippery path towards the Beaumaris ferry that started from Lavan Sands. It was both the fastest and also the shortest way back to Plas Coch. They were all tired and the horses were flagging. If necessary, they could eat in the town and then hire a gig to complete their journey home.

It was nearly a fatal mistake by the usually reliable steward. He didn't have much experience of the tides at this end of the Menai and the mists started to roll in whilst they were still a mile from the ferry. It made it impossible to follow the poles marking the winding route that avoided the quicksand. The horses' hooves were digging deep into the rippled sandbank, making the animals snort and buck as the visibility dropped to a few yards. The three riders had no choice but to dismount and walk side by side in the direction they thought they had seen the ferry, but the light was now fading above the murkiness. The squelch of their feet told them the tide was quickly secreting its way across the flat sands and filling the shallow trenches.

Elizabeth was scared, 'Owen? Is this the right way?' He hushed her.

Silly Elis started to blubber, 'I 'eard the drowned then Owen. Dead voices was talking to me, like they are coming to get us.'

'Be quiet man. There are no ghosts in this world, only idiots. Hush yourself immediately!' Owen motioned them to stop and walked forward alone into the gloom. They heard him shout loudly. 'Ferryyy...' The call drifted away into the clinging vapour. All they could hear now was the flow of the sea as it swished around their feet. 'Ferryyy...' They heard the fear in his voice. Seven times he shouted and then they heard the faint reply away to their left. A shadow appeared beside them. 'Quick, let's go.' It took another ten minutes of shouting and walking before the ferry lantern appeared before them. All three gulped in cold damp air in their relief to climb aboard. Half an hour more and they would have joined the hundreds sucked away into the night and involuntarily buried at sea.

The Bull Inn provided three rooms for the bedraggled and bewildered group. Owen's was on the first floor adjacent to Elizabeth. He located himself there to act as her protector, whilst Elis was with the servants in the rear. The inn was warm and welcoming; more so after their narrow escape. Low black beams sagged across the ceilings and a few colza oil lamps and candles burned merrily on the window ledges giving the burnt aroma of rape seed oil mixed with wax. A harp disconcertingly sounded its slow haunting songs in the snug behind the dining room as they ate ravenously. The harpist played old English folk songs in this bastion of England, but each note clung to them, reminding the pair of the sadness in the mist. Owen only took a single mug of ale, as he was determined he would stay awake all night to ensure Elizabeth was safe. As her steward he was deeply unhappy to be staying the night in Beaumaris, but nervous exhaustion made it impossible to travel the last eight miles. By 9pm all three were safe in their beds, with roaring fires set in each chamber to drive their fears away. Owen lay back against the bolster. He was naked as he had placed all his damp garments on a chair near the fire. A red light warmed the dark room and made him nod.

He jerked awake at the gentle sound of three knocks on the heavy oak door.

'Who is it?' He expected it to be a maid bringing more coal to the room but realised it was probably too late. He asked again. 'Who is there?'

The latch lifted and he reached for the dagger under the bolster. An angel's face appeared around the door. Lady Elizabeth stood in a borrowed white nightgown. 'Owen, I'm scared. Can I come in and talk for a moment please?'

'Of course, your ladyship.'

She walked across towards the bed and stood with her hands by her side a foot away from him. 'I was terrified, Owen. After the best day of my life, I thought we were going to die.'

He looked away from the violet eyes. The angel had a heavenly power over him. 'It was entirely my fault your ladyship, I'm so sorry.' He couldn't resist her look and turned back towards her as she lifted the sheets and slid naked beside his hard body. Her touch on his chest made him gasp and the first kiss stopped his breath completely. He eased onto his left side and closed his arms around her to make her feel safe again...

The perfect day and night contained no guilt and no regrets. If they had known the ferrymen had tipped off Rhodri Morgan about their passing... that one of his henchmen was told to stay at The Bull Inn that night, well then they might have been less carefree.

Chapter 8

Power Over People

The summer was consumed by a series of depressions with the bad weather and endless work making survival harder for the poor. Too soon, the autumn started to tinge the avenues of beeches at Plas Coch a dull caramel colour. The trees had expanded their girth far more than in a normal year having soaked up the incessant rain in the mild temperatures.

Lady Elizabeth and Sir John received a surprise invitation and argued continuously for a week prior to the evening of the event. Before they left for the dinner at Plas Newydd, he was adamant he wouldn't go. The reason was embarrassment over the rumours concerning Lady Isabel and him.

'I can't stand those damned Pagets showing off their wealth.'

'We have accepted their first invitation, Sir John. Their first one!' Her husband craved respectability and knew that social acceptability rather than his wealth would give him what he craved.

'They think they own the country. Strewth and zounds, our bank owns half their mortgages!'

She was looking forward to the event. Her friend Charlotte would be there with most of the other Menai dignitaries. 'Please calm yourself, Sir John. This is not for us. It is for George in ten years' time. We need to prepare the way for his entry into society. Money is not everything.' She smoothed her green satin dress as she sat upright in a leather chair in the drawing room. Elizabeth heard the crunch of the gravel as the coach pulled up outside. 'Come sir. You have no need to justify yourself. If you were in Jamaica or Liverpool they would be desperate to attend your dinner parties.'

He comforted himself with the thought and they set off for Plas Newydd, but he was determined to hate every minute.

The drive through the grounds alone dwarfed his ambitions. Every turn was on a grandiose style set with venerable beeches and luxuriant ash attracting pretty red squirrels. A procession of pines extended to the west to act as windbreak for the mansion. They were old, with trunks six feet in diameter. The stand leaned at a consistent ten degrees, with dark foliage on the outer extremes and bare spindly branches in the centre. These were swept skywards as if stroked through a giant's hand. As the coach passed, the sun caught the edges of the dark needles and turned them to bright green, illuminating the whole into a fantastical archway, gothic in the modern trend.

Plas Newydd, "the new place", was made from Penmon marble ripped from the coastline east of Beaumaris and transported by ship to the site. Its beauty was derived from its situation close to the straits, as it was set on a large mound commanding the sea. The reflections from the waters bounced from the many tall windows liquefying the very glass; the mirrored images of mountains, sea and sky in an ever changing kaleidoscope of colours. Closer to the house were expansive flower beds containing fuchsias doffing fairy caps in bright red and yellow stars of tall hypericum. Occasionally there were dramatic interventions of large gunnera leaves, which could be used by the fairies as an umbrella as they polished their stars.

The couple were formally greeted in the music room to the left of the imposing entrance via the Gothick hall. The portrait above the wooden fireplace was the 1st Marquess, staring down at his guests in full military regalia with his red face. The oak fireplace had been painted to look like stone, seemingly supporting the man who was equally wooden in his posture. A fashionable Broadwood piano was playing in the corner of the room, the sound resounding off the ceiling way above them. The remaining walls had huge canvasses by Franz Snyder depicting a gory bear hunt and scenes from butchers' stalls. They were rather dark and depressing, brutal and bloody like the family history.

After a fine dinner, the men gathered in the smoking room. The stewards and butlers had been invited but kept their distance from the gentry. They were there in case of trouble or to run errands. It was Sir John who started the argument with the Marquess.

'The damn press gang took twenty of my seamen in Liverpool last week. What right have they? Why should they ruin a man's business?'

The Marquess always smirked as he talked. 'The Navy has needs sir. We are heading into troubled times. It is a matter of choice.'

The Marquess took a pinch of snuff as if ignoring his neighbour. He was a ponce in his dark blue velvet and fine wig. Fluttering his hands with his head permanently tilted backwards to avoid the smell of lesser mortals.

'Business has needs too, Paget. A band of men armed with cutlasses took my men from an alehouse in the name of the King. The press gang rampaged through my city without any thought. They crashed into churches, boarded ships in the harbour and foraged wherever they could find innocent seamen. They did not choose sir, they just took!'

The Marquess deigned not to reply. As far as he was concerned, the King, the army and the navy always came first and always had the best as he was partly responsible for purchasing their assets.

The Earl united with Sir John. 'Come now, Marquess. What say you? Will you propose compensation for our losses?'

'Certainly not, Earl. We have always done it that way. Think about it. In five years' time we could be part of a French Republic unless the country remains strong.'

The Earl and Sir John consoled each other over another glass of port. They were benefiting from the high interest on the national debt after all. Owen heard none of this. The Marquess's steward had him penned in a corner, asking him to reveal his methods by which he had boosted the Plas Coch estate's farming output. The neighbours were jealous of Sir John's success and irked by his application of business sense to farming. Selling store pigs for 6d a lb by sending them to a central market and avoiding the travelling jobbers who only paid 2d. The use of more women labourers to decrease the charge on the poor rate. But the conversation was boring until the drunken gentry turned their attentions to pugilism. Bets were laid on the next bare fist fight between Tom Spring Gully and The Chicken. The Marquess's butler scribbled betting slips for each man who signed the foot of the papers. More than £200 was bet within ten minutes before they moved onto the big horse racing events for the season. After another happy and much louder hour, they all marched outside to watch the cock fighting. They roared and shoved each other and were as heated as the cocks that ripped each other to shreds. The smell of blood and sawdust mixed with the men's sweat and the fumes of alcohol. The final fight was for a bet of ten silver spoons and it was Sir John's cock that remained the last alive to defeat the Marquess. He was elated.

Calling Owen close to him, he shouted loudly, 'I believe you have a Welsh proverb, Owen?' Sir John stared around for the vanquished.

'Master?'

'In muck is wealth and indeed there is a lot of muck on Anglesey.' It was lucky the Marquess didn't hear. The slight was not very subtle, but the Marquess was some distance away, talking with the Earl.

'My dear Earl, we are the ruling class and see the country as it is and not what it wants to be. I know the Welsh are oppressed in their own country... they have lost their self-confidence; they do not believe that they can achieve much with the result that they attempt little.' They both guffawed and held each other upright before staggering back to the house. Owen had heard the Marquess. He wasn't drunk and the night had been an education in attitudes.

As the men drank and heatedly discussed fornication and cock fighting, the ladies sat and chatted in small genteel groups. Every few minutes they would politely swap places to talk to the other guests. A comic but thoughtful game of musical chairs. The winner didn't gain the prize in a parcel; instead they accumulated more tittle tattle than their peers. The richness of the dresses could be heard. The toile cracked as they walked, swept and sat. Black was predominant with lace ruffs around slim beautiful necks. An occasional horizontal band was in some exotic colour, a wide gold ribbon immediately below the breast. Some ladies sported Celtic brooches, almost as an apology to the Celts as they were bought in Caernarfon or Bangor to compensate for the fortune spent on the dresses from Liverpool or London. Elizabeth found herself alone with Charlotte and the two talked longer than was considered polite before returning to the gaggle. They cared for and supported each other now. They had shared the horrors of the legal rapes, the disciplines and constraints expected of a lady and Elizabeth kept her friend's lovers names as their secret. Charlotte had seen Owen earlier and was waxing lyrical about him.

'If only he was our steward. I do believe I would give him extra responsibilities. What do you say to lending him to the Earl, Elizabeth? He must be so bored of that little garden of yours!' Elizabeth coloured up; Charlotte had used the term to mean the Plas Coch estate not the convivial kitchen garden.

'Lending him to you, I think cousin? However, I do not believe he is available anymore.'

'For the nymphomaniac Isabel Paget or moi?'

Elizabeth had regained some composure when she replied, 'Owen is wedded to his job, his position and his responsibilities, my friend.'

Charlotte tilted her head gently. Her gaze exposed the depths of Elizabeth's heart. 'That makes him an unusual and attractive man. I do hope that he can keep his secrets close.'

'I hope so too, Charlotte.'

They strolled arm in arm back into the drawing room to retake their places with the loud company and watch Lady Isabel make her apologies before drifting across the hall towards Owen, only pausing to collect a glass of champagne from the silver tray proffered by the man servant.

'Steward, how delightful to see you again.'

His reply was a trifle curt. 'Lady Isabel.'

'Oh dear, what have I done wrong now?'

'I'm so sorry to cause offence ma'am. Please forgive me.'

'I would forgive you anything, Owen. That is your Christian name, I believe?'

'Yes ma'am.' Her casual use of his name worried him.

'Come then, I have something to show you in the salon.' He hesitated. 'Come, come.' And she swept him away turning back just the once to make sure he was in tow and then to latch upon his arm. Lady Elizabeth watched them depart and followed at a safe distance, and Lady Charlotte watched Lady Elizabeth. She decided to warn her later that her secret night of passion in The Bull was delighting her husband who planned to use it against Sir John. The steward stood arm in arm with Lady Isabel in front of a mural that stretched 20 yards across the salon wall.

Owen was genuinely astonished. 'That is so beautiful Lady Isabel.'

'As beautiful as me?' She turned and pushed her bosom into his chest. Her luscious full lips pouted a foot from his mouth.

Owen coughed and gently broke away from her. 'Your beauty is renowned across the country, your ladyship... are you in the painting?'

She stepped close to it and pointed, 'Yes, of course! My lovely artist created it for me. It is called a "trompe l'oeil" and tricks the eye as you move. Come, walk with me.' As they traversed the room, the footsteps in the centre of the painting changed their direction by 180 degrees and the mountains grew smaller. 'So handsome Owen, is it as beautiful as me or less so?' He was beside himself with fear of the woman's intentions. He knew without a doubt she had "taken" the Earl and Sir John and "took" whomever she desired. The sound of footsteps approached from their left.

'Steward!' Elizabeth didn't approach. As Owen turned she gave him an order. 'The master wants you immediately. Come!' And then she turned and walked away followed by Owen after giving his unwelcomed apologies to Lady Isabel. Left alone, Isabel started to waltz across the room, clutching her hot bosoms. She needed a man and felt frustrated as she wanted power over them, not just the sex. She also had some new gossip to share with her society acquaintances. A lady would never chase after a servant on behalf of her husband, unless there was a reason. It was the Earl who ended up in a guest bedroom with her later in the evening. After five minutes he had satisfied himself and was pulling away from the mad woman. He had to push her back onto the bed and virtually run from the room to escape her clutches. She had no morals and didn't care that everyone knew about her sexual appetite.

By 2am, the party subsided. The master was rampaging about his biggest competitor in the slate industry to anyone who was still standing.

'I will never set foot in any place bought by the Pennant family. How impertinent to construct a damned castle what! They were enemies in Jamaica and are enemies in Wales.' Lady Elizabeth had joined him and remained politely patient with her friend Charlotte stood next to her.

'We both have an invitation to the Pennant's garden party in Liverpool, my dear. If nothing else please let me accompany my cousin.'

He was unmoved, even in his excellent mood. 'I forbid you to speak about them ever again.'

She said her goodbyes to Charlotte, assuring her he would change his mind and then climbed into the coach. As they drove home Sir John continuously belched, bloated by the venison and turtle served by the truly rich. He said four words before falling asleep and snoring loudly.

'Damned good party what!'

* * *

The leaves resembled floating shavings of gold and brown, shimmering through the low beams of sunlight.

October is the time of the "Blood Moon" according to pagan beliefs, when the Celtic year, Lammas, draws to a close and the people prepare for the harshness and impending darkness of "Samhain". The circle of the year was closing on its round, and the sense of death overriding life was ever present. The Druids believed that the soul was taken to the west after death, in a ship made of white crystal and hence stored on the island of the blessed. A soul on a ship of fire went the opposite way, to the land of the damned. The Celts had a ritual where they drew a protective circle around a body. They would stretch out the right hand with a pointed forefinger and describe the path of the circle towards the sun to provide protection from darkness.

The leaves died and waited to be reborn into the lighter days. All Hallows' Eve drew closer and people's doors were locked that much earlier.

Owen was ready for church and sat on the settle in the cottage as tad and Cadell bustled around preparing for chapel. Cadell started the argument whilst Aeronwy was fretting over the twins who were in the bedroom knitting socks. She returned downstairs to the table as the argument heated up and recommenced washing and squeezing the freshly churned butter with two wooden beaters held in her red raw hands.

'Why don't you come to the chapel then? You are a true Welshmen still, aren't you Owen? Come and join the non-conformists man!'

Owen was pleasant enough as he replied to his brother-in-law, 'You know Sir John would object. Minister Evans speaks truly but somewhere along the line, men are being encouraged to revolt. Bolstered by the talk of The Union.'

Lewis was staring hard at his son, 'If I can go to chapel as his overseer, why can't you? You are betraying your family, Owen.'

His son was shaking his head. 'So many things have happened in the years since my appointment. There is no going back.'

Cadell and Lewis lambasted him about the conditions the men suffered at Dinorwic and Parys Mountain and all Owen could do was keep his head bowed in shame. 'I know! Now leave me alone as there are so many things you cannot know!'

It was tad who asked, 'Like what, Owen? We are your family. If you keep secrets when you live so tight to us, then maybe you shouldn't be here.'

Owen looked up. 'Do you want me out? Is that it, so you and Cadell can plot without interference?'

The three men stood breathing into each other faces. Lewis twisted his dirty turnover around his neck with a clenched fist that was ready to fly. The anger and bitterness had been brewing for years. If Aeronwy hadn't separated them, blows would have been exchanged.

'I'm off. I'll collect my things this afternoon.'

As he left the cottage he slammed the door and missed Cadell's comment, 'Good riddance, Englishman!'

Lewis grabbed his son-in-law's collar and spun him around to face him. 'That's my son you are talking about and my son is a part of me, so shut your face.'

After Owen had calmed down he walked purposefully to Saint Edwen's but was lost deep in thought. He wanted to help his people but how?

The Dean was waffling as usual. Owen listened reverently but knew he had more in common with the fire and brimstone service in the Salem chapel at Porthaethwy. He also knew he would never go there as it would be full of nationalists agitating for a Union in his employer's businesses. The rumblings had increased lately, spurred on by someone with money no doubt. He turned his attention to the service.

'In the beginning was the Word, and the Word was with God, and the Word was God. He was with God in the beginning. Through Him all things were made; without Him nothing was made that has been made. In Him was life, and that life was the life of me...'

It was delivered in a low incessant tone, uninspiring, and Owen listened as part of his duty to God, the King and fundamentally, his master. The master also had a problem with the sermon. He made things and if he didn't make them, then nothing was made and there was no profit. He believed in self-help; whilst his head was bowed and his eyes followed the perpendicular patterns of the slab joints, he decided he would tell the Dean to avoid this section of the gospel in future and focus on practical advice and stories. How Jesus cleared the temple of the money changers, an allegory to the newly established regional banks. After a while he decided that was also a bad topic.

They sang a hymn by Ebenezer, a great love song of the Welsh revival, but the English didn't understand the implication. Elizabeth avoided Owen's gaze, whilst William and Beth glanced at each other several times. Owen heard the words as a descendant of Glyndwr. In his mind he sang the Welsh version. He thought about the Welsh people, the power behind Cadell and tad's emotions and he resolved that one day he would use his position to help them all.

> *"Here is Love, vast as the ocean,*
> *Loving-kindness as the flood,*
> *When the Prince of Life, our ransom,*
> *Shed for us His precious blood.*
> *Who His Love will not remember?*
> *Who can cease to sing His praise?*
> *He can never be forgotten,*
> *Throughout Heaven's eternal days."*

The mortals of this world sang and pondered their own beginnings and endings.

At this time of year, the natural and the supernatural were greatly enhanced, with many rituals taking place such as All Hallows' Eve. There was a belief in the need to prepare against the gathering forces of dark, which could be seen in all forms. In visual glyphs and paintings, in decoration, and in the timing of the rituals themselves. Evil was evident in many stories, rhymes and songs, in traditions and in rituals. The harsh winter, the darkness, was something to be feared, as not everyone who had enjoyed the summer, sown and harvested, would make it through the winter either due to illness or starvation. The oral tradition brought an understanding of each other, of bird and beast, of plant and tree, of Creation and the spiritual world. It cemented communities through its teachings, information not stored simply for amusement but as a daily way of life.

The Beaumaris hunt ball was an exclusive event. Once again, Lady Elizabeth was pleased they were being incorporated into local society. After heated pennies had been tossed to the children from the balcony of the Bulkeley Arms Hotel, there were harpists and fiddlers to entertain the gentry. She wore a broad dark red band over her right shoulder made of the finest silk and clasped at the head with a silver Druid's head. She was positively blooming with health as her swollen tummy lay hidden beneath the folds of cloth.

Lady Charlotte stood next to her, enabling the Earl to lean forward and ask Elizabeth an impertinent question. 'How are your botanical studies Lady Elizabeth?'

'I enjoy them immensely, thank you sir.'

'I am so pleased, they must give you great pleasure but surely a lady does not entertain anything so... physical?' His sneer made her uncomfortable, but her friend squeezed her arm to make her bold.

'I plan and create sir, I let my steward organise the physical side.'

'Indeed madam, indeed. So I have heard in Aber and Beaumaris.' He bowed and left them taut with tension and went to talk to Sir John. Gathering a glass of champagne en route, he sidled up to his new "friend".

'I hear your steward has been searching for beautiful specimens John?'

The master was immediately wary. 'My wife follows the work of Hugh Davis.'

'From what I hear, they seem to be gathering a lot of specimens together and were seen late one evening in The Bull ?'

'Yes Edward. I know about their dangerous moments finding your ferry that night.'

Edward stroked his chin. 'We shall see, yes we shall see. Plants and seedlings can be so complicated I fear, so hard to make fertile. Anyhow John, business is business sir. I believe you offered me some warehouses in Porthaethwy?'

'Of course, Edward it would be a pleasure to sell them to such a confidential friend.'

'Excellent, in that case, can we say three hundred guineas?' The Earl was a charlatan. The location itself was worth more than that. Sir John considered whether it was a bribe or not. A bribe for a rumour to be quashed, an innuendo that could cause him issues in society circles.

'Three hundred it is, Edward. I hope you obtain great profit from the deal sir.' He walked away to find the toilet. As he crossed the room he stared at his wife. Business is business after all.

The following evening the couple were sat in the drawing room, alone with the newly fashionable aspidistras. Sir John was reading the newspapers. Lady Elizabeth sat demurely playing patience, with an occasional glance at her new red toile de jouy curtains and green wallpaper with its birds and flowers. As he drank more toddy, he ranted more and she nervously searched the cream ships sailing across the windows for some solace. She picked up the recent letter from George. At the age of twelve, he had been packed off to Eton after a shameful romp with a servant. If he were older and had professed his love for the girl, he would have been sent packing to the army.

"I miss you mamma, the regime here is brutal. Papa said it will make me a man, but I never saw the like on the steward's farms. Say hello to him please mamma. I fear I must stay in the London house to learn the real business according to papa. Love George x."

There was an outburst from Sir John. 'These damn sheets tell more lies than truths. Monday's *Observer* claims it is "unbiased by prejudice and uninfluenced by Party." How ridiculous, I know the Baronet who is telling the editor what to write. Pfur!' He was agitated, but she didn't know why. Calming herself, she waited for the explosion. '*The Daily Universal Register* is the only one to tell the truth, especially about the damn Frenchies.'

'I thought it was called *The Times* now, my husband?'

'Yes of course it is woman, stop contradicting me!' She lowered her head prepared for anything. 'The owner has been sent to Newgate prison for libel, what!'

'Sorry, Sir John. Why was that?'

'I said keep quiet woman. A 50-guinea fine and two years in jail over a damn woman by Christ! The Prince of Wales sued him for alleging he wanted to marry the crackpot Roman Catholic strumpet. The paper's article said George was a womaniser, a heavy drinker and up to his neck in debts! All the damn truth, what !' He stood and snorted. Walking to a window he yanked the curtains violently and brought them crashing down. He turned to Elizabeth and stood with his hands on his hips. Red-faced and breathing hard, his gut was hanging over his belt. 'There are rumours in Beaumaris, madam. Like the newspapers, a story to believe or disbelieve. What do you say woman?'

She carried on stitching but looked up every few seconds. 'I have no idea what you are talking about sir.' Her heart was beating fast, but she fought against the panic.

'My wife was seen with a commoner, seen to be talking like a love-driven doe. All eyes a fluttering.'

She knew she had one chance. 'I told you about my trip and how I was saved from drowning. If I looked relieved in The Bull Inn, then I think it is normal.'

'Relieved! Good God woman, what about my reputation!' He was spitting saliva as he shouted at the top of his voice.

'Can I ask, sir, who is spreading such lies?'

He strode across the room towards her. 'Lies, my Lady? Lies?'

'Yes lies. Who is spreading these lies? Tell me please.'

He was incandescent with rage, but she had given him doubts. 'It came from the Earl.'

'In that case, all is explained sir.' She stood and walked to the door; as she opened it he followed her out and up the wide stairs to her bedroom. The rape was the most brutal ever. His hands ripped at her clothes, tearing in fury and as he shoved his cock inside, he grasped her neck and squeezed. If he hadn't orgasmed so quickly she would have been strangled. Lady Elizabeth was tended by Beth and stayed in her room "indisposed" for more than a week. She sent a private note to Lady Charlotte via Aeronwy who came to administer arnica for the bruising. She asked Lady Charlotte to do everything possible to stop the rumours. It was through Aeronwy that Owen found out and therefore he adjusted his behaviour around his master to brook no lies or indecision. It was a close call, but they both survived their night of passion, when seedlings had been set.

Elizabeth had walked with Beth and Siân to the church on Halloween. Each woman collected three snails off the north wall and left them under leaves on the kitchen table overnight. Siân was happy for them both. She had heard the rumours about Owen and her ladyship and hoped William would propose to Beth. Now she was married herself, she could feel others' pain. Duncan was a good man and treated her well, but it seemed she could not have babies and that made her sad. In the morning, the three women excitedly lifted away their leaves and followed the snail trails with pointed fingers to spell out the first name of their lovers. Beth's snails had changed direction several times and there was merely a shape fashioned from slime that looked like a tombstone. The mistress was also out of luck; her name was the wrong sex, the trail spelt Rose. Siân was convinced hers spelt Duncan, but the others pointed out she couldn't spell and so they all giggled and laughed before turning their attention to making blackberry preserve.

Christmas, as usual, would be spent in London. Sir John was speaking to Elizabeth again and appeared to have forgotten the insults to his honour.

'Next year I want to create an "English garden" at Plas Coch. Something better than the Pagets in this monolithic madness called Wales.' He was striding around the drawing room the day before they departed. 'Like the house at Stourhead. Or a Capability Brown design with a temple of Parthenon.' She kept quiet, she was happy with her walled garden, the rest could remain natural. The location itself was more beautiful than anyone might create. 'You know madam, stylish and modern not rustic and backward like the damned Celts. Something to brag about on this miserable island.'

'I liked some Capability Brown gardens, sir but I can make our own design if you fancy?'

Sir John was aghast. 'A woman designing hundreds of acres, are you suffering from melancholy madam?'

'I'm sorry to be so forward Sir John. Maybe we can talk to a designer next spring.' He "humphed and pfur'd" to great effect before departing to his study.

On the day of departure, she walked around the kitchen garden. Two women employed to weed were chewing their tobacco and spitting the resulting juice on the grounds to kill the worms which were considered pests.

The wind swept through the trees with such a violence it felt like all the ghosts of the world were howling through the air. She pulled her coat close and bowed her head as she wandered and said goodbye to her beloved plants. On occasion she bent down to break off some dead growth and then smiled as she saw the fertile new shoots at the base of the plant. Her swollen tummy made it hard to bend but the baby would be born in London, away from Owen, away from suspicion. Poppies and antirrhinum seedlings had already fallen and sprouted from the pods moving in the breeze. She stood still between the giant waving gunnera and bare twigged acers and looked up at the scudding clouds high above. She sensed his presence before she turned to look. When they gazed at each other, they didn't notice how much they had aged. It was the same spiritual look of their first meeting, where time stood still. She spoke sadly, the years were passing too quickly.

'Taid. Another goodbye, another year done.'

'Be well Elizabeth.' She shivered in the cold. Her lips were blue as she spoke.

'He that will eat the fruit must climb the tree. It is a new saying in society.' Owen was sad she was leaving. Their meetings had been few since Beaumaris and her beating.

His words were soft. 'I look upon the pleasure, which we can take in this garden as one of the most innocent delights in human life.'

She turned away and wiped a tear from her cheek. 'Elizabeth, I know what is the most delightful part of my life—'

She interrupted him, 'But your innocence can be denied.'

He came closer. 'Stay well and return to me please, my love. The innocence of life between two who can never be together, is the only delight in my world anymore.'

'I want you Owen. My very soul yearns for your touch, but it has been touched by the devil.' Elizabeth's tears fell on the dusty paths as the specks of sand were swirled into the air and then she walked away without glancing back.

In the winter days following All Hallows' Eve, the negative forces on earth were believed to be stronger in the darkness. With daylight so limited, all portents were to be heeded, no messages ignored. The Menai folk adorned their homes with a vast array of natural objects like dried seaweed to predict the movement of the weather and God's creatures. To ignore the interpretation of any omen was to ignore experience, not of the immediate, but of generations past. The ghosts of the Welsh royal family roamed the straits and their descendants still unknowingly obeyed the royal whim.

"The Horned One stepped forward bringing darkness, and the end of the year."

Chapter 9

Lies and Deceit

A year in the countryside passes with a certainty that everyone can touch and feel. Emotions grow stronger, but nature stays the same. The wind drives the horizontal rain across the green face of mother Wales; the sun shines but briefly and dries the minerals of the heat-pressured earth. An invisible zephyr of moisture raises itself above the mountains and the wind scrapes the scudding clouds off the peaks before the rain returns yet again.

Whether it is light or dark makes a difference in all aspects of nature, and therefore in human beings with emotions it makes an absolute distinction. Spring came late that year and the swollen ewes hung onto their lambs before birthing into the sunshine. Elizabeth avidly watched them and rejoiced in the tenderness between mothers and their children as Henry Littleton-Jones struggled through the third month of his life.

Ovid states that June honours Juno but others connect the month to the consulate Junius Brutus. The name is probably an agricultural reference and originally denoted the month when crops grow to ripeness. Thus Henry survived into the warmth of summer and was loved by his mamma and tolerated as an heir by his papa.

Time would tell if the child lived to his second year. Time would see the shaping of his true character by his true mother and father.

Beth and Elizabeth were driven by Elis in the gig when they decided to visit New Borough's sandy promontory, a desultory finger wagging at Caernarfon. There were a great number of birds in the lanes as they passed. Warblers, linnets and yellow hammers were all relishing the abundance of summer food. The women headed towards the straits after passing through Brynsiencyn instead of turning inland for the town of New Borough. As they passed the church, Beth recounted a story told her by Owen. A human thigh bone was an ancient reliquary and if removed from inside the church it would always mysteriously find its way back. The Earl of Chester, called Hugh the Fat, had wrapped the bone in chains and had it thrown into the straits to break the hearts and minds of the local people. But Druid magic born before any Christian thought or idea was stronger than the religious sanctitude of the incomers. The bone reappeared in the church and was laid to a permanent rest by setting it in the mortar of a hallowed wall.

The women travelled close to the swirls of the Menai and followed a water-logged track until a bank of sand dunes required them to alight and walk. Climbing to the top they held their parasols above their heads but still needed to squint as the sun blazed from a perfectly blue sky. Across the silver sea and no more than two miles away was Caernarfon Castle, a monolith that was still magnificently guarding the entrance to North Wales after hundreds of years. Strong and defying in its exterior, but bereft within, a partial ruin, unused by the military and unattractive to visitors. They watched enthralled as a porcupine was towed by a small boat powered by four rowers as it went back and forth to clear away bars of sand in the bright distance. The ship owners of Caernarfon and Felinheli worked tirelessly together to improve their access, driven by the riches earned from the burgeoning slate mines a few miles inland.

Elis was out of earshot as Beth held her ladyship's arm, 'Does the master suspect, your ladyship?'

She shook her head negatively, 'I don't know. Henry is an heir. That is all he wants.'

'Why did you choose the name?'

'After a great King of the Tudor family.'

Beth could see the significance and tightened her grip on her ladyship's arm as they stared at the wondrous day. The tide had receded to its utmost position and therefore they could see four different shipwrecks in different states of decay.

'God grant their dead souls grace. The men who chart these waters are so brave.'

'Or foolish, my Lady.'

'No definitely brave. Imagine the fear in the dead of the night with the wind roaring like a dragon and the seas smashing over your head.'

They could see a dozen *Cored* on the exposed sandbanks, with mainly women looking inside the wattle fencing for any trapped fish. To their right was a group of morass workers, resplendent in their grass hats to thwart the rays of the sun.

Beth asked tentatively, 'And Owen? What does he think?'

Elizabeth lowered her parasol and laughed bitterly. 'He doesn't know, he will never know. That is a secret between you and me, just like your daughter.'

Beth sighed deeply, 'Maybe it is for the best. He has no concept of family, he is a mere man.'

Elizabeth motioned her to walk further. She wanted to see if there were any puffins this year. 'That makes him a father twice over, Beth. What an injustice for a man who would have made the perfect father.'

The subject was dropped and never discussed again.

In the evening, Elizabeth sat as a dutiful wife as the master read excerpts from *The London Chronicle*. The editor specialised in proceedings from Parliament which he memorised as note taking was banned within the chamber.

'Richard Pennant is quoted in Parliament. He said, "...were the House of Commons to vote for abolition of slavery, they would strike at 70 million properties, it would ruin the colonies and egad, by destroying an essential nursery of seamen, give up the domination of the sea at a single stroke". That is the first sensible speech he has made.'

'Yes, Sir John.' She wasn't interested; since the baby was born, her spirit was flat. Her life was humdrum. No more than a slave herself.

He continued, 'Josiah Wedgwood's medallion says on it, "Am I not a man and a brother?" Pfur!' He was disgusted with people attacking slavery. Elizabeth stared across at him. Until her life in Plas Coch she had supported the family and closed her mind to the trade. Inwardly, she too wanted abolition. She saw the parallels with the Welsh and therefore secretly espoused the non-conformists. Siân had shared some pamphlets with her. Speeches by the now great Jenkin Evans, but both women hid their views and avoided trouble with their husbands, who always knew best.

It was in a dark corner at the rear of The Bull Inn where the major events influencing the next century in Ynys Môn were decided. It was the coolest and most confidential place where they could meet on neutral territory. The Earl appraised Sir John after they had despatched three lobsters apiece. Four bottles of red wine had been consumed and they were now contentedly sipping brandy.

The Earl pouted as he spoke, 'Take me through the strategy again.'

The master slurred his words as he summarised their agreements. 'We work together on copper to create a cartel on sales and manipulate world prices. After all, we each own half the mountain. We build a joint tramway to Amlwch and share the port running costs. You take the north side, I take the south and we build our own kilns to calcine the ore into copper cake. I provide the coal from my mines in Saint Helens and Worsley through my shipping line. I will also bring the lime in as ballast on my ships and reuse them to take cake to Swansea. We are already using the same manufacturer in Birmingham so we can compare his costs for wage tokens, toys, wire et cetera.'

The Earl nodded, 'Agreed, John. I will use my contacts in Westminster to reduce the duty on coal when moved by ship. All the prices are in order and the contracts can be signed next week. But how do I benefit from the...' he searched for the right word, '... tax avoidance? You know, in principle, I hate exporting copper to England's enemies.'

'It may be banned by royal proclamation, but the opportunities are massive. These damn wars will blow over within a decade and we must create new markets in places like America.'

'So I benefit by selling increased volumes?'

'Providing you keep the customs occupied.'

Edward nodded his assent; the costs of the bribes were relatively cheap. He moved the conversation forward. 'We maintain the status quo with slate. I can use Felinheli at the agreed costs and we compare prices to beat any bids made by the Ashettons and Pennants.'

The master smiled, 'Absolutely. We satisfy the high quality market and leave them to fight over massive volume contracts. We can't possibly compete with the Pennants investment at Bangor.'

'What about your new warehouse developments at Porthaethwy, John? Why would you want to tread on my toes so close to Beaumaris?'

'They are a mere trifling to me, Edward. In fact, I would be happy to sell them to you like the last batch and also my contracts on that quay if it helps. That will help you create a monopoly on the trade in your backyard. I can certainly use the money to develop Felinheli; you can't believe how expensive it is when you are competing with the damn Ashettons.'

'Why is that, sir?'

'We have started to make margarine, cure bacon and even grind chicory, but they can't accept even piffling industries like those next door.' The Earl was completely taken in. The purchases in Porthaethwy would consolidate his trading interests locally and it seemed logical. Sir John knew it was a distraction versus the main event, the potential bridge. 'We have enough to do with beating the Ashettons and Pennants what!'

'I agree, but my nearest neighbours are the Pennants and I shall concentrate on making it difficult for them in Bangor. As for the Pagets, well they are too busy playing at war.' The Earl splashed more brandy into both of their crystal glasses before slurping back his own drink. 'So did you give the Paget woman cock?'

'Of course, didn't everyone?'

Edward laughed, 'She is one hell of a fornicator but she said you tried and failed.'

'I always try my hardest Earl, especially when it comes to cock and on important things I never fail.' In his mind he envisaged the first bridge over the straits and then he gulped some of his brandy as he contemplated a second crossing. A link that his brothers were already preparing for in the corridors of power in the capital. 'Remember, we can divide and separate the opposition as I will solely focus on the Ashettons at my end of the Menai.'

A self-satisfied Earl was never as good as his forbears about details. It was why his estate and businesses barely increased in value apart from the copper mining, which he constantly dithered over. He gripped Sir John's arm. 'That leads us to the crossing. We both know it will have to be at Porthaethwy. We have a monopoly on all the shipping from there, but neither of us has the building contracts or land rights.'

'My dear Earl, some things are never set in stone. Let us agree that we work together to have the damn thing approved and stay talking about the spoils my friend.'

The Earl sat back in his chair and thought carefully. His spies had yielded no information to the contrary. If Sir John knew more than he professed, well it would be an issue, but he had nothing, absolutely nothing to lose at the moment. So he agreed to focus on the permissions rather than the commercials. He held out his hand. 'Overall then, we are agreed sir?'

Sir John leaned forward to shake it and lied, but that was why he was successful. 'You have my hand in agreement. That should suffice between gentlemen.'

'Indeed, then we have an understanding John. But mark me. This island has been in my family's control since Edward I in 1284. One day we will allow it to be joined to the mainland and my country will finally lose its independence. It will be my bridge, my rights and to the benefit of my Anglesey.'

Sir John barely suppressed the glee he felt inside. The Earl would surely want him dead if he knew the agreements made years before. 'Of course, I am so new on your island. I am a mere businessman interested in the copper.'

The Earl reinforced his point. It was his pride that was at stake. 'The other owners of Ynys Môn, the Pagets agree with me. There is no contretemps in our loyalties to our island.'

'No Edward, you are not soft like copper in your dealings, you are as hard as slate.' The master was delighted with the meeting. He thought to himself how easy it was to split slate.

'Precisely my good sir, precisely! You should join us in the Whigs. You know we control the new politics and will come to power soon.'

'Unfortunately, I can change many things, Edward, but my political allegiance to the Tories is fixed with the family business and the church. Maybe one day though. After all... the parties always swap clothes every decade, what!' The drunken men guffawed loudly at the truth. 'But if you are you offering me your MP's seat at Beaumaris?' Sir John let the query hang.

'In time, when I have the rights to the bridge. I do believe you yearn for respectability. You are moneyed, but I own the mayor, JPs, bailiffs and burgesses. Therefore, the seat is mine to give and not yours to take.'

They shook hands vigorously again, clasping each other's shoulders. The Earl was driven home in the warm air, satisfied with his scheming as he blinked alternate bleary eyes at Venus shining brightly above him. Sir John crossed the street and strode purposefully into his room at the Bulkeley Arms Hotel. On the side table were two crystal decanters. One contained Madeira and the other white port. He choose the latter and charged a glass before pushing open the windows and walking outside to stand on the large balcony. He could hear the sea but couldn't see it in the full moon. The new promenade had created a visual obstruction, especially at low tide. He sat and watched the star inspired shadows play across the mountains above Aber and focussed on the future. He wouldn't be hung over in the morning and within a few years his dreams would have been achieved. Improvements to the roads and new bridges were vital. It allowed the circulation of new ideas. Fresh markets would be reached faster and people would move to the towns and cities as the country launched into the industrial revolution. He laughed at North Wales lying at his feet. It was the greatest double-cross of his business career. His sons George and Henry would be like him. His sons would have the ultimate power in Anglesey.

Owen, William and Rhodri had been asked to sit in a separate room as their superiors supped, drank and finalised their joint strategy. The three antagonists remained together for less than ten minutes. Rhodri only wanted trouble.

'Sometimes Smith, I accidentally step in some dog muck. Then as I wipe it off, I think of you.'

'You were always bitter and vindictive, Morgan. In the 20 years since I left the Earl's employ you have become even more cynical and bitter. I suppose it is because no one in Earl's Hill will let you give them cock anymore?'

Morgan slowly took his dagger from his belt and stabbed it into the top of the oak table. It quivered between the tense still men.

'Always full of bad judgements, always wrong Smith. I take Cadells's sister whenever I like. She is more of a whore than a cook.'

Owen stood slowly. 'Take that back.' He had to react, family was everything. If he didn't, Rhodri might suspect his source of leaked information and Lady Elizabeth's secret contact to her friend Charlotte. Morgan, touched the knife with one finger to stop it vibrating. He wanted to stab Owen and was barely restraining his anger, but the Earl was next door.

'The Earl wants to bargain, to be Sir John's friend. But you and I will always be enemies, Tudur.' Smith stood and stabbed a larger dagger into the table. He deliberately flicked it so it knocked against Rhodri's with a chilling metallic ring.

'Owen and I will always help Sir John and his agreements are our agreements, but if we can kick and piss upon you, then we shall do so at every opportunity.' Rhodri, pulled out the knife and left without a word.

They sat and relaxed. Owen told William about his dream of the future. 'Somewhere, in some way, I want to help my country before I die. Sir John and the family will always come first, but I need some justice. I need to hurt Morgan and the Earl and all the damned English on my island.'

William sighed, 'Years ago, I would have been upset but now... I agree. The Earl plays games with us. He encourages the nationalists, the Union and the non-conformists, but he doesn't believe in them. He doesn't want them in his businesses. As for Morgan, he is an old debt that I will settle one day.'

'My tad and Cadell hate me, William. I am banned from seeing Aeronwy's twins. You see man, I agree with what they want for the Welsh nation.'

'If there is anything I can do to help Owen... I will do anything for our friendship and so will my friend Ieuan.'

'Why Ieuan?'

'Because Sir John made him pledge his soul too. When Ieuan's family died, it seemed like an accident. The slaves rioted and his wife and children were found dead the next day. It was only recently that another captain told him a rumour. Sir John had instigated the riot and ensured the number of guards in the estate were at a bare minimum.'

'Good god. So they should have been safe?'

'Safe, yes safe Owen, but the master wanted half his slaves killed. He wanted to improve productivity, so the day after the riot all the older men and women were singled out for summary execution.'

'Is it a rumour or the truth?'

William had tears in his eyes as he answered, 'I confirmed it was true to one of my oldest friends the day after the incident.'

'To Ieuan? How did you know?'

'I was the master's agent and I carried out all of his orders on the plantation.' Owen was deeply shocked.

'So all three of us are heading for eternal damnation... the time will come William, the time to make amends to each other and to God, so be ready. You have the real power here. You know all of Sir John's secrets.'

'Truly, but on some days it makes my head spin. However, when you nearly died on the Sychnant Pass, I made it my business to understand why the master cared about nothing else except a secret letter.'

'You know about the letter? The one that nearly cost me my life?'

'Shush my friend, I know everything and one day I will give you the freedom to act as your heart desires.'

William went to his bed in the inn whilst Owen rode home with Elis as protection. William took the small wooden chock from his inside jacket pocket and placed it under the door of the bedroom, jamming it tight with his boot. He heaved at the door as hard as possible and noted with satisfaction that it only opened an inch. Barely enough room to poke a pistol through and they wouldn't use a pistol in such a public place. He knew he was on borrowed time and regretted falling in love with Beth. It complicated his practical mind. He settled down to read *The Times* and the latest about the war with France. King George had allowed William Pitt to increase taxes, raise armies and suspend the right of habeas corpus. The loss of basic rights for prisoners to question their custody was important to the agent. He cared for people but had always pushed the tenderness to the back of his mind. Of singular importance were the secret deals Sir John's brothers had negotiated with the French government for copper and brimstone. 'Business is business,' he thought, 'in love and war.' He started to read the summary of the Battle of Trafalgar. He was interested because of his friend Ieuan's intensity when discussing ships and also to see the effect of copper sheathing on the hulls of the latest warships.

"Napoleon's strategy was to have his fleet threaten the West Indies. Thence to draw the English fleet away from Europe, giving an opportunity for the combined French and Spanish fleets to beat the remaining English ships in the Channel. This victory would buy him the week required to move his troops across the Channel and invade his old adversary. But Bonaparte did not foresee the cowardice shown by his navy. Admiral Villeneuve, who was based in Toulon in the South of France, took his fleet as ordered to the Caribbean. Our wonderful Vice Admiral Horatio Nelson chased him across the Atlantic but missed the French. Therefore, Nelson returned to Gibraltar to wait for their next move. Villeneuve headed back to Europe and in Ferrol, northern Spain he met our Admiral Calder who badly beat him, forcing a retreat to Cadiz. Nelson blockaded him and Napoleon pressurised the French Admiral to fight at last. Before the battle at Trafalgar off North Africa, Nelson sent a message to all his ships. The flags read: *England expects that every man will do his duty.* There were three cheers from every British sailor and thus inspired, 32 British ships took on 23 Frenchies and 15 Spaniards. Our superior tactics, seamanship and courage allowed us to cut their lines and beat them hollow. With great regret we lost 1,600, including our hero Nelson, now Lord Nelson. But we killed 16,000 of the opponents. Rule Britannia, Britannia rules the waves.'

William threw the paper on the floor. The British advantages would be lost if more copper went to her enemies. The courage and commitment of the underdog had inspired him. He wanted to help the Welsh before he was murdered. He wanted to help Owen and Ieuan gain their revenge. He sat and thought about Beth. He thought about running away with her, but that was a coward's way. Nelson wouldn't have run away. Nelson did everything he could for his country before he died, and Wales had been good to William. He was as good as Welsh in many ways.

Aeronwy missed Owen. She worried about him, on his own, living in the servants' quarters in the great house. None of the staff would feel that they could talk to him as a friend and therefore, he would be lonely. Her family lived for life around the hearth. It was all of their life. The range was used for heat and food and was a constant source of welcome. Fresh bread was baked daily and eaten with homemade butter, strong cheese and raw onion. Now her twin girls were older they played riddles or conundrums in the red glow.

"What goes a long way on its head?"

"A nail on the bottom of a hobnail boot."

"What turns into every house on the way to Chester?"

"A path."

It was family life, a life Owen was missing, where neighbours were your only friends, where everyone in the community helped each other every day. They recited tongue twisters and composed complex oral sentences. They talked about the strife over corn, the new corn orders from Parliament. The landlords demanding an even greater share. The speculation on prices increased dramatically and the manipulation of already deprived people mirrored it. It affected the nation but especially the poor and especially in Wales. Local farmers sold corn covertly and her brother had to stamp on it. She understood why but it was harsh. Informers were offered bounty but the people, her people, starved. There was a food riot at nearby Llanfairpwll. A crowd of one hundred seized a shipment of corn bound for Liverpool on one of Sir John's ships. Owen became a hated man and he hated himself and was more estranged from his family. He talked endlessly to William about his concerns, as he felt they needed to do something. He shared some of them with Elizabeth, but she had already heard most of the issues from Beth. Both women were appalled by the greed of the landowners. Appalled as they attacked the Calvanistic Methodists, who as sectaries, started to control the people and advocate unionism. The English were worried about their profits, but corn wasn't the issue; their real wealth came from the slate and copper.

* * *

Jenkin Evans was kneeling on the bare floor in front of the clear chapel window. It was a wet Saturday evening and he was waiting patiently for his inner congregation to arrive. The rain beat a tattoo on the panes of glass, as though God was trying to draw his attention.

Three giant candles illuminated the front of the church creating shadows that danced around the white walls. The dark pulpit pulsed in the flickering light, a giant dragon ready to devour the Minister.

He spoke softly to the shadows. 'God forgive me for my sins. Money is the essence of all evil, but men can both take and give it to usurp or support your power on earth. Please guide me in what I do, with that I have taken and let me give, in a way that will help my people, your children.' The adulation of the Welsh people had given him a lust for power that he now realised was unhealthy and against his God. He had begun to feel like a revolutionary, a man who could make no mistakes in what he said or what he did. The people wanted him to be a figurehead. A nationalist marching with the throngs against King George III and his cronies. A leader to represent them, the poor. But Evans had read about the French and American revolutions and he realised he was not that sort of man. He prayed harder for forgiveness, his eyes were shut tight and hurt with the pressure. Jenkin had constantly sinned to gain his fame, bank-rolled by the Earl and now, in the twilight of his years, he felt guilty in front of his maker. The Minister heaved his massive frame to his feet and leaned against the pulpit for support. He placed a hand underneath his jacket to feel the erratic pump of his heart and knew the time was coming to go to heaven or possibly hell. He constantly weighed up his good and bad deeds but knew there could be no real balancing. Slowly he staggered to the nearest pew and sat heavily. He hung his head in his hands, the white hair glinting yellow in the candlelight. For the first time since he was a child he cried. The tears came from his heart as he repented his sins.

Lewis and Cadell were still battling into the squalls of rain as they followed the coast road high above the Swellies to their right. Visibility was poor and they could see no lights on Ynys Gorad Goch or Tysilio as they closed on Porthaethwy. Cadell was berating his father-in-law for the slow pace.

'We shall be late for the meeting at this rate. I told you we should have borrowed some horses.' Lewis kept his head down so that Cadell couldn't see the contempt in which he held him. He was out of breath and his chest hurt as he walked, but he was too proud to admit it. He quietly spat blood when Cadell wasn't looking.

'Save your breath for the Minister.' He slipped in the mud and nearly fell. He knew his world was coming to an end and wanted to help Jenkin Evans before they both died. They had planned the meeting a few weeks before and Cadell and Morgan were invited for effect. Cadell splashed ahead but turned to express his anger.

'I'm going to tell him a thing or two. The Earl and Morgan don't like his public change of tone. When the Earl buys you, it is for life.' Lewis grimaced. He had tried hard to be a good overseer for Sir John and protect his son, but also he had looked after his men. The extra money he had given them, turning a blind eye to the poor work of a man with problems at home; many little parts to make the whole better.

'Well life can be very short, Cadell, and money won't make it any easier for the Earl to reach heaven.' They arrived at the chapel in Porthaethwy at the same moment as Rhodri Morgan. He had also walked but was still dry and warm as his home was only 300 yards away rather than a black and wet six miles. The men sat next to Jenkin Evans at the front of the chapel and appraised each other quietly in the dim light. The Minister started the conversation.

'We have been friends working to a plan for many years and performed many great deeds. The new chapels and Sunday schools. Help for the sick and ill. The establishment of The Union and, of course, the spread of non-conformist nationalistic values. But...' he caught his breath and looked across at Lewis, 'the time comes when we can do no more.'

Cadell insolently interrupted. 'No more? We have barely started the revolution. The bastard English need taking down by force.'

Evans held up his hand to stop the tirade, but it was Morgan who asked Cadell the obvious question. 'And how are we to do that? Are you going to arm every Welshman and stand on the border? Are you going to murder the landowners and take control?'

Cadell stood in his anger. 'Why not? The English army are too busy enslaving other countries and the local militia are away enforcing the landowner's rights in Britain and Ireland. Yes man, now is the time to do more and not less. You are all spineless, damn you.'

There was a painful silence for a minute or two. They all thought Cadell was a hothead, devious and mean but essentially weak.

Lewis spoke slowly, 'Damnation Cadell. That is the point and Jenkin is right. We must not take the Earl's money and do his bidding like lap dogs. That is the first stage in becoming strong and independent. Everything else is in God's hands.'

Rhodri turned on him. 'You Tudurs are so pathetically weak. I have paid every one of you good money for years to do as you are told and then you say you want to stop. None of you can stop until you die. You have to deliver the agreements on the bridge or you are dead men before God calls you.'

Lewis stood above the steward. 'God will decide when we die. If you ever threaten me again, or insult my family, I will kill you and He shall judge me.' The Minister moved between the mean little man and Lewis.

'Enough, begone. I called you here to say the deceptions must end. No man is bound by money. That is my decision and it is I who control the people through the chapels.'

Rhodri spat his final words out before leaving. 'You have forgotten the last task the Earl gave you, gentlemen. Owen Tudur must be turned to our cause so that the Earl can manipulate Sir John's assets. Whether the steward is alive or dead.' Rhodri and Cadell left the others, leaving Jenkin to douse the candles. Lewis took his arm as the light dimmed.

'My dearest friend, I know that life is short for us both and I agree we must try to make amends for our sins. I am still with you. Never forget that, Jenkin.' Evans and Lewis walked to the door with their arms around each other's shoulders.

The Minister had the last word. 'Go with God, Lewis. We did our best and many would judge our deeds were good. The problem is God. He is the only one who saw how much evil we used to achieve them and therefore, only He can truly judge us.'

Chapter 10

Bryn Celli Ddu

Plas Coch sat in the ancient parishes of Llanidan and Llandeiniolen, which were the principal seats of the Druidical priesthood, and in which the Arch-Druid had his chief residence. Deeply shaded groves, ideal for the performance of the sacrificial rites, sat amidst numerous remains of Druidical temples, altars, circles, and cromlechs.

Bryn Celli Ddu used to be a tiny Neolithic community in 4,000 BC. The mound in the dark grove was a place to sacrifice and ritually bury the dead. The people would have been highly superstitious and their Druidic priests would have ensured that their perception of the world would have been one of wary fearfulness.

Religion has always established itself in reality and fundamentally in the hearts and souls of people by creating an enemy or exaggerating the unknown, both before Christ and in Georgian Anglesey. Equally the word sacrifice had now been termed murder.

Inside the mound is a single, rounded column with horizontal markings cut into its diameter. The site used to be part of a much larger astronomical instrument that had other ancient structures in alignment. The column is a shadow gauge and can be used to accurately calculate the summer and winter solstices and the spring and autumn equinox. It was a perfect place, *the Gorsedd* or high seat, where Arch Druid Morgan could meet his supporters. The Gwyneddigion Druidical Society in London supported the modern Druids and created the Eisteddfod, but long poems by bards using clever pseudonyms were not of interest to Rhodri. Nor were the farming competitions and new practices supported by the society who were well known in the local towns and bereft of secrecy. No, Rhodri believed in the ancient Druids in their white costumes, secret nationalists who were willing to terrorise people into supporting the old superstitions, whilst ironically supporting the new fervent ideas of the Methodists. His aim was to foment strife in all slate and copper mines except the Earl's. He constantly talked of ending the local slavery to his followers whilst perpetuating his control as steward of the family who thought they controlled the island.

His message to Owen came from Aeronwy when she was visiting Plas Coch. Her brother hugged her hard as they stood beside the coach house.

'I am so sorry Owen. I have tried to persuade your tad and Cadell to let you come home but they are dead set against you. The corn riots haven't helped you know.'

'Please don't worry about me sister.'

'But I do and they have requested you to attend one of their silly meetings.' She stroked his hair. 'Only a sister can say it my brother, but you are looking old and weary.'

'I have plenty of life left in me sister, don't worry so. As for a meeting! You know that is impossible.'

'Not impossible, just dangerous.' He placed his back against the wooden door of the stable with one foot stepped at right angles to rest upon it.

'They want you to be at Bryn Celli Ddu at midnight tomorrow, the night of the full moon.'

'To discuss what? The devil of lies if I ever have to justify it to Sir John.'

'They wouldn't tell me why. They said it was your duty, but your tad won't be there. He has bad lungs...' they both knew it was inevitable due to working in the quarries. 'Too much tea, as the bosses say, but there is no help from the company when he is ill at home.'

Owen ran his hand through his greying hair. 'Tell them both that I will attend. Let us call it research.' He kissed her cheek and added, 'tell Tad... oh forget the idea, tell him nothing.' He strode away without another word. She watched him go for a few moments. She knew he was in an impossible position. She knew he loved his father.

The following evening he armed himself with a dagger and pistol that he tucked into the waistband in the small of his back. He felt safe and in control because of the adrenaline. Owen walked slowly towards Llanddaniel and at the stone bridge he turned right to avoid the boggy area to the south of the stream. He paused to watch the flow of water. Lines of silver were gushing across black rocks, making the sound of dead souls who talked of his future. He remembered his father's words when he was a boy stood inside the dark of the burial mound. His tad had measured his height against the central green obelisk counting the cut marks from the floor.

'When you are taller than the stone itself, then you will be a man.'

He was scared that day but not tonight; it was his destiny, he was a man. His father had told him that there was a slab of stone covering a fire at the centre of the henge that surrounded the mound. Underneath was a human ear bone.

'And that is what happens to you, if you don't listen to me or your mam. Remember to listen my boy and not to the words, to the silences between them.'

Young girls had been burnt and buried by each one of the fourteen stones making up the henge. Female life was cheap even then, but it satisfied the gods. Tad had clipped him gently over the head and laughed at his fear, but Owen was in awe of the Druids and their history. Now this place of silent souls had been infiltrated by the living, the Celts and Druids supplanted by nationalist Methodists who were still fighting for the freedom of men.

As he closed on the Earl's farm he could see the mound to his right and an outcrop of limestone to his left as it shone in the moonlight. To his far right were the mountains of Moel Rhiwen and Moel-y-Ci, which hid the giant gash of the Penrhyn slate quarries, the largest in the world. His trepidation increased as he crossed over the stone wall marking the Earl's territory. He knew he could be hauled in front of a Justice of the Peace on any pretext, any trumped up charge, but he wanted to face the opposition to stand up for his own views without justification. Hushed voices of men carried through the air from the meeting on the entrance side of the burial mound. As he approached, their outfits shone a startling white in the moonlight and he realised the open situation was extremely dangerous. He looked for a possible escape route. Three hundred yards to the right was a stand of yew trees beside the farmhouse and stream. If he ran, nobody would expect him to head into the opposition's territory. It suddenly went dark as a cloud covered the moon then it brightened again as he stepped forward to meet the Arch Druid who spoke from beneath his hood.

'Tudur, a man uncovered! So you are here at last.' Owen noticed a Druid standing behind the crowd. By the height and shape he guessed it was Cadell. 'Ynys Môn is the last bastion, the last defence against the English invasion of Wales.'

'Your point is?' Owen rested his hands on his hips.

'You must commit to us of course.'

'I work for Sir John and the law and order of King George III and Britain.'

'So you accept their natural leadership? You, a descendant of our royal blood? You accept power in the hands of the English landed gentry?'

'You work for them too, Morgan.'

Rhodri tore his hood from his head in anger. 'Does that make them competent to govern when they want to rape and pillage our lands as if we are a mere Jamaica or India? You say we are part of Great Britain, but they treat us as like a colony.' Owen was shaking his head as Rhodri continued, 'Yes steward, a mere colony and we have been one since the Act of Union in 1543. Ruled as if we are culturally inferior and linguistically distinct.'

Owen opened his arms wide and talked to the rest of the apparitions. 'You all know me and my family. I have tried to make life easier for you all whilst accepting my responsibilities as steward. Isn't that right?'

It was Cadell who answered, 'No it is not, Owen. You have made your own life easier.'

Owen remained quiet for a minute, many of the men beneath their hoods would be his friends, but he appealed to Rhodri. 'You think you can stop the English, Morgan? Look around you man! They have thrust their way into Ynys Môn, bridged the river at Conwy and cantilevered their turnpike around Penmaenmawr. You of all people know what is coming.' He stepped forward and shook Rhodri hard by his left shoulder. 'Be realistic and give up your dreams. They own everything and want more. You can't work for them and betray them at the same time. The Earl would kill you.'

Rhodri roughly pushed away the hand and leaned in close. It was brighter than day. Owen smelt the disgusting, fetid clothes and beneath it lay the stench of body odour, but he didn't flinch as Rhodri stared into his eyes from a few inches away. 'You have betrayed your race and your religion, Tudur. You disgust me. The men thought you would join us as an insider in one of the bastard's houses.' He struck Owen across the face with the back of his hand before reaching inside his jacket. Owen spun away and faced the vision of anger and hate, his dagger in one hand and the pistol in the other.

'I follow the law of Britain and God's law.'

Rhodri had pulled his pistol out too and levelled it at Owen as he started to castigate him. 'You follow the master's law because of his mistress. Are you sleeping with the enemy?'

Owen hit him hard with a right cross that knocked Morgan to the ground and immediately turned and ran towards the trees. Morgan belatedly shouted at the Druids who stood still watching. 'Get him back and he can stay in the mound until his bones turn to dust.'

But Owen had a head start and the chasers didn't have the heart to catch him. The clouds covered the full moon as he closed on the yews and the darkness overcame the light.

* * *

The water diviner was followed by Elizabeth as she and Beth walked a few hundred yards to the seaward side of Plas Coch. The master was adamant that he should have a second lake to match that which fed from The Spout and despite Owen suggesting it would be impossible, he insisted on trying everything to find a new spring. "Magical" hazel was used for divining purposes and was best cut on the midsummer feast of Saint John, which is June 24th. So far, no water had been detected and it would need a miracle as well as some magic to find some.

Beth held Elizabeth's arm and happily chatted as she twirled a hazel twig in her left hand. 'Hazel signifies blessing and good luck, ma'am. When exactly nine hazels grow around a well and some of their nuts drop into the water, they create a bubble of mystic inspiration.'

'Beth my dear, firstly how can you see a bubble so far down and in the dark? And secondly, all these old tales seem to have no basis in fact.'

'Of course they do, your ladyship. You ate some hazel nuts last night I think?'

'Yes, but they were barely edible since we collected them before Christmas. What is your point?'

'The taste doesn't matter. They act as a love charm. They reinforce the power of contemplation and help to resolve disputes. In fact, did you know that hazel was used for magicians' wands?'

'No, but thank you my dear. I know you are trying to entertain me, but I am not in the right mood. Anyway, where have all the magicians disappeared to if hazel is so powerful?' They giggled and invited a nasty look from the rabid old lady and her divining twigs.

Beth had an idea. 'If William visits Malltraeth to see "the works", I was going to ask him if I could also go on the trip.'

'Lovely.'

'And then you can arrange to meet the steward at New Borough on the way to buy some... marram products?'

They faced each. Elizabeth looked happy for the first time in months. 'Maybe hazel has its charms after all.'

Owen accompanied William to Malltraeth a few days later. The first third of the embankment was complete and work was starting on the sluice. They sat on their horses peering seawards, where a small barque was arriving at the tiny port. They could see to the horizon in the perfect visibility. On their right was a narrow strip of deep water which glinted in the sun and on their left a vast expanse of tidal marshland. Behind them was more marsh but with taller grasses that released their seeds into the air creating a blue-green smoke that drifted across the brown-green carpet.

William was ecstatic. 'By next year, we will have a thousand men and women building the remainder of the embankment. Imagine that!'

'I can't my friend. What excites you so much about engineering? It is so tedious to move a bit of soil and plant nothing. You have already rebuilt it all twice after the storms!'

'Good god man, you are losing your enthusiasm in your old age. I bet you perk up when I give you an extra 3,000 acres to farm?'

Before he could reply a gig came careering down the track from New Borough. Elis was driving with two beautiful ladies hanging on tight. Lady Elizabeth quickly jumped down and mounted the spare horse that Owen had thought to provide and after a hurried agreement to meet in Brynsiencyn at 5pm, the couples parted company. She followed Owen at a trot as they headed towards Lovers' Island. Passing the *hendai* or cottages adorned with marram grass mats and ropes, they reached the last of the deciduous woodland fronting the sea and dunes. They heard the sound of the rooks attacking the buzzards before they saw them. A raucous cry from two and then three rooks as they chased the dominant buzzards away from their fledglings. The buzzards were always driven away unless they saw something to feed upon. Then they would dive from the sky, leaving the rooks flapping in their wake and take whatever they wanted. They slowed to a walk as the horses kicked white plumes of surf off their hooves. After a few minutes they commenced the climb to the shrine and fell in side by side.

She asked gently, 'Why are you so unhappy now? It's like a poison pervading your spirit that has taken hold of you Owen.'

'Because of circumstances, nothing more.' He changed the subject. 'We hate the English because ever since they came here, they have destroyed people's lives. It was Edward I who started it by moving all the people out of Beaumaris.'

'I thought it was this area that supported the Welsh royalty, the nationalists?'

'It had the principal court of the medieval Welsh Princes, but the town was overwhelmed by storms. It wasn't the sea damage that made it uninhabitable; the problem was the drifting sand. There was too much to move and anyway, it would have happened again and again.' They dismounted and tied their horses to a small rowan. Walking down to the tiny beach opposite Ynys-y-Cranc they sat on a rock and talked. Elizabeth leaned against his strong shoulder as she listened. He told her about the midnight meeting at Bryn Celli Ddu and the feelings the people had about *Mam Cymru,* Mother of Wales.

'Why is it called that, my love?'

'Because in the Middle Ages, its fertile fields formed the bread basket for the north of Wales.'

'I will help you and William, Owen. Anything you want. I hate seeing the poverty, but my loyalties are with the family until Sir John dies.'

'I know. You look very beautiful today.' He tilted her chin upwards and gazed in rapture into the violet eyes. Her red lips parted as he gently kissed them. They stood entwined and grasped the life from each other before Owen dragged her to the warm sand and took her to the sound of the sighing surf.

That evening, a satiated Elizabeth was talking animatedly with an unknowing Sir John. Over the last month he was in remarkable spirits and seemed pleased to chat and argue as he had in the first five years of their marriage.

'I like William Blake, he is anarchic.' She was defying him to argue.

'Tush woman! He is a commoner, hostile to the Church of England and professes free love. Egad he has ended up in corruption with an Earl's wife, what!'

'But people listen to him and are inspired by his ideas!'

'He was influenced by the revolutions in France and America, so he has copied their ideas. The man is not original.'

'But he has copied nothing concerning marriage as he says it is the new slavery, Sir John. Nor on the state abolishing its restrictions on homosexuality, prostitution, and even adultery.' She clammed up, realising this was dangerous ground.

'No Elizabeth, anarchy is not the answer. The Christian notions of chastity as a virtue are sacrosanct.' She picked up her book of Blake's poems. What her husband said and what he did were two distinct options. She started to read, "Why should I be bound to thee, O my lovely myrtle-tree?" Blake seemingly advocated multiple sexual partners and he castigated the "frozen marriage-bed". She let her mind wander; in *Visions*, Blake had written:

> *Till she who burns with youth, and knows no fixed lot, is bound*
> *In spells of law to one she loathes? and must she drag the chain*
> *Of life in weary lust?*

It was all true and many women knew it. She smiled to herself as she remembered the poet's "Marriage of Heaven and Hell" and then she excused herself from her master to take to her solitary bed and dream of Owen.

It was a busy Sunday in Porthaethwy. The Edward Lloyd-Williamses, the Pagets and the Littleton-Joneses were attending the first service of the new Anglican Church. The Dean was nervous as he gazed at the ships gliding along the straits. The sails billowed, cracking back and forth in the divergent wind that filled them from every direction. The boats were in the tidal flow and caught between the tall sides of the gorge. Only the skill of the helmsmen would save them from grounding on the treacherous rocks until they reached comparative safety after the Swellies, when the straits widened. The smell of the brine and call of the gulls should have steadied his nerves, but he knew the landholders would be incensed by Jenkin Evans' provocative visit to Salem chapel just a few hundred yards away.

Everyone wore their best clothes in both places of worship. Outside the chapel the men argued with Lewis and Cadell about the Union. They were vilifying Owen, how their family was betrayed at Dinorwic and Parys Mountain. The emotion of the conversation was carried inside the chapel, weighing like a coffin on their shoulders.

Jenkin Evans strode around the front of the chapel, ignoring the pulpit set on the bare earth floor. He was surrounded by a halo of light from the solitary tall window behind him. He shouted as he told them that damnation would follow for anyone not supporting the community. Thunder was his dwelling place, his oratory inspiring the congregation to believe in God but more importantly to believe in themselves. The place was full to the brim and overflowing with emotion. The quarrymen loved the rhetoric. The servants loved it, but an unemotional Rhodri sat and closely watched the men from Sir John's and the Ashettons' slate mines. The fool of an Earl had given him a task to disrupt the competitor's world, but he was only following his own heart.

Cadell leaned towards him and whispered, 'A revolution is coming Rhodri. First the Americas, then the French and now the Welsh.'

Morgan was growing tired of the overseer. Production in Llyn Peris had dropped, the slate was poorer quality than Sir John's and the transport to Felinheli was slow and costly. Cadell always had too much to say. His use as an informer had died when the fool had insisted that Owen leave the cottage at Brynsiencyn.

He whispered back, 'You know too much for your own good.' He added in his mind only, 'And your service will be esteemed long in this world and by God in the next'.

At the new church it was the opposite atmosphere to that in the chapel. The Dean was boring his guests. The rainbow from the newly donated windows did nothing to enlighten them. Sir John sat contemplating the effect of the abolition of slavery. He damned Wilberforce as the Dean urged them all to turn the other cheek. His brothers had failed to influence the man who had preferred mankind to party and given up his chance of becoming Prime Minister. They had informed him that Wilberforce had such sway with the middle classes. 'Unlike the Dean' thought Sir John. He had always believed his Negroes were happy on the plantations. He couldn't understand how Wilberforce had turned so many outsiders against the slave owners. He decided he still had much to learn. Was it the tracts, public meetings or subscriptions that had turned people's opinions? All new ways to generate propaganda and opposition. Wilberforce had generated a new way and he would learn from it.

He looked at his wife. She had changed over the years but was still beautiful. But her attitude was different and it worried him. She had learned the right tone of voice to belittle him about his sexual antics. It was never a direct confrontation about his brief fling with Lady Isabel all those years ago, nor a recent young maid. Just a gentle and guarded reprimand couched in coquetry.

The Dean droned on before starting to lambast the non-conformists. 'God is in His heaven. But whose? Must we turn away from all we have created over the centuries? Stability is the key to heaven and stability is what the Anglican Church maintains for all its communicants.'

Owen had arranged to meet Aeronwy and Frances after the services. He sat with them on a low wall near the island of Saint Tysilio. As he looked between their faces he knew he could trust the women implicitly. His sister had carried secret messages for Lady Elizabeth to Lady Charlotte. Frances had relayed Earl's Hill happenings and rumours to Aeronwy and she had told Owen. Both women had started to hate Cadell and his big mouth gave them valuable information that they could also pass on to Owen. The overseer was overbearing in his self-styled importance and when he started to beat Aeronwy, he lost all credence as a man. Owen knew he needed their help. The information about the new bridge to be built above them was still secret. Only William, Ieuan and Owen knew the details, but Owen needed to know immediately if the Earl had discovered that Sir John had tied up all the rights to build and run the new crossing. He explained his plan to the women and their part in it. He said he wanted to give something back to Wales before he died and asked if they were with him, no matter how dangerous it became. They parted as allies to return to the three abodes that had ruled their lives and wait for the moment to change their history.

Chapter 11

Coincidental Events

Human beings generally don't recognise the big changes in life. They only react to day to day circumstances, but 50 years on they may look around when close to death and realise the enormity of their lives and the changes that had occurred. Beaumaris was declining as the promised bridge over the Menai came closer to a reality. The A5 road heading south through the wilds of Wales was to become key to the development of the Holyhead to London route. Whether it was the importance of the mail coaches or whether it was the ideas and concepts of the politicians travelling on the route, no one will ever know. But what we do know is, the men who went to Ireland to continually talk over the Irish question continually created bad answers.

Strategic developments require great engineers like Thomas Telford and his friends, including William Smith, but they all needed visionaries like Sir John Littleton-Jones and the money from the new banks like Lloyds. A new bridge would be a massive change for Ynys Môn and for Wales, but when it opened it would be the imposing physical sight that outweighed the significance of the endemic and emotional change. It would only be celebrated with a small band and groups of local people promenading across the structure. The Lords of the Treasury had received many ideas for bridging the straits over many years and for many locations. Telford's second proposal at Porthaethwy had two towers which would be nearly 600 feet in height, with wrought iron chains supporting a crossing platform suspended beneath. This had to be 100 feet above the water to allow fully rigged sailing ships to pass underneath and so at 1,000 feet long a suspension bridge was an incredible feat for the Georgians. It would take seven years to build and employ up to 400 men. The wrought iron would come from Shrewsbury. Nine-foot links heated and varnished with linseed oil to prevent corrosion. Tunnels would be constructed to fix the chains into the bedrock on each bank. The bridge builders' lime kiln would be near Ynys Tysilio, on Sir John's land but adjacent to the Eisteddfod stone circle which was on the Earl's. Two powerful men with a verbal agreement, who were joined by lime thrown into the pits of the contagious dead and a circle to celebrate life. The small port of Porthaethwy on the Anglesey side of the bridge would lose its name and most of its trade until Victorian times when the tourists arrived by steamer to spend their excess money. "Porth" meant ferry or crossing place and "Daethwy" was the original Celtic clan that lived there. As Porthaethwy died, the mainland side of the new bridge lived. The new crossing encouraged the city of Bangor to expand out of the valley and two miles towards the east. All of this expansion was onto the lands owned by the shell companies of the Littleton-Joneses.

Change happens and people don't see it until they are dying.

Planning for change is easier than plotting for change. Plotting requires the time and the circumstances to be in conjunction.

* * *

Owen Tudur, now more frequently addressed as Taid, was looking at his reflection in the cracked mirror donated from the big house. It had been a cold and lonely night on his lumpy mattress with the blankets pulled up and over his head to keep out the bone-penetrating chill. His hair was grey and his face lined, but he saw the reflection of a young man with hopes and ambition. He was standing in his tiny cottage near Plas Coch which had been rented by a shepherd until the month before. The man had lived alone apart from a young collie dog who had shared his secrets. No one knew where the man had gone, but his personal items and the dog had abruptly disappeared with him. There were unconfirmed sightings of him crossing the ferry at Lavan and heading east towards Manchester, but he wouldn't be seen again. The shepherd was chasing an easier life, a richer lifestyle by looking for labouring jobs in the big city.

Owen considered himself lucky as now he had assets as well as a home. He had his own horse, a stone jug, pewter plates, a whetstone, shoe making tools and a spade. On his oak table stood an ink stand and on the Welsh dresser were three books about animal husbandry. He had two oil paintings, a decent bed, a guzunder, a settle, a range and bellows, and the luxury of enamel mugs and jugs. However, he had no cow or pig, as all his needs were satisfied by his grateful farm tenants who kept him well stocked with food. They always called him Taid – grandfather– a man who always acted with experience, mercy and compassion beyond his years. All his washing was taken care of by the housemaids and so he had no mangle, no galvanised tub and no woman at home to do any of his work. That was a sad thought, but it was soon dispelled as he preferred true love to convenience.

He finished shaving with the cut-throat razor and rinsed it in the cold soapy water whilst reflecting on how he was lucky to have so much. He was blessed to have water so close to the cottage as it helped to make life easier. The spring called The Spout was only yards away and he used wooden buckets to collect and store enough for his meagre needs. The thought reminded him to tell Mrs Jones her cow needed a minimum of three buckets of water a day to make one of milk. She would soon learn; a 15-year-old girl from the town shouldn't have fallen for the charms of a pig man, but it was better than a life at home with ten others.

He looked at the lead tobacco jar on his mantelpiece. It was red with a lion on the top. Aeronwy had brought it to him on the day he moved in. It was an emotional gift as his mother had given it to his tad on their wedding day. His sister wanted him to keep it as Lewis had stopped smoking and taken the container and hidden it away in their shed more than a year before. Owen averted his gaze and contemplated the day. He had to see Duncan first and that made him think about marriage. He knew the couple were happy despite having no children and that brought a lump to Owen's throat. He remembered the noise of his nieces before he was thrown out of the family home. Their crying when young, their questions as toddlers and now? Now they were young ladies with hormones to satisfy and so were interested in boys. That reminded him to ensure the tenant farmers put tar on the back of the sheep's hindquarters to deter the foxes. Spring was always a troublesome and busy time as the estate threw off its winter coat and rejoiced in the returning warmth and light. His mental list was endless. More limestone needed quarrying to be ready for the boat going to Liverpool on Friday. The quarterly rents were due next week, but the day clashed with accompanying some tenants to a public hiring mop in Conwy. He put on his black jacket. Could he persuade Sir John to drop the idea of building a windmill at Llangefni, as the site was too low, only a mound by a stream? But it was near the centre of the town and a good commercial plot. He would tell him that a windmill needed to be at Parys Mountain facing west. He knew if he persuaded the master, Sir John would then badger him about a woollen mill on the Llangefni site. Before he left the mean little cottage, he had one last thought as he glanced at his silver pocket watch. Spring enticed Elizabeth into her kitchen garden for another year's growth of hope and beauty. Pure pleasure for her and therefore also for Owen, as they would have to meet to discuss her botanical needs.

He was always thinking and always busy.

It would be a long day; the dawn chorus had only just started.

He slammed the cottage door shut and strode at speed towards Plas Coch, an endless path that must eventually end.

* * *

In the hills near Snowdon, 50 quarrymen had crammed into the *caban* to eat their lunch. They had an hour's break before resuming work and sat smoking and drinking tea. Lewis was at the head of the large table. His face was grey and when he coughed into his handkerchief, he could see the thickened blood. He knew what was going to happen; they had all seen it before, but with the vanity of Man he hoped for longer and had no choice but to stay working whilst he could walk. He had managed to introduce the Union at Dinorwic, after many arguments with Sir John and the agent. But production had increased during the year following its introduction and Lewis had also made sure the costs had reduced. The men were happier, their families would now be looked after if they died in an accident and they all received free medical treatment. It kept the giant quarry happy. With twenty galleries and up to 500 men it needed that stability and was therefore the envy of the other slate barons in North Wales.

The community spirit showed in the *caban*. Men laughed and argued, told their jokes and exchanged sermons from the twenty different chapels in the area. There was no keeping up with the neighbours; they were all in this life together and community meant everything. That is why they sang. It was always the same one or two who would start the humming. Their neighbour would join in and gradually the hum would roll around the table. The sound reverberated from the slate walls of the shed, each man assuming a slightly different tone and gradually the harmony would envelop them, lifting their souls and soaring through the roof to their God. And then, the words, a solo at first, the sentiments inspiring their day and the men would join in, a couple at a time, then half the *caban* and finally a crescendo of sound as they harmonised the words of a hymn by a local favourite like Owen Williams. It lifted their souls; they were proud men who loved their country, who helped their neighbours and workmates as they were their true friends.

They were also hard practical men behind this spiritual ascendance. There was the physical battle against the elements each day, but they had become hardened to it since starting work at the age of twelve. It became a way of life, it was purely physical. However, it was the mental hardness that made them old. The bargaining with the overseer at the mine, the compromises with their families over the inadequate money they had made and then the courage to repeat the stress day after day. A man might earn up to thirty shillings a month if he were lucky. Splitters would need to produce 400 slates a day on average. The men were paid for each 100 produced, but they had to give the owner 128 to cover the damages during transportation. And splitting was easier than the actual quarrying; at least that was what the quarrymen argued. Splitters sat next to their *Trafal* cutting horse in a comfortable shed. They used their serrated stick with its steel pin as marker before cutting the "Princesses" at 24 by 14 inches or "Ladies" or "Countesses" depending on the required size. The others slaved outside in all weathers and 70–90 per cent wastage came out of their bargains. It was soul destroying and that was good enough reason to sing... to save their souls.

Lewis blew heavily into the cold air. On the coast, the lambs were already frolicking, but the winter clung to the slopes high above the grey galleries. He laboured as he walked and then stopped and coughed, spitting onto the tough tussock grass. He watched the spittle and blood slide off the blades and then quickly moved on. Smith was due the next day and a decision was to be made on the location for a new gallery. He skirted an outcrop of rock and headed horizontally across the steep slope, making his way to the second trial site. A buzzard screeched high above him and he turned to watch as it hovered above a run of screed. His focus was on the bird and so he didn't notice Rhodri Morgan's henchman crouched behind a boulder to his left. The man worked in the Elizabeth quarry but was a newcomer. He had applied for a job a few months earlier, saying he had fallen out with Cadell. When Lewis asked his son-in-law, the story had been backed up by him and so Lewis employed him in good faith.

The overseer checked his ropes were secure around the large rock above the trial hole and then straightened the pulley blocks to make them easier to run. In his youth he would have used a single rope without pulleys to scramble down the face of a gallery. He could be down and back up within a few minutes and was the best in his day. He coughed and spluttered, then carefully placed both boots at the top of the cliff, scraping the hobnails and creating a spark. Easing the rope in his right hand he slowly lowered himself at right angles down the face so that he could inspect the potential new seam. He wasn't scared after 60 years of experience, but he was slower as his body was weakening. Tying off the rope around his waist, he used both hands to closely examine the green slate. He chipped away with his hammer and chisel. The shards fell 70 feet and landed on the rocks below.

The man kept low by the top of the gallery and looked around for witnesses. There was no one but a few rooks and the distant buzzard to see his deed. He took his knife from his waistband and started to saw at the taut rope. That night, he would meet Morgan in the inn at Aber to receive his twenty guineas and then he would take the road towards Birmingham to find a new job. Lewis felt the rope give an inch. At the top, the last three remaining strands sat taut under the knife blade.

Lewis didn't cry out as the rope gave way. As he plummeted down he admired the beauty of the sheer wall of slate; there was no time to think. Then all went black as his head split open on impact.

It took the men an hour to find his body and load it reverently onto a small cart. Everyone in the quarry stood in silence and watched as two of the workers drove it across the slate debris, eerily creaking and cracking under the wheels. Lewis was on his last trip to the Moel-y-Don ferry; he had always maintained everyone's respect and had always set an example to his only son, even in death.

It was William who retrieved the rope and saw the cut marks, but everyone was told it had frayed. However, he told Owen the brutal truth and only Owen knew about the absent worker and his references. That meant only the son planned on taking his revenge. The death was also a warning to William as it could have been him. It made him realise that his time was limited if he was to help Owen. The loss of their Union leader had an impact at the Earl's quarry further down Llyn Peris. Lewis had extended his power base by creating an unofficial version of the Union in the competitor's quarry. Cadell had always turned a blind eye to it but had soon started to lose respect from his workers because of his weakness and double-dealing. Now there was no father-in-law to protect and defend him anymore and men bear grudges. It was no surprise to anyone that Cadell lost his life in a blasting accident a few weeks later, but it wasn't instigated by the hate of the quarrymen; it was Morgan tying up the loose ends and eliminating a poor overseer. A loose cannon, leaving only Jenkin Evans and himself with the knowledge of their years of double-dealing.

The Tudurs mourned tad; he was buried with respect in the chapel grounds at Brynsiencyn, but Cadell's passing moved very few people who weren't his immediate family. He wasn't buried in a chapel; he remained beneath a few hundred tons of poor quality slate on the east side of Llyn Peris.

The slate quarries had developed fast and drawn everyone into a new future. More than a dozen ships could now be moored at Felinheli. There was no more lightering of the slate out to moored vessels in the deeper channel. The requirement to wait for the right state of tide and double-handling was soon considered as antiquated. The boats unloaded coal or ballast before taking the slate on-board. The mules with panniers on their backs had been replaced by a plateway, but horses still pulled the cars as William and Sir John examined the latest in steam engines. They experimented with velocipedes to help the workers commute. It was novel to see a skeleton carriage on the flanged cast iron rails rolling slowly on its flangeless wheels. They watched as eight men wound the two handles to make it move forward, but like the men, the bosses thought it was too slow and tiresome. But they did invest in "The Incline" behind the docks to drag heavy carts up and down the hill to the start of the plateway. William devised an endless chain mechanism driven by horses, but he and the master were planning ahead to the coming of age of steam. Demand for the Dinorwic products was accelerating as more houses and factories needed roofing in the burgeoning cities. Slate is mud, compressed and compacted then squeezed together and heated by the earth's forces millions of years ago. It is full of minerals – sericite, mica, quartz, haematite. The colours are beautiful and range from green and wrinkled, to redwood, bronze, and willow green. Some slate has copper inside it, the green deposits are pretty when seen, but there was not enough to make it commercially worthwhile to extract.

Life came from the mud many millions of years ago. Life returns to the mud at the very end.

Nash watched little Henry as he grew into a strapping boy of 11 years old. His long black hair had developed ringlets and turned mousey. He always wore a smile and was helpful, with an enquiring mind. Henry spent many hours riding out on the estate with Taid and silly Elis. Elizabeth would secretly encourage the relationship whenever possible and Owen thought it was his duty to help Henry in exactly the same way that he had helped George. Morgan had instructed Nash to monitor every event concerning the boy in case they could use it against Tudur. The Earl had forgotten about the rumours at the time of Henry's birth, but both Nash and Rhodri increasingly and vindictively took matters into their own hands behind their masters' backs. Nash had informed Morgan that Henry and his mentor were due in Amlwch and would be staying overnight in the inn called The Copper Ladies. All Rhodri needed was an excuse to cause trouble and it was the Earl who presented him with the opportunity. Lloyd-Williams required Sir John's signature on way-leaves for access to the new bridge. They were for passage across land owned by Sir John adjacent to Saint Tysilio Island. The Earl was planning to provide most of the raw materials for the work on the bridge and needed access to the lime kilns. Denial of access so long before the actual building work would indicate an issue with his plans, and therefore a problem with his partnership.

Henry and Taid held their horses steady as the crash of an explosion ricocheted around the Parys mine. It was nearly five years since Taid's last visit. He therefore couldn't explain to Henry about the rotten egg smell from the sulphurous fumes billowing skywards above the tall kilns. He also had no idea how they worked and it would need William to explain exactly how the copper ore was roasted. The agent rode towards them at a trot. Jumping off their horses, William clasped both the man and boy to his chest.

'How was your ride young man?'

'Good enough. Thank you for asking agent. But I don't think you should hug me like that.'

William was abashed. 'But I have always hugged you in greeting since you were a whippersnapper.'

The boy was serious for his age. 'I know sir, but papa wants me to become a young gentleman and follow in George's footsteps by going to Eton school in September. Therefore, he says I have to behave like an heir to The Littleton-Jones family.'

Owen and William stood with their hands on their hips in amazement. Henry had always been treated as their little boy and now Sir John wanted to take away the fatherly love they had shown.

Owen resolved the issue. 'I tell you what Henry. Whenever we are in a public place or in front of the workers or staff at home, we will treat you like a Lord. But in front of your mother and when we are alone or with Ieuan, we will treat you as an adopted son. How's that young sir?'

Henry mulled it over and after a few seconds he bowed to them, making them laugh. 'Indeed, egad. Strewth and zounds, it sounds like a damned good idea, what!'

They all clutched each other as they laughed uncontrollably. Henry's penchant for mimicry was endearing.

It was William who recovered first. 'Are you ready to see hell on earth men? The shagged arches of Virgil's entrance into Tartarus?'

They remounted their horses and followed him down the track and into the heart of the multicoloured mountain. The dust hung thick in the air and immediately gave a light yellow covering to their coats.

'My god William, what have you done to my farms?' It was the only question that Owen could think of as they went down the track into the opencast mine. On their right they could see vast caverns of varying heights along the sides of the giant hole. Above them were perilous 'whimsies' hanging over the man-made cliffs and busy hauling the copper ore to the top, 100 feet above.

William held his arms aloft as he preached to his disciples, 'Isn't it incredible? Soon we will have nearly a thousand men working here.'

It was Henry who asked a business question. 'And how many men are working in the Earl's Mona mine?'

'No more than 200 I would think. Everything we do is on a grander scale. Look at what we have achieved.'

Owen congratulated him. 'What *you* have achieved, William. Well done. I bet no one ever says that do they?' They shared a knowing look. Making hundreds of thousands of pounds profit each year didn't buy any thanks.

The noise of the winding gear and pick axes echoed off the overhanging rocks as a mockery of their deadness. Teams of workers followed the veins of ore into the walls of the gigantic bowl. They used pickaxes to clear the rock falls created by blasts that echoed throughout the bowl every quarter of an hour. A blast warning was shouted loudly and repeated around the mine. '*Tân, Tân, Tân*' – fire, fire, fire – and a deeper chasm was blasted open for exploitation with a resounding "crump".

Smith was delighted to show them around. 'Remember your last visit Taid? This was merely 100 yards long by 40 wide. Now we are half a mile across and that's before you see the pits.'

'But how?'

'Do you remember me talking to Sir John about bargain-takers versus piece-workers? Well he agreed with the latter, which has made us more productive. They are paid based on the amount and quality of ore after it has been assayed. The last I heard, the Earl has trouble on his side. If he doesn't change to our method of pay his workers will undoubtedly riot.'

They watched the women dress the ore in their distinctive attire. Throughout the island they were known as the copper ladies. Each had an iron gauntlet, a mallet, and a yellow shoulder bag. Around their waists were aprons and tied around their heads they all sported bright kerchiefs. The copper ladies and their children, who were as young as five years old, broke up the ore into walnut-size pieces. Each area had a few men sorting the ore into baskets before it was despatched up the side of the cliff to the mountain top. Most of it was then transported to Amlwch in hessian bags on large wagons driven by the local farmers who no longer farmed their blighted land. They were happy to earn more money carrying the ore to the port and use the proceeds to drink themselves to oblivion after each delivery. A little of the ore was washed, then calcined on site by burning it to remove the sulphur, but the majority of the kilns were located at the port where the raw materials were easier and cheaper to handle. The process interested Henry as it took months of heating to achieve sublimation and it still wasn't ready for its final use. He wanted to know what eventually happened to all the copper.

The agent talked to him as they walked. 'Copper is used to make brass and demand for brass items such as kettles and pans is increasing. This particularly applies to distilling rum or boiling sugar.'

'Is that in Jamaica where we own estates?'

'Yes, but also on the other islands in the Caribbean. In fact, we export copper out of Liverpool to places like Africa and send it together with cotton products coming from the Manchester area. That's Ieuan's job. Imagine the trip on his wherry that you took to Liverpool and multiply the distance a thousand fold.'

Henry's eyes were wide in admiration. He asked another question. 'Papa told me he makes money with the metal?'

'Not coins of the realm but these,' William drew a small coin from his waistcoat pocket, 'we give them to our workers as payment because coins are in such short supply. They are in the company name and on the reverse,' he flipped it over to show Henry, 'the head of a Druid with a wreath of oak leaves.'

Henry spun the coin into the air, 'Bugger me agent, how many a year?'

William looked sternly at his protégé to discourage the swearing. 'We have made millions of them, all payable on demand in major cities like London. That is how important and trusted your family have become.'

They turned for a last look at the gigantic scar on the hillside before heading the three miles down the mountain to Amlwch. As they approached, William pointed to the smoke hovering nearby. 'A five-foot pile of ore in the shape of an obelisk is set on fire with coal at both the top and the bottom. It burns for about four months to remove most of the sulphur and produces brimstone to make gunpowder.'

Owen commented ruefully, 'There's nothing like a good war to make money is there William!'

'Indeed. We are experimenting with the manufacture of copper rivets for the sheathing on the ships, but it's difficult to make them hard enough. We even make sulphuric acid as a by-product.'

As they slowly descended, Henry stopped by a series of ponds and asked what they were used for. William made it simple. 'We bring scrap iron to put in these pits from as far away as London and Swansea. Some of the whimsies are used to draw giant buckets of water out of mine containing saturated sulphate of copper and the water is placed in these precipitation pits. The iron dissolves and we dredge out the sludge, dry it and then we can smelt it.

Henry clapped in delight. 'You are a magician, Smith, much better than Merlin.' But as they rounded the corner of the mountain to give a view of the port, it dawned on Henry and Taid what the industry had done to the countryside. The copper dust and sulphur had devastated plant life for miles around.

The steward was shocked, 'My god man, we even have red rivers like the blood of crushed workers.'

Their approach to Amlwch was smelly and smoky. An easterly breeze directed the pollution into their faces and they retched and spat as they rode. They could see twenty giant conical kilns by the port. Henry dutifully learned about his father's business. William and Taid fielded dozens of questions as his imagination flew from one concept to the next.

The inlet that made the natural port was narrow but served ten ships without modification. The size and shapes of them were a mixture. Flats with shallow drafts, fast looking sloops, wherries and brigs and all with a different combination of masts and sails. The science behind shipbuilding was indeterminate and historical trends still governed the designs. However, the largest ship in port was a sizeable 150 tons and Ieuan Fardol leaned across the bulwark from this beauty to shout friendly abuse at them. He strode down the gangplank to warmly greet the group. As always, Ieuan was excited and energetic about his job. He had two new ports to develop with both Felinheli and Amlwch growing strongly, and ten more ships in his fleet in that year alone.

'I never thought everything would work out so well. God bless your father Henry. We talked about these things 20 years ago and now they are a reality. It's better than riding out a hurricane off Jamaica young sir. My god, I think I am enjoying the dry land again!'

The agent remonstrated with him. 'Steady on Captain, next you will be telling us you have stopped drinking rum!'

'I will never join these newfangled Temperance Societies. In fact, tonight you can pay for every damned round.'

'Well there is nothing unusual there my friend.' Ieuan clouted Smith over the head as if he were a 6 year old. Their friendship was certain until the day one of them died. The captain pointed at the opposite side of the harbour.

'You were right to urge the brothers to buy land on this side of Amlwch. We have room to build small boats and can easily widen the quay for extra lime kilns. Five will never be enough?' It was a rhetorical question to Smith.

'Twenty-five more like. Picture them marching towards the village. The latest conical-shaped sulphur extraction kilns, 30 foot high and 25 foot across. No one else has the imagination of Sir John.'

'Indeed, my friend, nor the money backing him. My ships support manufacturing in Holywell. Smelting in Saint Helens and Swansea and the odd trips to beat the bastard customs.' They all laughed, including Henry. The three friends agreed to meet for dinner at "The Copper Ladies" leaving Taid to escort Henry to their room. The two of them would share for the night as it was safer.

The boy was in bed upstairs as they sat in a dark corner of the inn swapping tales. They were careful to look around them to make sure no one was listening. Behind them was a thick wooden screen that had been taken from an old Catholic church. It had been used for hundreds of years to separate the priest and the person repenting their sins. William was telling Taid more about the town.

'Amlwch is a violent place, worse than a big city. It has more than 30 alehouses supplied by three local breweries. Many of our workers who make up the majority of the population are complete drunks. They live in places like the Turkey shore area, a maze of pubs and tiny cottages.'

Ieuan butted in. 'I know I like a drink but usually it's brandy or rum. In their case they have a pint of spiced ale.'

Taid looked blank as he shrugged his shoulders. 'Spiced with what?'

Ieuan was grinning from ear to ear. 'I know you won't believe me, but they spice it with an ounce of gunpowder. They say it helps to eliminate the rheumatism due to copper poisoning.'

It reminded Owen of his late father, and he asked, 'Is the copper dangerous?'

William stepped in, 'Yes, a danger to be denied, I'm sorry, but it's no different from the slate.'

Taid said ruefully, 'Too much tea affecting their lungs again. Isn't that right?'

Neither of the others replied in deference to his tad. After a few more slurps of their drinks, William continued. 'It's the hovels they live in that also make them so ill, but they are a tough bunch. You can't differentiate between the men and women; hard working, hard drinking and with a terribly hard home life.'

Ieuan chipped in 'Not as bad as on a ship!'

'No, but worse than the slate villages. Imagine living in a space 15 foot square, with two tiny rooms, a settle, two stools, rush mats on the earth floor and damp leaking through the thatch roof. They shit in a bucket and tip it away nearby because they can't be bothered to walk far. I was appalled as they don't care and even dump it near the drinking water.'

'Like when I visited Edinburgh years ago.' Owen remembered the squalor of the closes and constant sickness.

William added, 'And if the drink or work doesn't kill them early, then the cholera constantly returns.' The men mulled over their lives. They were privileged in their positions. He carried on quietly. 'I never imagined that by betraying the Earl all those years ago we would see all of this. A chance meeting with Sir John and a reward based on the promise of huge copper wealth 20 years later.' He swept his hair back and sighed, 'Instead of being rich beyond my wildest dreams, I could have failed and both Sir John and the Earl would have wanted me dead.'

Ieuan slapped his back, 'Well at least now only the Earl would want you dead if he knew the truth.'

'That's true, but I have personally created industries that kill their workers and have to live with that on my conscience and with my God.'

There was a scraping noise behind the screen to their rear. Taid stood quickly and stepped around it. He reappeared after a few seconds dragging a snivelling wretch of a man who was expecting to be beaten.

'We have a visitor.' He threw Rhodri to the floor and kicked him in the testicles. As he was going to kick him again, a pistol was cocked by his ear and two more of Morgan's gang covered his friends who remained motionless.

Morgan struggled to his feet, his eyes flashed with hate. 'Secrets, always secrets behind every conniving twist and turn of the Littleton-Jones. Even the boy upstairs is a secret between you and his mother, isn't he steward?'

Taid went to move, but he felt the pistol nudge the nape of his neck.

'You snivelling piece of scum, Morgan. Come outside and fight me to the death like a real man.'

'Why should I give you the satisfaction Tudur? My words don't dishonour her ladyship, you do that for me.' Morgan kicked Taid between his legs and then kicked him mercilessly half a dozen times as he lay on the earthen floor of the inn. 'One day I will kill you but not now, not like this. I want you to die slowly, not fast from a fall.' He and his men stepped away from the table keeping their guns aimed at the friends and then they were gone leaving Ieuan to help Taid onto the settle. Because of the incident they failed to notice the other spy located within hearing distance. William sat immobile with fear.

Ieuan broke the silence as they both watched Taid spit blood and two teeth from his twisted mouth. 'They will come for you, William.' He and Ieuan had known it for years, but the shock had drained the colour from William's cheeks. The agent was thinking of his beloved Beth as he replied. He was glad he hadn't married her despite their love for each other, despite the constant potential for scandal. Their positions in society had protected them so far.

'I have lived with deception for too long, my friends. Maybe we all have? But I also know it is my time to get revenge.'

Ieuan stated the obvious way out. 'Run. You can be on a boat leaving tonight and in Jamaica in a month.'

'What good would that do? I would rot in a place that I hate and eventually they would send word to kill me.' He grunted, his lips were drawn in a tight straight line. 'I certainly can't marry Beth... not now. I can't leave her a widow.'

Although Taid was in pain he leaned forward and grabbed William's lapel, staring deep inside him. He struggled to speak, 'This is another reason to get even. It personalises what we have all felt for years. The rich become obscenely rich, the poor become poorer. The landowners are bleeding our nation of its blood, from the very heart of Ynys Môn.'

Ieuan called for more drinks before addressing them both. 'If I'm lucky, I have another five years to live. Whatever you two have been concocting, I am happy to help. They will never find me if I run. The seven seas are too big.'

Taid quietly outlined his idea, but after the generalities about the bridge they moved upstairs to William's bedroom for privacy. William's help was fundamental to the success of the plan as it required knowledge of the documents and contracts about the bridge. By midnight, the future was set and the men fell into their beds.

* * *

Earl Edward Lloyd-Williams should have closed the study door when he was berating his steward the next morning. His wife always found his conversations interesting.

'So, Sir John's men have started to focus on the bridge over the straits. That leads me to think that my friend John is not telling me everything.'

'I'm sorry sir, I didn't hear all their conversation and neither did the man I left behind.'

'Pfur! You seem to have trouble pissing in your guzunder nowadays. Many years ago, I told you to eliminate any troubles caused by the incomers onto my land. Now you belatedly tell me that I may have an issue in Porthaethwy?'

'Yes sir.'

'In your backyard. The place where I gave you lodgings to look after my interests. The specific location I wanted protected from Sir John and his cronies?' The tone was condescending, the words spoken slowly and with anger and spite.

'Sir.' Rhodri had his head down. He knew he may have failed his master for the first time. The slap of the whip cracked across the room as the Earl struck out in his anger. The leather cut a swathe of white across the stubble on Rhodri's cheek before turning a vivid red.

'Get out of my sight. You have a day to tell me what you will do to retrieve the situation.' The steward called into the kitchens before departing to his cottage in Porthaethwy. He needed a pie to take home for his evening meal. It was Frances who calmed him down and used ointment provided by Aeronwy to dress his wound and soothe his honour. But it was Rhodri who said too much as his tongue was loosened by his fear of failure. The next morning Frances and Lady Charlotte sat in the drawing room reviewing the menus for the week. It meant the two conversations were made into a single coherent message that Frances could pass on to Aeronwy for Lady Elizabeth. William Smith was in grave danger, but Beth was never told. She was too love struck to be upset by her friends, but Taid considered the news with Lady Elizabeth. They decided the time was nigh for the double-cross, the time was right for the Welsh to strike back. Sir John was ailing with a distended liver and a bad heart and had only recently modified the amount of his drinking. Circumstances and timing were coming together.

Any women meeting with a man had to be extremely circumspect or she would lose her reputation. Indeed, being seen together and un-chaperoned was a course to disaster in the social etiquette pervading society from top to bottom. But sometimes, friendships can be extremely useful and William was grateful that he could spend the night with Beth at Owen's cottage. The lovers valued every second together. Beth urged William to marry her and although she enjoyed the night, her sense of disappointment was increasing. The cottage was quiet, it was isolated and it meant that Owen could use the time to stay at the house in the servant's quarters. Sir John was in Liverpool and everyone was asleep by 10pm, except Elizabeth. Owen met her in a darkened study. She couldn't allow him near her bedroom or the drawing room as there could be no excuse for his presence. Two floors of separation from the sleeping servants were safer. She stroked his face as they sat on the leather settee.

'We are getting too old for this.'

'I agree Elizabeth. In that case I will stop loving you from this day forth.'

'You know that was not my meaning.' She paused. 'Have you stopped loving me, Owen?' It was plaintive; a woman who had given her heart was asking a question.

'Never. I will love you until the day I die.' He gently kissed her on her lips and softly played with her grey hair. The wig she wore during the day made her look much younger. 'You are the most wonderful part of my life. Without you, I would not have lived.'

'That sounds ominous, my love. When you talk to me now, it reminds me of my favourite novels by Sir Walter Scott. Your words have a depth and meaning that I don't understand.'

'Surely not in books like *Ivanhoe* or *Rob Roy*?'

'No my silly Owen. In a poem like *The Lady of The Lake*.

'I am sorry to sound so depressive; there is a weight on my mind.' He kissed her on the neck below her eye and sent shivers down her spine. 'What happens in the poem?' She leaned into his neck and breathed gently.

'Three men battle for a lady's love. A king feuds and then reconciles with his enemies in a tale of the highlands versus the lowlands. Do you recognise the plot?'

'Ma'am I see the English monarchy and Wales against England as a parallel, but for the life of me, I cannot see the contest of love.'

She hit him hard on the chest with her delicate hand. 'The master, the son and the steward are in the contest. Are you with me?' He touched her bodice and slid his hand lower.

'No I am not, but that is the correct question and the answer is: are you with me, my darling?'

She murmured softly, 'I love you deeper than the deepest sea.'

'I know.' It was a beautiful night, special to them both. It was an ending in the place where Owen had made his pledge.

It was never to be repeated, but they had true love and that was all that mattered.

In a small cottage a mile away, the same depth of love was experienced by a younger couple.

Two women and two men, friends and lovers had touched each other's souls but could never be together by accident, only when events coincide.

Chapter 12

Accidents Happen

The worse sea conditions on the Menai Straits are invariably experienced around Michaelmas each September. The feast of Saint Michael the Archangel is on the 29th. This angelic day occurs near the equinox and is therefore associated with the beginning of autumn.

Michael was the greatest of all the archangels and according to the Bible he defeated Lucifer in the battle for the heavens. Folklore suggests that blackberries should never be picked after Michaelmas Day because when Lucifer fell from heaven, he landed painfully in a blackberry bush and so he cursed the prickly brambles. The locals near Plas Coch were convinced that Lucifer, whom they called Satan, must have landed on the banks of the Menai. Perhaps the fallen angel's anger was fuelling the brewing storm as Owen drew close to Felinheli, but "good" men have nothing to fear as angels are always there to protect them.

Rhodri Morgan clambered aboard the smack at Porthaethwy and sat on a thwart by Captain Temple. The seaman had worked for the Earl for many years and had always been the one trusted to act with Dai Jones and Rhodri on any smuggling runs. On this occasion, Jones was busy leading his men astray around Red Wharf Bay to the east, whilst Morgan and Temple were taking contraband from the warehouses in Porthaethwy to Caernarfon in the west. An open subterfuge that all the participants happily understood, whilst pocketing their guineas. Time was of the essence. A deal had been struck and the customs men would return from their wild goose chase the next morning. Temple was chewing tobacco as he nonchalantly leaned on the polished wheel.

'How furious and wrong-headed a trip. Damnation man, doesn't the Earl listen to good advice?'

Rhodri yawned before replying, 'I asked if we could postpone it by twenty-four hours because of the damned weather, but he was adamant that we should proceed.' He didn't add that the Earl was punishing him at every opportunity.

Temple was unimpressed. 'Twenty- four hours delay on a profit of a hundred guineas. Pfur! If he lost the boat on this foolhardy mission, he would be truly piss'd.'

'Shut up and let's be off. I would rather be in bed with a good whore than sat in the rain listening to your claptrap. We need to join the tide and make passage through the Swellies whilst we have time.'

The captain hollered his orders to the four man crew and the smack was pushed away from the quay and immediately swept westwards. Within a few minutes they were going faster than a trotting horse as the tide swirled its way around the rocky outcrops in the centre of the channel. Morgan sat back, confident in the captain's skills. Temple was one of the best; he knew every swirling whirlpool and hidden rock in the central section of the straits where many ships had come to a calamity. Using two small sails to give him some leeway, the captain swung the boat left and then right to ensure he was in the exact position for the next 100 yards. The art was in the anticipation and not in the doing.

In less than an hour they were riding in the broader stream past Plas Newydd and hoisted a little more sail to give an extra two knots. Temple relaxed and sat on the thwart with one hand on the wheel. It would be half-an hour before they hit the nasty chop at Moel-y-Don where the channel narrowed and hidden sandbanks lurked.

The timing was perfect; they would land the contraband in the dark, wait a few hours and sail home on the inbound tide with the wind behind them.

The steward was exhausted after his long day visiting the master's farms around Dinorwic and knew it was due to his age. He had spent no more than ten minutes with William at the quarry, barely giving enough time for a convivial mug of tea. The weather had turned damp and cold immediately after Taid's departure for home and now all he wanted was some hot food from the kitchens before retiring to bed. He had been irked by all the farmers he had met during the day. They had obviously been conspiring together as he had received the same story from each one.

'We can't afford an extra five guineas a year rental. The grass has stopped growing as well since the quarry was expanded. We don't have so many lambs as the blasting scares the ewes and makes them miscarry.'

Therefore, he had been harsh and judgemental, using cuttingly short sentences and brooking no reply. 'I will send men every quarter to count your sheep and keep a tally. The rent increase applies immediately. Those walls adjacent to your cottage need to be repaired within the month or I will evict you for not taking proper care of Sir John's property.'

The farmers' attitudes had annoyed him as he knew they were having a good year. He stopped his horse on the promontory by the boatyard and stared into the abyss. It was already 8pm and the light was poor. Visibility varied from 200 to 400 yards and there was no sign of the larger ferry. Behind him were a gaggle of 40 people who were waiting to cross. Babies were screaming as they were cold and hungry. Mothers were trying to control the children who were playing tag perilously close to the 20-foot drop from the quay to the sea. There were only a few men waiting in the crowd as it wasn't one of the slate miners' commuting days. Most of the passengers had been to the market in Caernarfon and clutched brown paper parcels containing their purchases. Lengths of wool, tools for the farm such as scythes and grind stones. Some had bought a luxury item for which the family had saved money for a year or more: a Bible, a candlestick or even a box iron.

The wind howled down the straits, a huge gust disturbing Owen's horse and making it skittish. He dismounted and stood on the leeward side of the animal as a wall of rain slanted eastwards towards Porthaethwy. The ferry was slowly approaching but was still caught in the rip tide that was emptying the waters westward. It crabbed across the white caps, with the small sail filling in the gusts and making the boat heel hideously and then emptying suddenly to roll it the opposite direction. Four oarsmen could be seen fighting to reach the Felinheli inlet as the wind clashed with the tide. After a few minutes they were safe as the boat came out of the main channel and into the shallows to moor by the steps cut into the quay.

'Taid. What you doin' getting that 'orse wet? Poor sod deserves better than that!' Grace Parry was always endearing with him.

'Is that true Mrs Parry? And I don't suppose I saw you rowing on the leeward side of the sail to stay out of the squalls madam?'

'Maybe sir, maybe your eyes was mistaken, but Satan is certainly in the deeps tonight.' She and her husband were taking fares and hurrying everyone on board. They wouldn't attempt another crossing after this one, especially after dark. It wasn't until the heavily loaded ferry left the shelter of the shore that the passengers realised the difficulty of the crossing. Even with a small sail, the boat heeled in the gusts and buried her gunwales into the cold grey sea. There were gasps and cries every time she tipped sharply making the children cling to their mothers and behave for the first time in the whole day. The rowers angled the ferry 45 degrees towards Plas Newydd and it progressed on a straight course heading for Moel-y-Don.

As they hit the vicious white horses there were shouts of terror. The boat bucked and shimmied, the cracking of the sail and creaking of the beams drowned the noises of the passengers as they clutched their belongings with one hand and their seats with the other. Owen tightly held the reins of his horse in the centre of the boat. He had been riding the Grey for more than four years and he had never seen her so scared. Stroking her nose and patting her flanks he encouraged her to remain still but her every movement gave inertia to the rolling of the boat as the crew fought their way into mid-channel. Grace was scanning the sea around them and bellowing orders to the oarsmen as they eased their way across. She saw the smack coming from the direction of Plas Newydd at the same time as her husband.

He shouted a warning, 'We have right of way. Keep to the heading yes?'

She looked at the dark shadow which was emerging from the curtain of rain that had covered them a few minutes before.

'Heave away lads, no change of direction. They must have seen us by now.' The rowers pulled harder, gasping for breath from their exertions and blowing away the mixture of salt and rain water that was flying into their faces. The ferry dug its bow into a wave and the Grey was jolted forward. Her flailing hooves landed on two women adjacent and cries and shouts of anger and pain added to the commotion. The wind blew harder, whistling above their heads with an ominous sigh.

Temple nudged Morgan to make him stand. He pointed to the struggling ferry no more than 400 yards away, maybe two minutes with the speed of the tide.

'Poor bastards on a night like this. The damn thing is lying too low in the water with all the weight. Anything for a fare I would guess.'

Morgan was staring intently and picked up the captain's telescope. The Grey advertised Owen's presence and then Morgan spotted him holding her still. He gave a direct order to Temple.

'You didn't see them sir. Ram it.'

'Good god man, are you mad?'

'I said ram it. That is my order and my decision. Don't ever dare to contradict me.'

The captain swallowed hard; there would be little chance of any survivors. He had to ask, 'Why? Give me one good reason.'

The smack was a minute away from the ferry and on a direct collision course. A few degrees to port and they would easily miss it. His hand twitched nervously on the wheel.

'I want Tudur dead. The Earl wants Tudur dead and Tudur is on that ferry.' The captain had to make a quick decision. Do as he was ordered or forfeit his position and probably his own life.

'On your head Morgan, may God forgive you man.' The smack stayed on a collision course and now was only 100 yards away from the floundering ferry.

* * *

Both Grace and her husband stopped rowing and stood to holler and wave their arms. The rest of the passengers raised their heads and realised a collision was possible. Many of them followed the ferry crew's example, exciting the Grey and making the boat unstable. As it plunged first to port and then to starboard, she took on water that made her wallow deeper into the ferocious chop. Only Owen remained calm with his legs astride. He tried to balance the boat by pulling his horse left and then right in quick succession and then he looked towards the smack as the passengers screamed as if with one voice. There was a moment's quiet before it slammed into the rear planks of the ferry, tearing them open. The two boats writhed alongside each other as the smack pinned the ferry into the surface of the water. Grating and splintering in a tangle of broken bones, the crushed passengers died a quick death, sucked between the hulls. Owen's last view before he too plunged into the icy water was Morgan's leering face leaning over the gunwale. Rejoicing in the carnage with a satanic stare and then it all went black as the steward plunged into the depths.

The crew members on the smack rushed to the starboard side and leaned over to see what they had hit, but their speed had already left the wreck of the ferry wallowing behind. A squall of rain hit the boat and their captain shouted for them to return to their stations as he wanted to tack. The episode was over within two minutes and all the men could question was how many souls had been on the ferry. There was a timid query to the captain about returning to search for survivors, but he sloughed it away with excuses about fighting the rush of the tide and the gathering gloom.

Within an hour they were unloading at Caernarfon and the rumours spread thick and fast. William was sat in the Coxswains Inn when he first heard that the Moel-y-Don ferry had been hit and sunk. Within half an hour an old salt came from the port and confirmed the sinking and the exact time. His heart beat faster; it was the only ferry that his best friend could have caught. Donning a rain cape, he quickly walked to the quay to stand and wait for news. He felt helpless for the first time in his life. What extra could he do to help? A boat was despatched in the general direction of Moel-y-Don as he stood in the cold and dark. There were four oarsmen and a total crew of nine who were willing to be sent into the hellish night. It pulled away from the quay with one man at the bow as lookout. The boat was buffeted by the wind before it even reached the tide, making the lookout hold the knotter rope attached to the Samson post. It gave him some stability, but he still bounced in the air as they hit the swell. Their only chance to quickly reach the scene was by using full sail and staying close to the shore to keep out of the tide. The mission was dangerous and time was running out for the brave men to find any survivors as it was already past midnight.

Owen loosened the horse's reins as the beast was dragging him deeper. The shock of the cold temporarily stopped his breathing as he remembered his fall into the lake behind the house. He saw Elizabeth behind his closed eyes, she was shouting for him to kick with his legs and pull with his arms. He wriggled out of his cape and heavy woollen coat and kicked hard. The breath he had taken before going under was still in his lungs and now he used it to fight his way to the surface. Gasping for air, his head emerged and then immediately went back under the surface as the chop was nearly three feet high. He could see her violet eyes, deep violet and full of love. He kicked himself to the surface again and luckily found that he had turned away from the waves as his head re-emerged. It helped to temper his panic as he struggled to breathe between a few seconds of oblivion as he fought Satan beneath him.

There were no screams anymore. Something touched his arm and he looked down to see the white face of a dead baby as it floated by, swaddled in a blanket that gave it some buoyancy. He could see that there were no more than a dozen heads around him. No one shouted to each other as they strove to stay afloat with the wind howling and the waves crashing over them. Owen glimpsed the shore at Moel-y-Don, a solitary light shone outside the ferrymen's cottages and then it was gone as the tide pushed the dead and living towards the sandbanks off the salt ponds. A feeling of dread gripped his mind; below him was something waiting to drag him under. As the light disappeared, the dread became deeper; a prehistoric fear that "it" would grab his feet and pull him to his death at the bottom of the sea. The water felt cold, but he knew that in September it was warmer than at any other time of the year and then his feet hit the bottom. Struggling forward he lurched onto an emerging sandbank, heaving his legs out of the sand that sucked and strained at every sinew. Within a few minutes he collapsed gasping on his knees and cried with relief, sobbing like a baby.

The sea washed around his arms and legs as he crouched on all fours, shivering with the shock and cold. There was barely enough light left to see where the others had landed. Pushing upright with an effort, he staggered towards the nearest woman. The sands were still sucking at his boots and so he bent and threw them into the shallows to make it easier to move. Gradually five others joined him, a silent group of adults hugging each other in relief to be alive, but no children had survived. There were four women he didn't know, himself and Grace Parry: six survivors out of 44 passengers and crew.

The temporary lifeboat heard their plaintive cries at 5am. The women's long drawn out calls for help were wailed every five minutes and were only heard when the wind dropped. The rescuers shouted loudly to encourage them to hold on; they were only half a mile away. The group hugged each with joy as saviour was at hand, but as the boat closed on the sandbank the shallow approaches prevented them coming close enough to effect their rescue. Three women tried the short swim towards it, but all three were swept to their deaths by the strong incoming tide. As the waves started to break over the bank itself, Grace grasped Owen's collar.

'The only chance is to swim for the shore. Do you understand Taid. Swim for *Yr Ynys Dwyll* or perish in the vain hope of rescue.'

'No Grace, don't do it, you can't survive!'

'If I don't, then only you know it was murder by that bastard Morgan.'

He grasped her shoulders, 'Attempted murder, Grace. He would be acquitted by the Earl's JPs who would be more likely to hang him for stealing five shillings from a local store.' He drew a smile from her before almost certain death and then Parry was gone. She was a strong swimmer and headed towards Anglesey which was no more than 500 yards away. After a few minutes he lost sight of the dark bobbing head. Grace was better than any man who had ever lived a life at sea, but that night the sea took her life.

Owen was transfixed with terror; the sea was running fast and up to his waist. In the distance he could see the lantern on the boat, temptingly close but an impossible dream as it rode in the fiercest of tides. For the first time in his life, he couldn't make a decision and knew he would die because of it. He started to pray to God, to the angels and to his Elizabeth. As he prepared himself to die, a huge piece of wood smacked into his side, knocking him off his feet. Grasping it as he fell, he realised it was part of the mast from the ferry and he clung to it as the ebb swept him back towards Moel-y-Don.

A beautiful dawn broke over the sole survivor, but by now the lifeboat had reluctantly returned to Caernarfon to share their news of the disaster. There was no strength left in Owen now; he only clung to the spar because he was dreaming of his love who lay asleep in bed no more than a mile away.

William Smith had ridden his horse along the shore from Caernarfon to Moel-y-Don and back again. He stopped by the quay and stood talking to the captain of a local boat that had just arrived from Ireland.

After explaining the situation, the kind man gave him the only sane advice possible. 'Go back to where the accident occurred and wait. The ebb and flow will bring any bodies back to the same place within the next few hours.'

'Bodies?'

'There is no chance with the conditions overnight, so go and bury your friend. They are all dead and there is nothing we can do except pray for their souls.'

William felt sick with fear as he retraced his steps eastwards. He stayed on the small paths close to the shore, constantly looking for shapes in the gathering dawn. As he closed on Felinheli, he saw a mound of clothes lying on the mussel beds behind the promontory. Jumping from his horse he rolled the body over. It was a woman whom he didn't know. Crossing himself, he said a quick prayer before throwing her in front of his pommel. He remounted and carried on his hopeless search.

The sparrows were chirping in the hedgerows to warn their family and friends of the approaching invader. As the first glint of sunlight threaded through the leaves of the trees, he cried unashamedly. The body in front of him was a dismal reminder of the dreadful night. At last he was opposite Moel-y-Don, where the sea was tranquil, the tide slack in the wide channel and then he saw something moving in the water. He pushed the body off the horse and let it drop to the ground with a thud so that he could gallop along the sandy spit towards the object. The horse was bucking and rearing, fighting the reins as they cantered through the surf, but he was determined to reach it. Spray flailed from the horse's hooves as he reared to a halt in a foot of still water and leaped down to help the man grasping a long piece of wood.

His voice cracked with emotion as he spoke through his tears. 'My god Owen, I thought you had perished, my friend.' He grasped him under his shoulders to help him sit. 'Oh lord, what have they done to you? The Earl's men tried to kill you for god's sake!'

Taid couldn't open his swollen eyes because of the salt, but he could smile at the friendly voice. 'No, not his men, they aren't at fault. It was Morgan. I saw him.' William patted his shoulder as

Owen coughed up more seawater. The Welshman tasted the bile in his mouth as he spoke again. 'Do not...' he spat, 'do not worry about me, William. I have been spared for greater things. It is you who should worry; they will come for you next.'

Rhodri cowered in front of the Earl as they stood near the lime kilns adjacent to the island of Saint Tysilio.

'That is the deal, sir. I have paid massive bribes to Sir John's people and they will receive double if we succeed in changing the bridge contracts. This land will be yours and most of the bank opposite. But...' his skin crawled as he knew there was one flaw and the Earl would not accept it, 'they could still double-cross us.'

'Methinks not at that price!' The Earl was confident in power from his wealth; these were his people, on his island.

Rhodri drew himself more upright. His relief was palpable. 'Tudur must be dead. The deal in Porthaethwy is done, I can do no more.'

The Earl grimaced at him, 'You said you suspected deceit by some of my servants? Who might that be exactly?' The Earl's anger was ready to boil over. He had started to think that his steward was becoming senile and was therefore dispensable.

'The cook, Frances. She talks to Aeronwy, sisters talk to brothers and there is always another...' The Earl's head whipped around at the accusation. He already knew the insinuation to follow because he had suspected it himself. 'I believe there have also been messages between their ladyships that have hurt us...'

'Get rid of the cook and the Tudur woman. Don't ponder on a whim like "suspected deceit". I want no spies in my employ, proven or not. You "did" the brother now "do" the sister. They all know too damned much for my liking.'

It suited Rhodri as he was bent on his personal vendetta. The cook could be sent to the London house and not arrive. Lady Charlotte was the Earl's problem.

* * *

It was 3am in the cottage at Brynsiencyn and Aeronwy was fast asleep, curled like a foetus on one side. She was in one bedroom and her girls were in the other. She uncoiled and turned onto her side as the neighbour's dog barked at the squeak from the pantry window. It was a small window that was invariably left open all summer. The wood had distorted and required hammering hard into the frame to keep out the winter draughts.

A small dark figure started to inch through the small opening, struggling as their waist popped through before lightly dropping to the bare earth floor. The intruder listened carefully, letting his eyes adjust to the gloom. Moving forward, the shadow disappeared in the light of the embers from the opened range. The flames flickered higher as Rhodri added wood inside it and also because he was making a bonfire unhindered by the black metal at the front of it. He waited until he was sure the wood had caught fire on the hearth and then encouraged it further by dragging the settle into the flames. He piled a cushion and some coats onto the blaze whilst holding a piece of cloth over his nose. The smoke billowed upwards and the flames flared towards the low ceiling with its tarred beams. There was no sound from upstairs; they were dreaming of the games they played in front of the fire on a winter's evening. Carefully he let himself out of the back door and returned to his horse that was tethered on the outskirts of the village.

There was no proof, of course. The fire had destroyed all four of the terrace cottages that formed a single block. The neighbours all survived, but the billowing smoke and roaring inferno prevented any attempts at rescue. Owen buried his sister and his two nieces in the same grave as his tad, in the grounds of the local chapel. Jenkin Evans kindly came to officiate and walked in the graveyard with Taid after the burial. The grass had regained its greenness after the dry summer and had been recently scythed to make a sweet smelling carpet.

'I am so sorry for you, Owen. I can't imagine how you feel. The accidents to your family have been terrible events. Please accept this as God's will.'

The steward leaned on a low stone wall that bordered the road to Llanfairpwll and shook his head. 'Jenkin, I don't believe in that many accidents in a year. God has worked in mysterious ways or man has been helping Him.' He turned to the preacher and could see his genuine concern.

Jenkin stroked his white beard and tugged at his dirty dog collar. 'Your tad and I talked many times, my son. He was more sensible than Cadell; Lewis was a true rock of a man. One day we sat by the sea in Porthaethwy. It was a warm and a beautiful day like today, so we sat for an hour or two. We talked about Wales and its people and what we were doing to help them. He was very merciful and compassionate, your tad.' Jenkin glared up at the bright sun before gently closing his eyes. 'We both knew that the English landowners on our island are evil men in the sight of God and we both strived to bring good into our friends' lives.'

Owen's eyes were moist, 'Please help me, Jenkin. I am the master's steward, but life cannot last forever. I pledged my loyalty and forgot my God. You know that I want to help my people.'

Jenkin sighed and placed his hands together in supplication. 'I know that Taid. I have always known it. We are alike and no man is ever innocent.' He sighed as he looked at the tall mountains away across the straits. 'We have great ideals but take our pay from bad masters. Although there has been a long battle on this earth between the Earl and Sir John, well man, I don't think either of them will reach heaven. Sometimes it hurts me as I know too much you know.'

'Please help?' The Minister took his arm and strolled for an hour around the graveyard. He trusted Taid to do the right thing.

Taid had always helped everyone whenever he could, his father had been proud of that.

But only the dead heard their conversation.

Chapter 13

Shipwreck

There were 29 days that February, a leap year when women can traditionally ask a man to marry. But when two women love their men more than their own lives, they would never ask. Asking was an impossibility, not even a leap of faith.

Februare – to purify – or Februa, the Roman festival of expiation, which was celebrated at the end of the month. It was certainly a time to make amends.

> *"If Candlemas day be fair and bright*
> *Winter will have another flight.*
> *But if Candlemas day be clouds and rain*
> *Winter is gone and will not come again."*

Ieuan remembered the rhyme halfway between Portrush and Liverpool. He stood next to the helmsman as they beat into a freezing northerly that was laced with snow as they plunged into the next large wave. Freezing sheets of spray crashed upward from the bow before the ship reared high into the air ready to immediately plunge down again. Both men ducked to avoid the worst of each soaking and then quickly stood tall to view the dangers of the cruellest of seas.

Ieuan pulled out his pocket watch to check the time before verifying their bearing on the swaying compass in front of him. A landing at Cemaes to unload the contraband from Roscoff seemed tight, unless the weather improved. He had read the line in a news sheet, "Two fools, one rogue, one bully and one numbskull" describing the coast-waiters off Anglesey and decided he was the latter to attempt any such delivery. The large schooner had more precious cargo than the tea, but they were bound for Liverpool. Twenty immigrants from New York sat retching below. He knew their lives were at risk in such a storm and therefore in his mind the smuggled tea could wait. He had also read that the Prime Minister had recently claimed that less than half of the thirteen million pounds of tea consumed in England had duty paid on it. William Pitt was, of course, totally accurate on his calculation of the amount of smuggled tea; it was, after all, Ieuan's job to know these things. The captain grimaced; he knew he was expected to rendezvous with Taid no matter what. However, the PM had no idea of the pressure on the smugglers. As well as the monetary pressure from Sir John, Ieuan couldn't afford to arrive at Liverpool with the contraband and face the customs men. His company's reputation and his bonus relied on the safe delivery of the tea to Anglesey. He shouted a warning to the helmsman as he saw a rogue wave approaching fast on their starboard bow. Lady Louisa Littleton hit the wave bow on and shuddered to a halt before sliding across the crest and planing down the face. She was a beautiful ship and deserved the name of Elizabeth's courageous and tenacious cousin who was battling with the brothers to be trained in the family business.

The storm made him realise he was mortal for the first time. He was tired of being at sea. He was questioning his orders. Both were a sign of age. "Coincidental events" was William's expression, a time would come for action and now Ieuan knew he was ready. The years after Jamaica had been lived in oblivion, but now that William and Owen had a plan to double-cross the master, he wanted his own revenge on the man. His red eyes hurt from the salt grinding into them. After all, what sort of a man would risk the lives of 20 fellow human beings for a few chests of tea? He slapped the bulwarks hard with both hands, but the pain didn't help. He knew "that sort of a man" was exactly what he had become: Captain Ieuan Fardol, lapdog, money-grabber, a complete bastard.

The weather was worsening as he tried to make out the horizon. There was no real danger in the middle of the Irish Sea; they had enough visibility to see any other ships before a collision. The danger was in rounding Anglesey, where most wrecks were to be found on the north-east coast. This was exactly where the delivery was to be made.

He asked for God's forgiveness and prayed that his friend's plan would soon come to fruition and then he would sail away and never return. He had argued over the details with William, but eventually it had all made sense. Making Sir John sign away the bridge agreements to his son, Henry, who would be suitably controlled by Lady Elizabeth, must ultimately benefit the people on Anglesey. It was an easy administration task as William knew the documents, which required just one of the brothers' signatures. Whilst maintaining their secrecy, the three brothers had compromised on the safety of their investments. Owen had assured Ieuan that the profits would fund Welsh schools, help the poor through institutes and libraries and develop free medical care accessible to everyone. The captain didn't doubt Lady Elizabeth's promise to help as William had hinted at her love for Owen. But the timing and the method were crucial and still undecided.

As Fardol battled towards the rendezvous at Cemaes, the master was entertaining the Dean for tea. Sir John was grey-faced and spoke slowly as he struggled for breath. He had stopped drinking alcohol and that meant he had far more good days than bad. He knew his heart was causing the problem and was thankful that Elizabeth could administer a little digitalis on occasion to reduce the palpitations.

'Thank you for coming, Dean. As you know my health has taken a turn for the worse over the last few months and therefore I wanted to talk to you about death. I just want to be certain in our minds, that is, if it happens what!' He was planning for the worst whilst expecting to live another ten years, but that was how he had become a successful businessman.

'My dear Sir John, I do hope you make a speedy recovery. You are such a young man to feel the need to discuss funeral arrangements.'

'Well, it was not the spiritual side I was concerned with; more the business side that we have developed over the years.' He laughed at the Dean's discomfort. 'Tush man, mirth is the best physician, what!' The Dean tittered nervously. He was worried that Sir John was going to ask him for a giant favour or to repay some of the "offerings". 'No Dean, I am concerned about your… umm… your sole role of many years… your guidance of your flocks concerning my tax avoidance schemes.' The Dean took orders from his rich parishioners and gave them to Tudur to supply the contraband. He wondered what was coming. 'You see, whether I die or even if you die, I have to understand who will continue this profitable relationship.' Thomas Runcie breathed a sigh of relief. He gave Rhodri Morgan all the details of Sir John's smuggling trade each week so that the Earl could compete with the deals and maintain his ascendancy throughout the island.

'As you know Sir John, I have a duty to God and man. I have never condoned smuggling, though it helps our parishioners through your kind donations.' Although he only used a tenth of the illicit money on their behalf. The rest was kept under the floor in his rectory or transported to the bank at Chester when he visited the cathedral. 'But as any act of God could change our relationship, I have a trustworthy vicar in Llangefni who might be able to help us out. That is, if I can persuade him.' It wasn't a very subtle way of asking for a bigger cut, but Sir John was happy to fund a little more to safeguard the future for his sons. By the end of the meeting the Dean was happy with his extra ten per cent and the vicar from Llangefni would receive less than a third of this increase. After all, he was already well paid to meet Morgan each week.

* * *

Eight miles away in Beaumaris, the Earl was also taking tea. Jenkin Evans dwarfed the chair he sat upon and was tapping his feet in unison with the hymn reverberating in his mind. The Earl was boring the Minister.

'We have a duty to man and God. The income from smuggling gives me the means to help your congregations and through you, we obtain God's forgiveness.'

Jenkin brought all of his presence to bear on Lloyd- Williams. 'Dear Sir, I made it plain to Morgan at our meeting in the chapel that our business relationship is finished.'

'Egad Evans, I am personally asking you for a tiny bit of information and you have the front after all these years to say no?'

'You are asking me to find out the details of Sir John's latest tea run and tip off Dai Jones so he can arrest Tudur and the like. Firstly, I understand the same trick failed ten years ago and secondly, I have my peace with God to think about now.'

The Earl was bright red with anger. 'Circumstances change Minister. I have been too close and too lenient with Sir John when it comes to business and now I need to teach him a lesson. You know the details as your parishioners around Amlwch are intimately involved.'

'Circumstances have changed indeed.' Evans stood above the Earl and looked down into his weasel-like face. 'Our business is limited to God alone from now on. Do your own dirty work henceforth.' He turned and strode out, slamming the heavy door behind him.

When Rhodri noticed the Minister's gig trotting down the driveway, he immediately went to see the Earl.

'You were right, steward. There is no persuading Evans. The question is what should be done?'

'I could arrange an accident.'

'You are a stupid idiot at times. This is not a cook, a nobody. The man has a huge following and no accident would be credible. No, at least not yet. Make a direct approach to Nash for the information and then pass it onto Jones. I want to slap Sir John as hard as possible.'

'Yes sir and I will ask Jones if I can attend the arrest.'

The Earl walked up to him and smashed his right fist into his nose. The steward sat on the floor with his sleeve pressed against his face to staunch the blood. 'Really Morgan, stupidity has become your strong point. I don't want to be associated with the arrest and confiscation. Now get out.'

Behind the paper thin wall, Lady Charlotte lowered the glass from her ear and considered what to do. The issue was the reason why the Earl wanted to attack Sir John. She and Elizabeth had talked about what they could do for the local people before they lost their limited influence over their husbands. Both men were searching for an excuse to divorce their wives and marry to their benefit in society. They both still believed, in their dotage, that they could have more sons as heirs. It was an easy decision. She would inform Elizabeth about everything she knew, including Rhodri's conversations with the maid about the bridge. The steward had found a maid to bed and told her information to make him appear important. The maid was happy to receive his money and even happier when Lady Charlotte trebled it.

However, neither woman had heard the part of the plan where Morgan would ambush and kill Sir John's men after the customs raid.

Many of the worshippers in the church of Saint Edwen's had never contemplated the meaning of God. They couldn't conceive Him as real or an essential part of their lives but attended the Church as they were expected to. God was a hidden entity who would protect them and always be there no matter what their actions. They arrived, they prayed and sang and then they congregated outside to participate in the rich tapestry of life. God was a thought in the distant background whilst they lived a microscopically small span compared to the age of the universe. But they believed in themselves, their lives and their inaction, as they thought they were important in the grand scheme of things.

Owen Tudur was one of them. He coveted his beliefs in life and carried through with them whether God existed or not.

Lady Charlotte's lone attendance was a surprise to everyone who was present that Sunday. She made a point of chatting privately with her friend Elizabeth before returning to Earl's Hill.

'You must stop the smuggling run, Elizabeth and in addition, as discussed over many months, you must warn the agent that he is in imminent danger. It all makes sense now. Frances's disappearance, Aeronwy's death, the attempt on your steward's life.'

Her friend took her arm and walked her to view the straits. 'Calm yourself cousin. All those are terrible deeds and you and I will never know the truth, but why does the Earl want to attack Sir John now? Smith has known for years that eventually they would want him dead. You have to trust me my dear. Everything you have found out I can use. But... I worry so about you Charlotte.'

'If only I could run away from Earl's Hill, I would. The steward and my husband scare me so much.' She kept her head down, but her friend could see the tears dripping down her cheeks.

'We are too old for these men, Charlotte. They think they are still young and cannot accept a wife who is aged like us.' They strolled past the wrought iron gate leading to Plas Newydd. 'Remember Lady Isabel. The belle of the ball and now dead, with no children to keep her memory alive.'

Lady Charlotte gripped Elizabeth's arm. 'I am so sorry, I must go. The attack must be a warning about something. A shot across the bows of an ill man?'

They parted and promised to meet again in late October. Elizabeth idled towards Taid. She stood looking at the glassy mere surrounded by bare willow trees.

She spoke softly, 'What does the Earl know about the bridge agreements?

He too stared straight ahead. 'Nothing. I know he has bribed many of the locals thinking he can influence the outcome, but as I have promised them double the money that is now a closed path.

He definitely knows nothing about the agreements made all those years ago.'

She left him to return to the house in the gig driven by silly Elis, leaving William Smith to join Taid and walk back to Plas Coch for their lunch. Siân had promised them beef as a special treat.

The agent chatted to Taid as they walked. 'We have new copper smelters at Saint Helens and Macclesfield now. It is an attempt by Sir John to reduce costs, but he may still be in trouble.'

'Surely not?' Taid couldn't contemplate any grave financial issues affecting the family, but he had noticed that William spent more time at Parys Mountain lately. Now he realised the pressure he was under and the new stress on the family business.

William continued, 'The businesses in North Wales support the bank and cash is required. My God man, we have had the end of the Napoleonic wars and the abolition of slavery to contend with. Do you realise how much cashflow must be generated?'

Taid stopped to look at him, 'Maybe this capitalism idea will eventually fail due to its own greed?'

William nodded, 'Or it fails for a few years and returns stronger than ever? After all, it improves people's lives.'

'Not in Anglesey, William. At least not yet.' The friends despatched the dire thoughts and concentrated on their forthcoming lunch.

Elizabeth left the master's bedroom and walked towards the kitchen to order some chicken broth for Sir John. She needed time away from her master as she hated him more each day. In the ground floor corridor that linked the front to the rear of the house she saw Owen approaching in the gloom. She stood beneath the silent line of bells and mystifying wires that gently chimed to call the servants to the room requiring service.

'How is he your ladyship?'

She leaned back against the wooden panelling before she replied. 'It is a bad day for him, Taid. Yesterday he was out on his horse and went to the docks at Felinheli. I think he overtired himself. Anyway,

I have given him some more digitalis to stabilise his heartbeat, so by tomorrow he should be feeling better.' She twisted her hands together with pent up anger and hatred. 'Every day, of every week, of every year, I have to be there for him and never once has he cared about me.' She realised it wasn't a private place and surreptitiously looked up and down the corridor. Neither end was darkened by a body and so they were relatively safe to talk.

Owen spoke very softly from a foot away. He could smell the lily of the valley perfume. 'Please be careful. Not too much digitalis, not yet. His heart could stop at any time but you need to keep him going. We need him alive for a few more months.' He took a deep breath before moving away.

'If only Aeronwy were here, Owen.' They silently contemplated the emptiness around them.

'But she isn't. What we are doing is partly revenge for her.'

'Then you must give up the smuggling run tonight and stay with him. You can judge matters better than I and frankly, I need you here.' She swamped him with love as he hesitated. 'Please stay tonight, Taid.' It would enable her to stay away from her husband for the night. The success of their plan was a secondary consideration.

Owen sighed deeply, 'I will stay and I will visit him later. Leave the dosage to me tonight. I'm sure Duncan is competent enough to fetch the tea with the same team as usual. Dai Jones is still in the master's pocket and so they won't have the customs men within five miles of them.' They separated without a smile or the touch of a hand. Each walked from the dark towards the light.

* * *

Dai Jones met with Duncan Thomas alone. It was twilight as the two horses sidled towards each other on the track between Llanfairpwll and Porthaethwy. Each man checked behind them for any other travellers before they stopped to talk. Duncan handed over a small leather pouch and was questioned by Jones.

'Where is Tudur?'

'Indisposed at this moment.'

'And tonight?'

'I doubt if he would trust anyone else to do his job. There is nothing to stop him leading us.' Jones was pleased. Rhodri and his men were going to lie in hiding. After the customs had seized the contraband, Jones would let the smugglers escape and Morgan's henchmen would take the responsibility for killing them all.

Duncan was impatient to be off. 'It is all in guineas, the usual price.'

Dai opened the pouch and quickly counted the ten coins. 'The amount is correct. I know the landing is tonight but when and where do we not patrol?'

Duncan never usually had discussions with Jones and was more specific than Taid would have been. 'We have tea coming into Cemaes about 2am. So you will make yourself scarce then?'

'Of course, nothing has changed since Bull Bay all those years ago.'

Duncan was laughing; he was becoming senile in his old age. 'We beat you bastards that night Jones. What a trap!'

Jones never knew who led the ambush at their rear. 'So it was you behind us Thomas?'

'Of course, but thankfully our business agreement has meant it was the first and last time.' Tudur was the target in the early morning, but Jones was pleased Duncan would also die.

The customs comptroller turned his horse to head home and saluted Duncan. 'Goodbye coachman, enjoy your trip.' He galloped off and made sure he stopped at Morgan's home to receive another 10 guineas for the detailed information.

Off the coast of Cemaes the schooner pitched and bucked like a tiny rowing boat. Despite her 200 tons, the captain knew they were in danger. On the shore Duncan and his men could vaguely see the light from two lanterns and the smudge of grey for the sails above a darker shadow. They lit the tinder in the iron cradle to help the captain judge their location. On the hillocks above them, the customs officers lay on their stomachs waiting for Jones's orders. Whatever happened, they had been told to approach from the north allowing the smugglers to race to safety in the south, which was the route to Amlwch and their homes. Ieuan was tied onto the thwart behind the wheel so he could help the helmsman steer.

'Get ready to bring her into the wind.' He shouted at the top of his voice to the mate halfway down the ship. 'Prepare to drop anchor on my signal.' The mate relayed the order to the four men suffering at the bow as the waves crashed over them before escaping in a white swirl through the gunwales. Ieuan looked at the blackness he knew were the headlands. 'The devil has us man, we are too far south. Quickly now, head into wind so we are in irons.' He raised a fist towards the mate to tell him to drop anchor, but as the schooner broached on a giant wave he saw the white surf on the reef. He knew there was no chance and so he started to pray as the boat crashed at full speed onto the sharp rocks. The shriek of the wind didn't blot out the screams from below and as the timbers caved inwards she heeled to starboard and both masts crashed into the sea. The ship was immediately on her side and he was left hanging off the wheel as the helmsman plummeted overboard to die on the rocks. Instinct took over as the adrenaline pumped through his veins. Reaching for his dagger he cut his safety harness and clambered onto the heaving side of the ship and made towards the stern. As she rotated sideways, spinning on the pinnacle of rocks, he saw clear water and leaped as far as he could towards it – and then it went black as the vicious current dragged him down.

Dai Jones and his men could see more than Duncan because of their vantage point. The officer was white and shaking. Several of his men were mumbling the Lord's Prayer under their breath.

'Let's go you bastards. Remember, make a lot of noise and light the torches. Then regroup below and wait to help any survivors.'

Duncan and his men saw them coming and easily escaped to head south towards home. On the windswept beach the customs men dragged ten bodies out of the surf and threw the five that were corpses into a cart. The others were tied together and made ready to walk to the gaol. There were only a few cases of tea on the beach and therefore less for the customs men to steal before handing the remainder to the Justices in Beaumaris. Overall, it was a furious and wrong-headed night that made them sad to be in their jobs.

Ieuan lay still on the beach. He was exhausted from the swim ashore but glad to see the customs men gathering a few survivors together. They could only be his crew who were on deck like himself. A torch approached from one of the search party and he heaved himself slowly forward on his stomach until he was hidden behind a large rock. Clutching his dagger, he waited patiently, but luckily the customs man turned away and went to rejoin his group. Within a few minutes he watched the procession move out of the bay. The dim light cast shadows of the horses, carts of tea and men which were strung in a long line, but he was puzzled to see none of Owen's collection party. As they rounded the cliff face in front of him, he felt safe enough to stand and that was when he heard a dozen shots on the hill to his left. He hugged the overhang at the rear of the beach and headed towards the noise. A mile along the track towards Amlwch he found the bodies in a tight group, including Duncan, but there was no Taid or Elis.

He slumped on the floor, wretched with the sadness of it all. At least 30 dead to make a few guineas potential profit and now the tea would be washed away and ruined. The skeleton beams of his beautiful ship would stand proud on the reef for all to see, with the hidden bodies picked clean by the crabs.

It was a young man's game and he decided he should stop playing.

Drawing himself slowly onto his knees and then to his feet, he trudged with a heavy heart towards Amlwch, where he would borrow a horse and immediately ride to Plas Coch.

Chapter 14

Death and Demise Are Different

It was still dark outside as Siân rolled around the kitchen preparing breakfast for the servants in the dim red glow from the fire. Catrin had already tried to sympathise with her but had been despatched to the parlour to scrub the boarded floor with soft soap and silver sand. The back door creaked open and a grey-faced steward made his way to a chair set by the warm fire. Her heart missed a couple of beats and she steadied herself against the table, but still she kept her head down.

Taid looked across at her. Grey thin hair, a large red face, swollen by the years of food and inactivity. Her massive bulk and her air of solidity hid the kindness of the woman within the misshapen body.

He spoke quietly, 'Please forgive me, Siân. I would rather it had been me.'

The cook stifled a sob and wiped her eyes with her sleeve. 'It should have been you.'

Taid leaned on his knees and stared into the embers. 'Do you remember when I used to come in here as a young steward? You always made it difficult for me.'

'I made you earn your breakfast with a little chat. A few precious moments to keep a young girl happy.'

She moved closer to him, but this time it was his turn to keep his head down. She saw his shoulders heave from the sob and then he spoke through a sigh. 'Duncan was a good man, always trustworthy. He was my friend and he saved my life on the Sychnant.'

Siân clasped his shoulder and patted it gently. 'I always wanted his baby Taid.' The steward and cook sobbed silently in unison. They comforted each other as he stood to hold her tight.

After a few moments she pushed him away. 'Goodness me sir, what would the maids think if they walked in on us?'

'They would think that the wife of my late friend was going to serve me the heartiest breakfast he has ever eaten in his life.'

The small inn where Morgan met Nash was south of Llangefni and close to Plas Penmynydd, the royal home of the Tudors since the 1500s. They sat in a dark corner away from the handful of other drinkers and supped their ale. Frances's cousin placed his pewter mug on the table as he watched a phial handed over by Morgan which was swiftly pocketed by Nash. He watched nonchalantly; the sudden deaths in the family had concerned them all and news of this meeting might entice Taid to provide a reward.

Morgan grasped the butler's lapel to reinforce his quiet words. 'The deadly nightshade will kill him within a few minutes. So make sure you are not around when he eats his food and act surprised when you are summoned.'

'How do you know?'

'Know what idiot?'

'That it is so concentrated it takes only a short time.'

Morgan moved his hand onto Nash's collar and put his stinking mouth a few inches from his face. 'The next time you are clever with me, I will slit your throat.' The butler stayed quiet, he had no doubts the threat would be enacted. Morgan thrust him away. 'Sometimes I wonder if your information is worthwhile anymore; maybe you are surplus to requirements after this...'

Nash swallowed before nervously asking for an explanation. 'I am happy to make this a last job, steward. Make it a 100 guineas and I will disappear south.' He knew Morgan might give him the money and then kill him to retrieve it, but he had lived with that threat for years.

'So you want to run anyway?'

'Let's say I can give you Tudur's life as well as Smith's to tidy up loose ends. Sir John won't last much longer and I need a change of air.'

Morgan slurped some ale spilling a few drops down the front of his greasy black jacket. 'Fifty guineas if Tudur and Smith die and I will ask the Earl if we will let you leave after the deed.'

'With an extra fifty?'

'With your life.' Morgan slid the bench backwards and stood to leave. He placed his bowler hat on his head and ended on a haughty note. 'Do a good job and we will consider your request to bow out.' He left without looking back, leaving Nash to sup a few more tankards and contemplate a double murder. He wanted to leave; this would be his last act before he ran, whether the Earl let him or not.

* * *

William Smith arrived at Plas Coch late on the Friday evening. Sir John had summoned him to an urgent meeting before William headed to London to see his brothers.

The master sat behind his desk in the study and contemplated his agent. 'You and I have been through many dangerous times, Smith but there has never been any more dangerous than now.' William appraised his master of the last 50 years. 'They killed the coachman and our men at Cemaes last night. So why do they want to antagonise me now?'

'It can only be over the rights to the bridge.'

'My steward is dealing with that issue. He has bribed the essential people.'

'In that case they feel the need to put pressure on you to test your mettle.'

The master coughed uncontrollably for a few minutes; after sipping some water he spoke again. 'Do they know about the agreements all those years ago?' Sir John distrusted his agent for the first time ever.

'No, of course not. Please have no doubts about my loyalty.'

The master closed his eyes to help overcome the wave of pain in his chest. It was his spiteful and devious nature that prompted the answer. 'The Earl had no doubts about your loyalty at one time.' William stayed very still as he stared into Sir John's piggy eyes. The boar dropped his gaze first and shuffled some papers on his desk. 'The copper business is failing and I want your opinion on the problems besetting us.'

'Sir John, I have spent all week at the mine and Amlwch, but we have reduced the costs as much as possible. The infrastructure was built to support a market that is now shrinking and so our fixed costs are too high. In addition, our workers have been caught up in the general malaise.'

'Because of the Earl managing his side of the mountain so badly?'

'That is half the problem. Rio Tinto and South America are undercutting our prices. That is the conversation to be had with your brothers.'

Sir John always spoke quietly now and without anger, in case it stopped his heart. On some days he wished his maker would take him and have done. 'Then that is the issue they can address when you arrive in London on Tuesday... William?' He never used his agent's Christian name.

'Sir John?'

'Have you any ideas how we can solve this problem?'

William was tired of everything. 'There is no solution. The world has turned and we are on the wrong side of it.'

The master waved him away, too exhausted to speak further and William hastened to the kitchen as he was famished. The maid called Louise was waiting for him.

'Sir, we have some cottage pie left in the oven. May I serve it sir?' He slumped into a chair. For the first time in his life he was failing the family. He ate with gusto and Louise disappeared to the attic to take to her bed. As she passed the butler's room, she knocked his door and went in. Whispering, she told Nash that William was eating the pie. He passed her a fortune, ten guineas in total. He re-emphasised the need for secrecy and knew the money would keep her quiet long enough for him to make his escape. Louise started to lift her skirts ready for sex. She had nice long legs and his cock stiffened. As a second incentive for keeping quiet he ushered her away to bed with a frustrated push.

William lay on the slabs in the kitchen. He stared absently at the fire as he convulsed again. A pool of urine seeped into the cracks between the granite. He saw Beth walk past him without saying a word, and Owen brought coal for the fire.

Owen spoke, 'This slate doesn't burn well, engineer. Should I try some copper instead?' But William Smith, the great engineer had lapsed into a coma before he could reply and was dead within a few minutes. At 5.30am the next morning, Siân found his corpse and immediately sat on the cold flags to cradle his head in her arms. She rocked backwards and forwards in her grief. Firstly, her husband and now their friend, all within 24 hours. She didn't need to wait long before Taid arrived for his breakfast. He too held William tight and cried without making a sound as he lifted him into a chair. Owen sat next to William and gasped for breath, the emotion had seized his heart and bands tightened across his chest. Their battles had always been fought together, but now it was time for Owen alone to win their war. By 6.30am, Elis had removed the corpse from the house. It would be Lady Elizabeth's task to tell Beth and hold her close in her grief. In some ways it made it easier for Beth to reconcile herself to leaving Plas Coch.

Owen went missing for three hours before he came back to share his condolences with the women. As the ferryman stood up to his waist in water to load his horse, Taid's mood darkened. He remembered how he had once managed to cheat death at this very spot. The thrashing of the beast's forelegs as the ferryman lifted one into the small boat made Owen shiver. He crossed the ferry to Felinheli and climbed the incline so he could admire Smith's achievements. He didn't want anyone seeing him cry and only he and Elizabeth knew who could be the murderer. That made it even more personal.

Taid had finished the rent collection in the parlour and ushered the tenants out quickly for the first time in his life. They put his rudeness down to his age and forgave him this once. He was in a hurry to find Elizabeth; now William was dead they needed to put their plan in motion. None of the maids he passed had seen the mistress and so he marched out of the rear of the house and headed for the walled garden. He found her by the brew-house as she fingered a twig of the apricot tree.

'Taid, you startled me. We should give up on the idea of apricots fruiting here and try inside a conservatory. Somewhere warmer than the hot air flue across this wall.'

'We don't have time, Elizabeth.'

She walked away and he followed. After a few paces she turned to him, the vapour from her breath quickly vanished into the cold air. 'That makes me very sad my friend. Knowing we can only try to help others because our own time is limited.' She carried on walking but allowed him to come alongside her and speak.

'We have had our lives. Let your boys take over the future.' He couldn't understand why she was crying. She could never tell him that Henry was their child. Elizabeth sighed deeply and wiped the tears away with the back of her dirty hand. 'Look, you have made marks on your face.' He wiped them off with his handkerchief, gently and with love. 'You know that time is of the essence now that William is dead. I have arranged to meet the Earl and Morgan in a few days and will promise them I will double-cross Sir John on his death providing they give me five hundred guineas. Fardol is in Felinheli and so I have sent him a message to come here this afternoon.'

She shifted nervously from one foot to another; ostensibly it helped to keep them warm. Sir John had exercised his power over her for too long and it was hard to shrug off. 'God forgive me, Taid, but he is a monster.' She stooped and broke off a handful of spindly pink anemones turned brown by the frost. As she held the stalks and crumbled them through her hands she drew on her courage. 'Let me know when the captain arrives. Beth and I will be in the drawing room most of the afternoon.'

Shortly after tea, the four of them gathered together. Elizabeth and Taid immediately went to the master's bedroom and Ieuan stood silently with Beth waiting to be called. All four of them were nervous. Beth moved around the drawing room looking at the paintings and picking up objects like the tea caddy to closely examine. Ieuan thought of his dead wife and children as he stared out at the black still lake.

The bedroom was dark with the drapes already drawn and a single candle flickering by the bed. Elizabeth sat by the master's head and whispered quietly. The digitalis kept his heart steady, but the opiates she had given him an hour before were making him hallucinate.

She took the documents from a side drawer. 'You must sign your last will and testament John. This is important to assure your sons' futures.' She signalled to Taid to fetch the others.

Her husband answered but wasn't lucid. 'Yes my boys, bad heart what.'

Taid and Ieuan lifted the master into a more upright position. He warily looked at all four of them before grasping the pen that Elizabeth put into his hand. Carefully, she opened the addendum to the bridge agreements and guided him to the spot where he must sign. As the four of them watched, they held their breath. He looked at the pages and looked again. There was surely no way he could read the codicil giving his wife control over a single son.

'Come on my dear, you need to sign these for our sons, for their future. Come now, they give you the respectability on Ynys Môn that you have always craved.' She clasped his hand and guided the pen to the spot once again. Twice he signed, clear and legally and then he fell back and closed his eyes. As they left to countersign the documents as witnesses, they heard him snoring happily.

Taid turned to Ieuan, 'Now that leaves me to deal with another piece of the puzzle. Nash needs to help you and me this evening as the master is so ill.'

Ieuan answered grimly, 'I think a short boat trip across the straits to fetch some help may be in order?'

'Indeed captain. I will meet you at Moel-y-Don at about 8.30pm and you can provide the boat as the ferry will have closed for the night.' They exchanged knowing looks and then Ieuan went to meet with Siân. He wouldn't be attending the two funerals, but he wanted to share some of his happy memories about Duncan and William over a cup of tea.

* * *

Two hours later and only Taid sat by Sir John's bed. Ieuan had returned to Felinheli as quickly as possible and Beth had taken a walk to Brynsiencyn to visit her family.

It was the last time she would see them.

Sir John was awake and sipping tea, the opiates had made him thirsty, but he was still very relaxed. Taid was deliberately telling him some news to occupy his mind. They wanted him to retain no memories, however vague, of the afternoon. The master was as strong as an ox and could last for months. Only the drugs kept him stable and made him remain in his bed. The opiates made him pliable and that was what the plotters required.

'There were riots in Amlwch again and the militia were called out to quell them.'

'Was it the Earl's lot again?'

'No, it was the general population. Unemployment has increased as the copper trade has declined and there is little food in the area. Your indiscriminate shipping of corn from the port was one of the causes, sir.'

'My corn dammit.'

'But people are starving, Sir John.'

The master dismissed it as insignificant with a wave of his hand. He spoke confidentially, 'I need to check my will, steward. Can you fetch our solicitor?'

'Why?' Owen was nervous.

'My boys, I may need to make some changes.'

'I believe they inherit everything, master. I don't believe there is anything wrong with your will on that score. In fact, you told me you had it redrafted and signed it last year.'

'Did I steward? I could have sworn there was something recently.' He went quiet and handed Owen the cup as he collapsed back onto the pillows.

'You have been very ill; possibly you have had some strange dreams.'

'Yes dreams. I do have strange dreams lately.' And then the danger was passed, 'Are the copper men in league with the slate Union? Is that why they are rioting?'

'No sir, the Union and the nationalists aren't the cause. The people want justice; they need the basics in life'

'Pah! What do they know?' He caught his breath and paused for a few minutes. 'Look after my sons if I die Taid. They get everything.'

'What about Lady Elizabeth? Will she receive any of your wealth?'

'Damn no, she is but a woman. She can go and live elsewhere; my sons will provide a pension.'

'You would make her leave Plas Coch?'

'Damned right, I took the dowry and gave her some status. If I die, she is useless to the business.' The master was hard even when desperately ill. He cared nothing for people. He fretted about hurricanes in the West Indies damaging the sugar crop and the increases in import duty rather than the hundreds of dead Negroes.

Owen sighed before he spoke, making Sir John stare hard at him. 'There is a human need to accord significance to death and the passing of the soul to another place. It reflects our sense of ego and cultural megalomania.'

The master ignored the twaddle. 'A great change is coming, steward. The strength of the economic growth means the people want more and are not content with the likes of me controlling their destiny.' Owen thought at least the master had recognised the change that was brewing. 'Pass my ointment, my arse hurts.' Sir John had developed terrible piles over the years but swore by the concoction made by Amy Rowlands, an old woman from Caernarfon. It consisted of black lead scrapings mixed with honey which had been placed in an oyster shell set over a fire. The mix was then fashioned into a suppository.

As Taid left to leave, the master had one last comment. 'If I die, you must do one last thing for me steward.'

'I pledged everything for you sir.'

'Kill the Earl for me Taid. That would be my last order to end your pledge of loyalty.'

Owen turned back and shook his hand. 'That Sir John, would be my pleasure.' But revenge could not be taken quickly as the master fought to stay alive for a few more months.

* * *

That evening, after the servants had finished eating the lamb stew, they all sat on the long table in the kitchen and watched the butler pick at his food. Owen had also finished but waited patiently whilst Nash exerted his power on the staff.

Taid spoke to everyone, 'I am sure you all know Sir John is failing from his bad heart and would ask you all to please be extra courteous and kind around the mistress.'

Nash wiped his mouth with the back of his hand and belched before speaking. 'I will make sure of that steward. The girls always do what I say.'

Five maids' heads remained lowered. The youngest, Louise, showed a little spunk. 'Taid, will we see his brothers and sons comin' ere?'

'I would think they will arrive next week, Louise, if business allows.'

Her eyes danced, 'I can't wait. Catrin ere says them boys are handsome chaps.'

Catrin elbowed her, 'No I didn't. I said they are rich and unavailable to the likes of you!' The girls started to laugh but were cut short by Nash.

'Quiet, that is enough insolence. You can clear away now and then go to your room.'

The maids indolently cleared the wooden trenchers off the table allowing Taid to make a request of Nash. 'Lady Elizabeth couldn't find Beth to ask you butler but she wants you and I to go to Bangor straight after our dinner.'

'Why the hell would I want to do that?'

'Because her ladyship has asked you.' Taid delivered the order again in a cold clipped voice.

'So why are we going?'

Owen used all his charm to put the butler at ease. 'There is a new doctor from London, a modern man, who lives near the cathedral. He specialises in heart conditions and I have to collect him by boat and bring him back tonight as the master has taken a turn for the worse.'

'So why do you need me?'

'Dear Nash, I must return immediately but her ladyship trusts you with the money to buy any medicines he suggests. Therefore, we can obtain a list of items which you can buy in the morning and then bring straight back to Plas Coch.'

The butler pondered for a while. A night out in Bangor was enticing; he could stay in the new George Hotel and fritter some of the money on a good prostitute. 'In that case, I am privileged to help her ladyship and I shall go and pack a small bag.'

The two men met half an hour later and walked to Moel-y-Don to meet Ieuan and take a boat to Bangor on the ebb tide. Nash wheedled and whined in the small sailing boat as they set out from the quay. It wasn't too dark under the half-moon, but the captain was navigating by experience.

Ieuan was facing Nash who sat on the rear thwart but it was Taid who started the questioning from the bow. 'A distant cousin of mine told me that you met Morgan in Llangefni last week.'

'No, why would I?' Nash was thinking fast and wondering who had been sat in the inn.

'In that case, why was it confirmed by Lady Charlotte to Lady Elizabeth?'

'It is all poppycock, steward.'

'I don't believe the ladies have ever lied to each other? In fact, Lady Charlotte said that Morgan had given you three things.' The butler shifted uncomfortably in his seat as the boat hung mid-channel in the slack tide. Ieuan let the tiller swing free. He sat and glared at Nash with his hands resting inside his jacket, to keep them warm.

'I may have accidentally met Morgan, but we never talked.'

Owen laughed. The sound carried across the straits and scared the roosting birds. 'That is true Nash. You never talked over many years, you exchanged messages instead. Of course, I would surmise that little Jenifer or Louise helped on occasion?'

The butler started to plead. 'I did nothing wrong Taid, please believe me. A little information that's all.'

'Morgan gave you three things.'

'No, he gave me nothing, we just talked.'

Owen's voice was deadly calm. 'He gave you an order to kill our best friend, some deadly nightshade to poison him with and fifty guineas for doing the deed. Is that correct Roger Nash, erstwhile butler to the Littleton-Joneses?'

As Nash couldn't swim, he was helpless as he looked around. The boat slowly spun through 360 degrees as the whirlpools flowed over the sandbanks below. He started to plead with them. 'Morgan would have killed me—' Ieuan's knife slit the butler's throat before he realised where the pain came from. The captain quickly tipped him backwards to splash into the dark sea as he didn't want the man's blood in his boat. He tossed the man's bag over the side as an afterthought.

'Go and feed the fish you bastard.' Ieuan swilled his hand and the knife in the water to remove the blood.

'Ieuan, he may have given us some valuable information.' Owen didn't mean it seriously and the captain didn't take it seriously.

'Yes, but could you stand the snivelling lies any longer?'

Owen shook his head as Ieuan tacked the boat back to Moel-y-Don and delivered him safely home.

The strong women of Plas Coch were feeling weak as they walked on a cold afternoon. They were unable to cope with the events of this ancient month of purification. Beth and Elizabeth walked arm in arm from the house towards the physic garden. To their right the lake was inert; a small patch of water surrounded by a ring of blackened algae where the ducks and coots waddled as they lifted their feet from the clawing mass. Beth copied them, her bump moved from side to side.

A few leaves were falling from the beech trees on the avenue and floated into the lake. When the wind veered it brought with it the sound of the lambs being slaughtered, a plaintive cry for the loss of their short lives. Beth was sobbing as she leaned on Elizabeth's shoulder.

Her words were blurted out between large gasps of air, 'I had nothing to show...to show for Saint Valentine's Day... I didn't propose...to him in the...leap year.'

Her ladyship rubbed her back gently as she stared at the grey sky with its low scudding clouds. The condensation of her breath hung in the air as she replied. 'It is at a single moment that you realise this. You thought you had everything you wanted, but in fact you had nothing. A single moment of crisis in the humdrum of life.' Beth was still as she listened. 'A fracturing of perceptions, like a broken mirror, where your own reflection cannot be seen anymore.'

The garden walls kept most of the gale off them, but the roar of the wind was an absolute power that scared mere mortals. The south-westerly was ripping through the branches and vibrating the leaves in a manic shake. A crescendo of the gods who were housed on Mount Snowdon, roaring like the breath of the red dragon across Ynys Môn.

The women's bonnets barely reduced the chill from the wind. Elizabeth gently lifted her friend's face with her gloved hand, 'What will you call the baby?'

'If it's a boy, it must be William.'

Her ladyship prompted her, 'And what if it is a girl again?'

Beth hugged her close and whispered, 'Elizabeth of course. What other name is there?'

They clung to each other, united in their thoughts of birth and death, of happiness and sadness. 'But I can't give the baby up this time, it would kill me.'

'You won't have to, my dearest friend. No matter what the scandal, we will find a way for you to be a real mother.'

Chapter 15

The Tide Waits For No Woman

The Anglo-Saxons called September "gerst-monath" – the barley month – but there were no farmers growing the cereal on Ynys Môn; that was the reason they drank ale rather than beer brewed with barley. They also had an old saying, "September dries up wells, or breaks down bridges". In 1822 it was dry and on some places on the island they could have grown cereals, but it belied the usual wetness of the summers. The brake fern on the slopes of the mountains was beginning to turn bronze and yellow in the distance. The scent on the way to the slate quarry was exquisite. Touching the fronds released their essence which caught the back of the throat and gave a unique taste of Wales. Bulrushes at the western end of the lake at Plas Coch had reached a tall standing ripeness and if the soft brown heads were touched, they sent a cloud of white fairy umbrellas into the air. Further down the valley of The Spout, the red fruit of the wild guelder roses cowered beneath the pink-leaved bushes, hiding from the voracious birds that would come and feed in the early winter. But the insects for their food were still plentiful as the birds sat in the huge box tree planted by an ancient Welsh Queen. Others perched on the shaded boughs of the heavily fruited chestnuts, where they sang in happiness, enjoying the end of the summer.

Lady Charlotte had unfortunately died in her sleep and was found clutching a copy of Lord Byron's poem *She walks in beauty, like the night, Of cloudless climes and starry skies.* Her heart must have stopped beating late in the evening and she must have had no more than a minute to contemplate the end of her life.

They say your whole life flashes before you when you realise you are dying. Lewis hadn't experienced it as he died quickly, but Lady Charlotte saw everything as it was much slower. You also smell your past, as vivid aromas pervade the dying senses. But the only scent in that last minute of her life was her husband's cologne on the hands that held the pillow used to suffocate her. Charlotte's first thought in her flashback was whether she could reach the dagger under her pillow in time to kill him. The Earl had two thoughts. Firstly, the satisfaction of revenge for her betrayal and secondly, whether he was still young enough to sire an heir with a new wife.

Shortly after the death, Elizabeth and Owen agreed that time and circumstances had converged. Sir John was visibly failing and pledges died with the men who made them. Owen immediately arranged to meet the Earl and Morgan to complete the double-cross and so the day before her beloved's meeting, Elizabeth accompanied Owen from the house at Plas Coch to the peninsula at Moel-y-Don. Although only a mile's walk, it had taken them nearly an hour. They clasped each other's arms for support and tottered a few steps at a time before halting to regain their breath. There was no escort for the first time and it was a joy to be alone. They walked across the estate fields and avoided the busy track which led to their secret place half a mile from the ferry. It had always been special for Owen as it was where he and Beth had happily played in the innocence of their childhood.

'I love this place, Owen. It is the most beautiful spot I have ever been privileged to see.' They searched out a rock that was comfortable, shaped by the tide into two seats that had been side by side for thousands of years. The view went beyond the horizon, across the exposed sandbanks, past Caernarfon and Lovers' Island. The shrill calls of the oyster catches created a descant above the raucous noise of the rooks and the screech of the two marauding buzzards. A line of four shags sped their way up the strait towards the new column erected to commemorate the Marquess's heroic part in the Battle of Waterloo.

'We have lived, haven't we Owen?' They watched the sea creeping towards them over the mudflats. It pushed a line of brown foam in front of it as the sea repossessed the earth. She clutched his hand tightly as they watched the flow of the tide, which was as inevitable as the rise and setting of the sun. He was too quiet and she asked again. 'Owen?'

'We have, my beauty. We have lived and loved and that is all we could have asked for.'

'Will you come back to me after the rendezvous? Will you?' She hugged him tightly and dug her head into his neck. She felt his fingers ruffle her curls and his soft lips kissing her hair.

'If I can, my love. Our paths are set in heaven and on a day like tomorrow, I will hold heaven in my hands. If I fail and drop it, then I will be going to hell.' He opened the picnic basket and poured the claret into the crystal glasses. They clinked them together at head height, refracting the rays of the sun into a myriad of images of the sea cocooned by the mountains behind. A thousand images representing a thousand different universes, of different lives and loves that could have been. They slowly chewed their bread and cheese and watched the sun go down. Its rays reflected on the shallow water seeping in front of their feet, turning the rock pools from bright white to a dull red.

* * *

Llanfairpwll was a tiny hamlet set beneath a bare hill and on the summit was the folly to the Marquess. The tall stone column was an act of pompous pride. It said:

'Look at me; I am important, I own the Menai and control the lives of the Welsh.'

The locals saw it differently:

'Learn to bow down before your betters. Accept the English dominance of your lands as you are nothing, you are nobodies.'

But the column wasn't visible from Plas Coch; you had to be on the shore of the Menai at Moel-y-Don to see the long English forefinger beckoning the Welsh into submission. Elizabeth and Owen had walked around the promontory and were standing next to the small wooden quay. To their right, the red orb of the sun occupied the whole of their visible horizon as it touched the sea. In front of them was a small rowing boat scything through the water from Felinheli. The broad shoulders stretched the white cotton of his shirt as Fardol approached, his long grey hair shaking up and down at each stroke. He expertly tied the boat to the jetty and smiled grimly at his friends as they waited for Beth. There were no more ferries due that evening and so they were safe to assume no one would see them. After a few minutes Elis appeared down the main track in a gig driven at walking speed. Beth sat beside him and waited for the other three to approach. As they drew nearer, Elis wandered away from earshot and busied himself skimming stones across the surface of the red sea.

'I am so sorry I am late ma'am. It was the baby; I had to finish feeding him.' They all gathered close to look at William's face swaddled in a navy coloured blanket to keep the evening chill away. Elizabeth sat in the gig next to her and gazed at the large baby; she could already see the face of a young William Smith.

After a few moments contemplation she started the meeting. 'We must be quick, William should be inside and I don't want to advertise our presence. However, I wanted to summarise what we have agreed.' The rest nodded their assent. 'Taid will meet with the Earl and his steward tomorrow afternoon and conclude his business.' She hesitated briefly; it was too much to contemplate without dread. 'Sir John has signed the bridge documents with us all as witnesses and therefore upon his death... the rights of the shell companies all revert to my control via Henry.'

She looked up at Ieuan as he asked, 'Lady Elizabeth, it should be me and not you. For my family and my revenge.'

'No Ieuan, his heart is very weak and only I can be seen to be with him at the end. He should have died in the summer, but his bitterness keeps him alive.'

'Please my Lady?' Ieuan pleaded again.

'No captain. We must minimise suspicion. The brothers will be difficult to handle afterwards, but I can do it.' She also thought about her own revenge for the rapes and adultery before continuing, 'He will die soon anyway and Taid's meeting is crucial.'

Owen stepped in, 'Which means you both have to leave on the ebb tide tomorrow afternoon.'

The captain was happy to run away at last and he would be helping Beth and his best friend's son. He wanted to know one last thing. 'We will anchor in the channel off Plas Newydd ready for an instant departure, but as we will never see you again, we would like to know if the double-cross worked. Anything would suffice, for example a smoke signal?'

Taid clapped his shoulder, 'It will work my friend, trust me. After all these years I will make it work, come heaven or hell.'

'Please Taid, any signal for our piece of mind.'

The steward agreed, 'There is a flag of Saint George at the house. On my way back from the meeting at Saint Tysilio I will display it at the top the Marquess column for a few minutes. That is the signal that the deed is done and that we have helped the people of Ynys Môn.'

Beth was surprised, 'How ironic, the raising of the English standard to celebrate another Welsh repulsion of the invaders.'

Owen held her gaze as he replied, 'To celebrate our freedom too, Beth. All of us will gain.' The baby started to cry, a quiet mewing for the attention of his mother. Elizabeth called for Elis to take Beth home. As the gig went slowly up the hill, the last rays of sun illuminated the faces of those remaining.

Her ladyship shook hands slowly with Ieuan, 'Please look after her, captain. She is like a daughter to me.'

He hugged her close and pulled Taid into their group. 'She will be safe with me; I will treat her as my daughter and the baby as my son. Look after yourselves.'

He lowered himself into the boat and pulled away from the quay. The last they saw of Captain Ieuan Fardol was a brief wave of the hand before he was swallowed up in the darkness. They turned and started to walk towards Plas Coch. Before they reached the first incline on the track, they heard the jingling of a harness as someone approached.

Elis had kindly returned for them. 'Come and jump in missus. I don't want an old crock like Taid slowing you down on a dark night like this.' They mounted the gig and within five minutes they were safe and sound at the house. Owen held her hand tightly during the journey and kept hold of it as she alighted outside the porch.

After Elis had driven away with a cheery goodnight, they walked the 50 yards to the top of the mound in front of the house and stood in the moonlight staring south towards the sea and Snowdon. The serpentine band of the Menai Straits glinted, reflecting the moon back towards the stars. The waters dominated the view, supporting the black mountains and the starlit sky.

Owen turned to Elizabeth and placed his hands on her shoulders as he kissed her gently. 'I won't see you tomorrow before the meeting, it's not safe.'

She stifled a sob, 'Please Owen, just in case.' Her pale face seemed more beautiful than ever as he stroked her hair.

He nodded towards the straits, 'This is our gift to each other. I will remember this moment through eternity and beyond. You are my love and my life.'

He kissed her for the last time and walked away.

As Taid galloped his horse towards Porthaethwy to meet Morgan and the Earl, Lady Elizabeth sat by Sir John's bed and held a cooling cloth to his forehead. She looked in wonder at the different colours in the room, as if seeing the objects for the first time. The shining bright boots and the matching tan of his suit. Dark blue curtains with threads of vertical gold. The bright white enamel of the guzunder and yellow-green urine lying inside.

'John? Talk to me John.'

He lay deathly still, afraid to move and initiate a heart attack. The voice was low and breathless, 'Lizbeth, I am dying.'

'Yes you are. What are you thinking about?'

'The boys, I want the boys to be like me. A success.'

'They have no choice, John. You took them from me, they lost the loving care and guidance of their mother and they have lost their mercy and compassion.'

'Best for them, ma'am.'

'You think so? I don't agree. I don't want them to be brutal and uncaring drunks who rape their wives and maids and think that money is everything in life.'

'Damn you woman.' He could barely speak, her words had stressed him. 'God will guide and protect them. My God will let me watch them from heaven.' He was dry and motioned for some water. Elizabeth stood with her back to him as she emptied the whole phial of digitalis into the water. She lifted his head to help him drink. The stench of piss and sweat made her want to retch.

'Drink deeply my dear, very deeply and remember how well I have looked after you although you left me to die all those years ago.' He swallowed three gulps, struggling to breathe in between. She still held his head. More tightly now and keeping it close to the glass. 'Come on my John, take a few more swallows. Water is the basis of all life.' She forced some more into his mouth, making him choke. After placing the glass on the side table she watched the drops trickle from his mouth and dampen his nightshirt. He was an ugly man, with broken red veins across his white skin. The eyes were small and protruding and his bald pate was shining between the remaining few hairs. He gasped as he couldn't draw his breath and weakly grabbed her wrist. Elizabeth picked up his hand and laid it back on his chest. By now his heart had stopped and he knew he was going to die. He jerked twice, fighting against the pain and the lack of oxygen. She had to watch him die to be sure and despite her hate, she felt ashamed.

'Your God will judge you, not me. But I doubt very much whether you will see him and his heaven. Think back John, remember the pacts you made with the devil and look forward to hell.' His eyes rolled to their whites and he lay still. Elizabeth waited by the window and stared at the straits and mountains before checking there was no pulse and then she went to find Beth in the garden.

The head housekeeper walked with her arm around the old rheumatic lady dressed in black. 'Owen is a great man, Beth. One hundred times the stature of my ex-husband. A real man.'

It was Beth's turn to comfort her mistress this time around.

The bright September sunshine defined every colour of the island of Saint Tysilio. Taid could see the walls of the stone church were etched with fine veins of grey, white and black. The solid tussocky grass had turned brown on the ends of the blades and as he stared down from above the sea wall onto the waters of the straits, he marvelled at the liquid repetition of the greens and browns. The seaweed had started to flow horizontally as the tide increased. He looked up. If he squinted he could see the Marquess's column in the distance and prayed he would climb it later on such a beautiful day. Ynys Gorad Goch sat low to his right, an artificially angled rock with its blue haze of smoke merging into the silvered horizon. As his gaze moved to the east he noted the two horses rounding the promontory and waited patiently without dismounting. The Earl was in the lead and reined in a few feet from Taid, with Morgan stopping close to his master's side. The haughty commanding tone of Edward Lloyd-Williams derided Taid without a greeting.

'You have the way-leaves?'

'No.' He decided it was their conversation to lead.

'Morgan paid hundreds of guineas to secure them from your people and we will pay you five hundred more.'

'Did he?'

'Do not play games, Tudur. Where are my rights?'

Taid looked across at Morgan before he answered, 'You paid hundreds of guineas to Morgan and not my people.'

The Earl understood the implication that his steward was corrupt but continued abruptly, 'Hand them over now!' He had realised the shortcomings in Morgan over the last few years. Taid would be a good replacement; his whip gently slapped Morgan's arm, 'He bribed them. They, "your people", to do what their Earl pays them to do.'

Rhodri urged his horse in front of his master and came closer to Taid. He snarled at him as he drew his pistol, 'You double-crossing bastard. Now I can settle our scores.'

'Wait!' The Earl was thinking.

Taid kept his eyes on Rhodri as he spoke. His voice was strong and unafraid, 'There is nothing less important in the world than money, sir. The emotions and loyalties of the local people, count for everything.'

The Earl wanted an explanation. 'They told you about our bribes?'

'No, they told Jenkin Evans. It was a matter of conscience and country and so they wanted their God to know.'

Morgan spat his words out. He was desperate to finish him. 'That bastard has double-crossed me, he will die for this.'

Taid stood tall and proud as he replied, 'Like all the others you have killed? My tad, my sister, my brother-in-law and nieces. I wonder what happened to Frances?'

'Let me kill him, master?'

The Earl didn't reply as Taid continued, 'Have I missed anyone out?'

'Only you, Tudur.' As Rhodri lifted his arm to shoot, the Earl placed a pistol to Rhodri's head and pulled the trigger. The body thumped to the floor, scaring the horse which bucked away. A patch of blue smoke remained in the air as the grass turned red.

Lloyd-Williams looked at the body with disdain before haughtily addressing Taid. 'That solves a problem for you, steward. Now we can do business.'

'My name is Owen. Owen Tudur. My ancestors have ruled Ynys Môn for thousands of years and beaten all its invaders.'

'Your point man?'

'My point is that you and Sir John are imposters, invaders to be fought by my people.' Owen looked at the man who thought he was the most important on Ynys Môn. 'Dear Earl, if only you really knew and understood your people like Saint Tysilio. You stand on his island and know nothing.'

'Get on with it, steward. How much do I have to pay you above the five hundred?'

'My point is that, before his death in 640 AD, Saint Tysilio was a great evangeliser in this area. He directed local affairs and that is very apt.'

'Why, you fool?'

'Because I have been directing affairs concerning the new bridge rights.'

The Earl shouted in his rage, 'You have what?'

'Another great evangelist called Jenkin Evans finally came face-to-face with God and served the people.' Lloyd-Williams was speechless as Owen told his tale. 'The hundreds of men who will live and die whilst making the bridge, work for just three companies. He told me that you had bribed two of them leaving Sir John with one in his pocket. But people who can be bribed, can be bribed for more, and workers in a Union can be persuaded by their leaders and their chapel to act in a certain way.'

'You bastard, Tudur. Sir John denies my rights with his secret dealings and you attempt to control my labourers. I won't let you get away with any of it.'

'Precisely, you won't let me get away with it.' Owen laughed loudly. 'But that is a tiny part of the double-cross. The ownership agreements will belong to Henry Littleton-Jones who will be controlled by Lady Elizabeth when Sir John is dead and she will ensure Henry helps the people of the island.'

The Earl was confused. 'What are you talking about man, that could be years away.'

'Or he could be dead by now.'

Edward Lloyd-Williams realised he had lost. 'Pah, you are an imbecile. This is my island; I rule it and you are nothing. I solved your problem, now solve mine.'

'Rhodri was never a problem.'

'He hated you steward.'

'He hated everyone, but I never lowered myself to his level. I had two problems and now I have one.'

It dawned on the Earl that he was in danger, but his sheer ignorance made him ask, 'What is the remaining problem?'

'You.' Owen aimed the blunderbuss at the Earl's head. He saw the eyes widen with fear and then he pulled the trigger. 'Now I have no problems in my life.' Owen dismounted and grabbed the torso. The bloodied head was unrecognisable and lay a few feet away. Without remorse he dragged the body to the low stone wall that kept the swirling tide away from the church. With a final heave he launched the Earl into the Menai and staggered back to the head. He was breathing heavily and he felt the pains in his chest and left arm. Bending slowly, he grabbed the head by the wig and it dropped to the floor leaving the white powdered hair in his hands. He leant down again and used both hands to grab the bald mass of bloodied skull and then he flung it all over the wall. The pains were increasing, but he had to dispose of Morgan.

Before he dropped him into the sea, he looked into the dead staring eyes. 'God forgive you Morgan.'

He pushed and heard the body splat into the mud barely covered by the shallow water and then it was sucked away towards Caernarfon. He watched it float away and crossed himself in supplication. 'And God forgive me for what I have done today.' He wanted to wash the blood off his hands in the flow of beautiful sea water, but he couldn't find the energy to climb over the wall. He called to his mare and she came close enough for him to grasp the saddle. Using a large rock to clamber laboriously on top of her, he rode holding the saddle and leaving the reins loose as he let her wend her way towards home. Owen slumped, constantly nodding off and then jerking himself awake. It would take half an hour to reach the column and display the flag.

The tide took the two bodies towards Ynys Gorad Goch, the island of red weirs, where a haze hung on the water next to the smoking chamber. A loud bell was sounded from the shore on the Bangor side and the old man walked from his comfortable seat in the sun towards the rowing boat. He placed his hand over his eyes to reduce the glare and could make out four people waiting for collection. His wife was already preparing the visitor's whitebait tea, the fish freshly caught in the wattle fences in the early morning before dawn. It wouldn't be until the next morning that she and her husband would find the bodies of Morgan and the Earl.

A garden can be a wonderful place when all your friends have left you. The scents salve the mind and free the conscience. Elizabeth bent to smell an apricot-coloured rose, she recognised the delightful scent as "Whisky Mac" and bent close again. A thorn pricked her wedding finger, so when she twisted her hand she could see there was a band of blood. After a moment's contemplation she placed her finger to her mouth and kissed the blood away.

Under the trees to her right, she could see what remained of the summer's biennial foxgloves. A handful of tall spires supporting pink tubular bells shone in the dappled light of the shade. They had other names: "dead man's bells" and "witches' gloves", but she had preferred foxgloves since she was a child in her mamma's garden. She vividly remembered placing the fairy caps on each of her fingers and showing her mother who made her remove them because of the poison.

It was time to rest and so she sat on a wooden bench and watched the butterflies and bees working hard before the winter. It would suit her to manage the funds generated by the bridge. The almshouses and schools... there were many nice ways to give instead of take. As her head drooped and she started to nap she felt happy and at home. There would be many things to plan and discuss with Owen tomorrow.

* * *

Beth clutched baby William as she stood on the stern of the newly built Lady Louisa Littleton anchored off Plas Newydd. A new ship launched by her ladyship as part of her new role in the empire of the three brothers. Ieuan placed his telescope to his right eye every minute and focussed on the top of the Marquess's column, solitary on the bare hill a mile away. He glanced over the side at the still waters, squinting to reduce the glare. The sea was perfectly flat and sparkled silver in the afternoon sun. He watched a branch float leisurely by and then looked up at the column.

'The ebb tide has started, Beth, we must leave in less than an hour my dear.' The baby whimpered and squirmed in his sleep and so she leaned down and kissed the perfect skin on his cheek.

'Calm yourself William, have no fear, I will always be there for you.'

Ieuan touched her arm, 'Look, the signal.' He watched a man, half-hidden by the flag of Saint George. The flag was draped from the platform near the top of the column and he clearly saw the red cross, a sign of the crucifixion on the white background. But then it fell. Fluttering in the light wind, it was caught on a zephyr and dropped onto the surface of the sea. Ieuan looked back to the man, but there was nothing certain, only a black heap that may have been Owen. 'He did it by God.'

She had only seen a brief image, a detachment that had ended in the sea. 'God is the right word, Ieuan. Thanks to God and to Owen and now we are free to start a new life.'

'I promise I will look after you both Beth. There are no conditions. I owe it to my friends and whilst I live I will make your life safe and happy.' The captain shouted forward to the waiting crew and ordered the anchor to be lifted and the mainsail set. As the schooner joined the last of the tide he grasped the wheel and brought her onto a reach. Within a few minutes they were heading westwards at six knots. Beth leaned on Ieuan for support as they passed Moel-y-Don and looked up at the hillock that hid Plas Coch and Lady Elizabeth who was asleep in her garden.

It was a beautiful day to start a new life in the Americas. They were sad to leave their friends, but Ynys Môn would look after them.

"The Mother of Wales" always remembered those who helped to repel the invaders. Crossing the Menai Straits never guaranteed victory.

Only the island itself could do that.

Author's note

Most of the story is historically factual, but I have bent dates and events. A historical timeline is given below.

BRIEF TIMELINE for THE EBB AND FLOW

The novel starts in 1767 and ends 1822.

1756 – 1763	The Seven Years' War in Europe. Britain and Prussia versus France, Austria, Russia, Sweden, Saxony and Spain. It was a major military conflict that lasted until the Treaty of Paris signed on 10 February 1763.
1760	George III on the throne.
1763	End of the Seven Years' War.
1765	Turnpike road built between Porthaethwy (now Menai Bridge) and Holyhead. A well-maintained road where you paid a toll but reduced the journey time.

1765	The Isle of Man becomes part of the Crown jurisdiction. Agitated for by customs and cost paid from customs-derived money.
1768	The Royal Academy formed – nobles purchased fashionable pictures e.g. Turner and Constable.
1770	Captain Cook becomes the first European to reach Australia.
1770	The Watt steam engine introduced at Parys Mountain.
1772	The Druidical Society of Anglesey founded.
1774	A new safer road around the Penmaenmawr headland was created.
1775 – 1783	American War of Independence.
1776	Bangor to Felinheli turnpike road created.
1779	French fleet ruled The Channel. Great danger of invasion of England.
1779	The song *Amazing Grace* first published. On hymn sheets the lyrics were accredited to John Newton.
1780	First stagecoach between London and Holyhead.
1780 – 1810	Rapid spread of country banking in England and Wales.

1783	Committee formed for navigation of the Menai Straits to block a bridge.
1784	"The Warehouse" a non-conformist meeting place built in Beaumaris.
1785	First mail coaches on Menai ferry. Objections against a timber bridge.
1786	Pompeii became fashionable with many famous visitors. Eruption was 79AD.
1787 – 1817	Privately-issued tokens become common in Britain instead of coinage.
1788	*The Times* owner, John Walter scandal. The newspaper falls foul of the Prince Regent for telling the truth.
1789	Malltraeth near New Borough. Embankment and sluice started.
1789	The French Revolution worries the rich of Britain.
1792 – 1802	French Revolutionary Wars. Continuous war with Great Britain to 1803.
1792 – 1815	The above merges into the Napoleonic Wars.
1793	France declared war on Great Britain.
1798	Attempted uprising Ireland and a French landing.
1800	Union of the Great British and Irish parliaments.

1800	Caernarfon port has 250 slate vessels, 2,000 coasting vessels, 1,000 foreign ships per annum.
1800	Felinheli starts to develop
1800 – 1830	Trinity House lighthouses on Anglesey. 1809 South Stack, Holyhead. 1830 Semaphore Station at Point Lynas on the N.E. coast.
1801	34,000 persons on island of Anglesey. Many in Amlwch because of the copper industry and four times the number in Beaumaris, the county town.
1801	Horse-drawn trucks from Port Dinorwic to the Llanberis slate quarries.
1801	Food riots in Llanfairpwll.
1802	End of French Revolutionary Wars.
1805	Battle of Trafalgar – part of the Napoleonic Wars. Lord Nelson dies.
1807	Slave Trade Act passed in British Parliament, making slave trading illegal throughout the British Empire. However, it was not fully abolished until 1833.
1809	Marquess Paget elopes with Wellington's sister-in-law, Charlotte Wellesley, and leaves the Plas Newydd resident, Lady Caroline, in the lurch.

1810	Prince Regent takes over from mad King George III.
1810	Telford asked by the Lords of the Treasury to review the best method to bridge the Menai Straits.
1811	Telford report to Lords of the Treasury.
1811	Calvanistic Methodists arrive on the island.
1811	Copper dominates Anglesey's industry. By 1821 it is declining.
1811– 12	The Luddites break frames in a systematic plan of action. Soldiers suppressed mobs in Notts. and Lancs.
1812 – 14	War between USA and Britain.
1815	Telford's iron bridge at Betws-y-Coed. The Battle of Waterloo.
1815 – 1846	Corn Laws. Post 1815 major crash in corn prices.
1816	A starving poacher would be transported for 7 years if caught with nets.
1817	Marquess column erected.
1819	Menai bridge started. 4mph walking pace max.
1820	George III dies.
1821	First steamer ships - Dover-Calais.

1824	Port Dinorwic tramway completed between the port and
	the slate mine.
1826	Thomas Telford suspension bridge completed over the Menai Straits.
1829	Following the Metropolitan Police Act, the first police – or Peelers – in London.
1829	First lifeboats, but there were coastguards before this.